I0684364

The Sour Orange Derby

Kristina Circelli

All rights reserved. No part of this book may be reproduced or utilized in any form, or stored in a retrieval system or transmitted in any form, or by any other means, without the written permission of the author, except by a reviewer for quoting or brief passage to be printed in a newspaper, magazine, or journal.

All characters in this book are fictional and have no existence outside of the imagination of the author. All uses of names and incidences are purely inventive and have no relation to anyone bearing the same name or story.

First Edition

1 2 3 4 5 6 7 8 9 10

Copyright © 2012 Kristina Circelli
All rights reserved.

ISBN: 0-9763-7283-5
ISBN-13: 9780976372837

Dedication

For Mema and Papa,

who fill our lives with magic, love, and endless imagination

Prologue

It was a rare day that the old man felt the weight of his long life crushing down on his shoulders. In his mid-sixties, he still enjoyed a brisk walk through the park, a boat ride down the river, a few sunny hours of gardening. He prided himself on keeping his body healthy, his heart strong, his mind sharp; but now, with his thinning dark brown hair, deep lines etched across a sun-roughened face, and arthritic limbs, his age had finally caught up with him.

But this wasn't an old age brought on by time and its unfortunate consequences. This was the old age of sorrow, and for an entire year, that sorrow had beaten him down.

As he sat on the back porch, feeling the warmth of the summer sun against his leathered flesh and keeping his eyes trained on the tall, grand orange tree in the middle of the yard, K.B. reflected on his troubles. It had been just over a year since his world changed, since his family suffered the tragic death of one of their own, and he still, no matter how hard he tried, how hard he searched, couldn't find a way to move forward in life, couldn't find a way to remember the way his grandson deserved to be remembered.

In fact, none of them could.

K.B. rose from the plastic chair and made his way across the grass, feeling every single burden of not only the past year but of his entire life suffocating the air of the world around him. As he neared the house next door, he saw his teenage granddaughter stretched out on a hammock, absently petting the fat orange cat lying across her stomach as she stared up at the clouds.

"Where's your momma?" Kariss Standridge turned her bright green eyes to her grandfather. The look alone spoke every word that the old man needed to know.

"Papa?"

"Yes?"

"Do you think the reason why it's so hard to move on is because we don't know how to stop being sad?"

"...Could be."

"Then how do we stop feeling sad?"

That was the question K.B. had been trying so hard to answer for the past year. How does one stop feeling sad, when all around are constant reminders of an event so painful that happiness seems impossible? He thought about that as he turned his attention to his beloved orange tree, the tree that never lost its beauty despite the ugliness that surrounded it, and he realized he may have the answer. The way to stop feeling sad was not to mourn, but to celebrate, and celebrating his grandson's memory was what they needed to do most, what he needed to do most, and what he had failed to do thus far.

When he turned his attention back to his granddaughter, he saw that she, too, was staring at the orange tree, an expression of hope crossing her young face that told him they were thinking the exact same thing.

"Get your mother and brothers outside," he ordered, heading for the tree. "We got a game to play."

Chapter 1

Twelve Years Later

"There ain't nothing quite like the feel of a sour orange bursting beneath the swing of a baseball bat."

Rod Jenkins, a middle-aged New York reporter, scribbled the quote on his pad of yellow, wide-ruled paper. He was an old-school reporter, and preferred the feel of pen and paper in his hands rather than a cold metal recorder as he covered the biggest event that Barton County, Florida, offered once a year.

The comment amused him as he attempted to imagine the skinny and seemingly unthreatening woman before him swinging at a big, sour orange. And even though he had no desire to experience the feel for himself, there was something about the way she spoke that created an atmosphere of both nostalgia and mystery.

The woman, Kariss Standridge, turned her steely green eyes from the reporter sitting on the hard aluminum bleachers to the baseball dugout, where her friends and family, all members of Team Colly, were debating over the lineup. She toyed with the end of the French braid that trailed all the way down her back, a smile tugging at the corners of her small mouth and lighting up her face—a bright, unpainted face that deceived the years it had seen. To any glancing eye, she looked like she was seventeen, with a heart-shaped face framed with dark brown tresses, cat-like green eyes that saw everything, high cheekbones that accented a tan yet somehow creamy complexion, and a petite frame, but Rod knew she was pushing thirty. He wondered if her love of oranges and fresh air kept her young, then silently ridiculed himself for thinking such foolish thoughts.

Rod followed her eyes to the field. On the pitcher's mound was a pile of oranges, sour, no doubt. They lit up in the sunshine, looking delicious and juicy despite their bitter nature. On the field, the opposing team was anxiously waiting to begin. Smiles flashed as jokes and laughter echoed throughout the park.

The first player was up to bat. At home plate, he dug the toes of his cleats into the clay much like he'd seen professional baseball players do before a big hit and practiced a few swings. His bat was painted a gaudy neon orange, with his name and number scrawled along its length in dark green. Turning before the first pitch, he waved to the large, enthusiastic crowd gathered on and around the bleachers, where sat Kariss and the reporter, getting them riled up for the hit. Kariss offered a loud shout of encouragement, pumping a fist into the air, while children milled around with hot dogs and Cokes despite the fact that the clock was yet to hit noon. Meanwhile, their parents wished other players wandering about the throngs of people good luck on their upcoming game. On the second field, the first orange had already been thrown, the umpires adding up and awarding points. A scoreboard lit up with the time and inning.

The games were beginning.

Eager to get on with the article that focused on a game of sour oranges that was beginning to gain nationwide fame, Rod shifted so that he had a clear sight of both the field and Kariss. He pulled a camera out of his bag, double-checked to make sure the flash and shutter speed settings were right, and snapped a couple pictures of the first member of Team Colly as he taunted the pitcher from home plate, which, oddly enough, was a metal trashcan lid. The sight was strange, but Rod was expecting strange, considering the fact that he was in a small town not far from the Florida-Georgia border that regarded an annual game of oranges as the high point of the year. If his boss hadn't of personally requested that he cover the story as a test of his diversity as a reporter, and if Rod, a somewhat seasoned newspaper man yet to have his big claim to fame, wasn't hoping for his own regular feature column, then he wouldn't have thought twice about the Annual Sour Orange Derby.

But he was in Barton County to get the story of the Derby, and in order to do so, he went back to Kariss' statement about the feel of hitting a sour orange.

"So how did you come to discover such a thing?"

"Oh, I reckon the same way anyone comes to discover such a thing."

"And how is that?"

"My Papa." There was a distinct touch of reminiscence in her southern-twanged voice, a hint of memories still fresh and joyful and ready to be relived.

"So, tell me how all this began."

Kariss leaned forward with her elbows on her knees, squinting as she watched the field. The wide bill of the baseball cap made it hard to see her face, and even harder to determine where her concentration was directed. "Well...that's hard to say, really, 'cuz there ain't a specific date. It didn't begin in one place or at one time. This...all this...has been more than ten years in the making."

"Begin where you see fit, then."

"How about I begin in nineteen sixty-three?"

"Or maybe a little closer to the origin of the game."

Taken aback by the comment, Kariss slowly turned, lifting her face to the reporter so that their eyes met, placing a hand on her hip. Her stiff body language and lifted brows suggested insult. Rod leaned back a bit when her piercing glare seared through him, and he was instantly aware that while the woman seemed pleasant, she certainly packed an attitude.

"Look, Mr. Yankee," she said with her southern drawl, taking only a second's glance at the middle-aged man. He could almost hear her sigh inwardly at his close-cropped black hair, thick glasses that sat on a long nose, and inquisitive if not arrogant blue eyes, before turning her head away so he could see only the profile of her jawline. "I know you probably don't like having to come down here from New York. It's hot, it's the south, you'd rather not get your fancy suit dirty, it's a small town with people you probably don't like or probably think are simple, and so you want to hurry up and get your story. Maybe you look down your nose at us because we play the Annual Sour Orange Derby. It's happened before." Kariss shrugged and gestured to the field. "But we ain't just a bunch of people standing around hitting oranges with baseball bats. This ain't a simple story filled with simple people. It's so much more. And like I said, it doesn't begin in one place or at one time, so if you want the story, then you're gonna have to settle for gettin' it my way."

It was a story she longed to tell, a story filled with family pride, tinged with fate, tradition, and magic. It was a story worthy of legend and legacy. But she wouldn't cheapen it by cutting to the chase. Her family deserved better. Her brother deserved better.

"Alright." Rod nodded in defeat, a bit embarrassed by receiving such a verbal berating in public. No one looked their way or spoke a word in agreement, but that didn't stop the snickers that worked their way through the crowd. He nervously adjusted the collar of his new shirt. She was right—he didn't want to get his suit dirty, and while he prided himself on keeping his body in shape and his wardrobe looking crisp, he nonetheless didn't want that holding him back from his article. "I didn't mean to upset you. I was only making sure we stay on track."

"Whatever I say will be right on track, I guarantee you that," Kariss promised, chewing on her bottom lip as she thought about everything she had to say. "But this story...the Annual Sour Orange Derby...it ain't always so easy to talk about. Despite its appearance, this ain't all fun and games for some of us, as I'm sure you know."

He didn't, as he hadn't bothered to do much research prior to his arrival in Barton County. He'd been sent to Florida last minute, with less than a day to pack and hop onto the flight south. Upon a brief inspection at a few websites along with his boss's initial description, there wasn't much reason, in his opinion, to further his research. Now he was left wondering what exactly he didn't know that was so important to the game. "We'll start wherever you wish."

"Thank you." She thought about her story, and decided she wouldn't start from the beginning. That part was for later. But she couldn't start at the end, or even somewhere in the middle, either, because first she had to establish a foundation. She knew exactly how to do that, as she was a writer and story-telling was her specialty.

"For generations, my family was known for their orange trees," she began. "But in nineteen sixty-three, a frost swept through Barton County, Florida, turning almost all of the orange groves my family owned sour. The trees still stood, still grew, but the fruit couldn't be saved. My family's business was in those orange groves, or what was left of them after a rare snowfall in nineteen fifty-nine destroyed more than half the acres of orange trees. They lost their business, their income, everything. Even worse, they lost the Standridge family tradition."

Kariss held up a hand as though to emphasize the tragedy. "So, they cut the trees down, all except what was left around the house. Those, they let live." She smiled a proud smile.

"Some twenty years later, by the time me and my brothers were kids, my Papa," she gestured to the old man with broad shoulders and a wide grin sitting on the top row of the bleachers, dressed in a pair of torn jeans and an Atlanta Braves T-shirt, "had to cut down almost all the rest after they died. Eventually, only one tree remained, the one that still stands behind the family house. The oranges were always sour, but they were beautiful, serving no purpose, as Papa always said, other than to represent the magic of nature." For a moment she seemed lost in time, her eyes taking on a faraway look as her mind took her back to the days spent playing around the orange tree, listening to the wind rustling among the leaves, leaping from tree to tree on their makeshift wire-and-rag swing, watching her grandfather collect the fallen fruit for their annual celebration.

Kariss' attention turned suddenly to the game as the second batter swung hard, spraying sour orange juice all over himself when the orange burst into a dozen pieces. The crowd cheered and hollered out encouragements. Her smile widened at that, snapping her back to the interview.

"Then my brothers and I came along, and Papa found a new use for the sour oranges, called it The Annual Sour Orange Derby. The Derby is…a combination of all of our childhood moments, like a series of crazy, magical snapshots of everything that ever mattered to us."

She focused her attention back to Rod.

"The Annual Sour Orange Derby is more than a game, Mr. Yankee. It's our way to heal. It's our way to remember…It's Papa's way to make us a family again. And it all begins with one little boy and his grandpa."

Chapter 2

BLUTO STEALER

It wasn't often that Colly got the TV all to himself. With two older brothers and one older sister, he often found himself on the bottom of the totem pole, right next to the crazy dog and fat cat. He got last pick of what movies to rent, had to go to bed the earliest, got pushed out of the bathroom the fastest. It wasn't fair at all.

This time, though, it was different. This time, *he* got to make the rules.

His favorite baseball team, the Atlanta Braves, was about to play, and as a reward for getting straight S's on his Kindergarten report card—S for "Satisfactory"—his mom decided that tonight, the TV would be all his. He could watch whatever he wanted, whenever he wanted, and, his favorite, as loud as he wanted. As his mother had predicted, he chose the Atlanta Braves baseball game to watch, and nothing excited him more.

Minutes before the game started, Colly Standridge, a scrawny, energetic child with unruly brown hair, tanned skin, and a wide, toothy grin that stretched up to big chocolate-colored eyes, set up his TV station so that he wouldn't have to get up and miss any of the action. On a tray that he carefully placed on the brown-carpeted floor was a can of soda, a hot dog that his sister heated up for him and loaded with ketchup, a candy bar, and a bag of Blutos, his own nickname for his favorite Ranch-flavored chips that came in a blue bag. On the glass coffee table was an autographed picture of Chipper Jones, a good-luck charm for the impending game. A well-worn Braves hat topped Colly's head.

For a five year-old boy, this was the life.

None of his other siblings liked baseball. Tony was into cars and the only sport Christian watched was basketball. Kariss would occasionally toss the baseball with him, but she would rather read a book, just like their mom. But it didn't matter. He could watch sports all by himself, or with his Papa, who lived right next door and was always up for a good old-fashioned game of baseball.

"Hey Doodle, game start yet?"

"Shhh, Papa!" Colly hushed his grandfather as he walked in the back door, frantically waving a hand. "It's on! And my name's not Doodle!"

Papa, better known to most as K.B. Standridge, only grinned. A retired newspaper worker with a hearty laugh, young soul, deep love for black-eyed peas and boiled peanuts, and the sturdy frame of a man not afraid of hard work, had been calling his youngest grandson 'Doodle' ever since he was born. It was an endearing moniker that stuck ever since he first heard his daughter say 'Colly' as a nickname for the boy's birth-name, Collin. Even now, K.B. couldn't help but sing the catchy yet annoying song *Polly Wolly Doodle*, only his version was sung *Colly Wolly Doodle*, much to his grandson's irritation.

But despite Colly's protests, K.B. continued to call him Doodle, as he had nicknames for all his grandkids, and even his daughter. "Hand me one of them chips there, Dood," K.B. said as he settled himself down on the couch. Colly held up the bag of Blutos, so called after his usual rapid-fire way of speaking jumbled up the name of his special snack, but refused to let go as his grandfather reached in for a handful. Teasingly, K.B. pulled the bag in his direction as though trying to take them away, but Colly only tightened his grip and shot a warning glare at his grandpa, his big brown eyes narrowing cautiously. No one stole his Blutos.

"Collin Adam Standridge, you share those chips with your Papa."

Colly looked up at his mother as she passed through the narrow kitchen. June Standridge regarded her son with a chastising yet playful eye, her curly brown hair highlighting her glare, when she saw the tight grip he had on the bag. More so than anything else, Colly guarded his Blutos with his life.

"Ah, let him have them." K.B. waved a hand, releasing the bag after snagging a few chips. "Boy's gotta protect the thing he loves from the Bluto Stealer."

"Bluto Stealer?" June, a trim, petite woman in her mid-thirties with bright brown

eyes that matched those of her youngest son, lifted a brow and leaned against the slightly chipped kitchen counter to hear her father's crazy made-up tale.

K.B. huffed, pretending to be stunned, though both he and June knew that he was only joking. The old man, with his jet-black hair, tanned face with wrinkles etched at the corners of his eyes, and hint of a potbelly, loved to tell his wild stories.

"Yeah," he said pointedly. "You mean to tell me you never heard of the Bluto Stealer?" June only crossed her arms. "Well, he's a tiny green creature with ten legs and a big ole' gut who likes to steal Blutos right out of people's cabinets, then take them back to his invisible cave to pig out. He's very well-known, and very feared."

"Like the boogey-man," Colly muttered to himself, eyes trained on the television and ears trained on the story, listening for any sounds of this scary Bluto Stealer he now had to fear.

"Worse than the boogey-man," K.B. replied, still speaking to June. "He's fat and stinky with a big ole' spike on the top of his bald head and likes to make people pass out with all his bad breath. You really mean to tell me you never heard of the Bluto Stealer?"

"Silly me."

"Besides," K.B. munched on a chip, "it ain't everyday the boy gets something all to himself. He deserves at least one thing."

It was true. Being the youngest meant Colly rarely had anything to call his own. He shared his bedroom, his TV time, his snacks, his sports equipment, even his Black Labrador puppy, Latheena, that was given to him on his fifth birthday. Most of the time, he didn't mind sharing. After all, his brothers and sister always shared their things with him, so he couldn't complain.

But when it came to his Blutos, he would fight to the death. Even if that meant facing the Bluto Stealer.

"Don't encourage him, Dad. He needs to learn to share.""Oh, I seem to remember a certain little girl who refused to pass the creamed corn at Thanksgiving."

"Yeah, well, that's...that's different," June stammered, hiding a sheepish grin. "Y'all were a bunch of creamed corn hogs and I wanted to make sure I got my share. Plus, I was just a young 'un."

K.B. raised his eyebrows. "You were fifteen."

Colly blew out a frustrated breath. *"Will everybody please be quiet so I can watch my baseball game,"* he cried out, his five year-old voice frustrated and frantic and anxious as he squirmed in his seat, terrified he would miss the opening pitch.

K.B. winked at his daughter, then settled back against the pale, pastel cushions to enjoy the game. When the first pitch of the game was hit deep into left field, both he and Colly exploded into cheers.

Tucked away in a tangled mass of the natural world, surrounded by woods and dirt trails and hidden from the busier streets of bustling society, stood the two Standridge homes. Three acres of trees and undergrowth had been cleared out several decades ago for the houses, and with each generation the little oasis transformed from a landscape of mere grass and trees to seemingly endless rows of orange trees to a charming display of gardens and scenic flowerbeds that wrapped around the yard. It was a landscape that boasted of careful and skillful gardeners who cared deeply for the earth, one that the family took great pride in each and every day.

Stretched out in a hammock beneath the shade of an oak tree, Kariss Standridge opened the latest book she was reading and dived right into the story, an energizing tale about a blonde-haired, blue-eyed child adopted by a clan of cavemen, and her eventual journey to find her own people. Kariss longed to be in that world, a world where adventure and danger were just a step outside the cave, where literally anything was possible, other worlds where people weren't considered strange or weird to believe in dragons and demons and other creatures of fantasy. Her mother was finally letting her read books that were more adult, believing that her daughter was mature enough, even at the tender age of twelve, to move past the storylines of baby-sitting teens and goosebump-rendering encounters, and Kariss was thrilled that she now had permission to pull books off the shelves of June's bookcase, books that told the stories she loved most.

She tuned out the noise in the background—her two older brothers working on June's car with a neighbor, attempting to get the oil changed by the end of the weekend. Tony, her eldest sibling with a long, lanky build that mirrored that of her second-eldest brother, Christian, was hoping to be driven to the mall on Sunday. He wanted to hang out with a girl from school, but no one was supposed to know about it, as her brother was secretive about his friends and even more so about girls. Kariss only knew because she happened to be walking past his room when he was on the phone with the girl, but she hadn't said anything. It wasn't any of her business, and besides, she didn't really care. Her book was more interesting than her big brother's love life.

In fact, anything was more important than her big brother's love life, or anyone else's love life either.

Kariss shifted a bit when her cat, a fat and furry puff of orange, jumped up to settle down next to her. He padded around the hammock, meowing pathetically every time his feet fell through the holes as he tried to find a comfortable position. Finally, he stretched across Kariss' legs and instantly passed out, tail swishing slightly. Turning back to her book, Kariss prepared to enjoy the next few hours of reading.

Her peace was disturbed when Colly, still bouncing with triumphant energy from his team's win last night, came tearing out of the house with his baseball glove in hand. He ran straight for his yellow plastic basket of base-balls, grabbed as many as he could carry, and raced for the metal trashcan lid that served as home plate.

"Kariss!" he shouted, wide brown eyes hopeful. "I'll be Chipper Jones! You be an enemy pitcher!"

"I'm busy!" Kariss yelled back.

"Please?"

"No!"

"Please?"

"No!"

"Please?"

"No!"

"Pretty please with a cherry on top?"

"No, Colly!"

Colly stomped a foot and put his hands on his hips, his young face squinched together in a huff of annoyance. "But Kariss! Kare-Kare? Kare-Bear? My bestest sissy ever? The smartest, most prettiest girl in the whole wide world? Please, please, please, please—"

"*Colly!*" Kariss looked up from her book long enough to stare down her younger brother. "Jesus Christ, dude! I played with you for like four hours yesterday! Stop with the hissy fit!" Out of the corner of her eye she saw her grandfather walking down the dirt driveway that the two houses, her own and her grandparents', shared. "Ask Papa!"

K.B., who was coming back from his long walk to the mailbox, headed into the yard after hearing his name and passed his granddaughter. "Being lazy today, are we, Stinker?" he asked, using the nickname he'd given her after an unfortunate incident with a smelly diaper when she was a baby.

"I'm exercising my brain," she answered, and K.B laughed. His granddaughter may have a tendency to be lazy, but she always had a snappy comeback. Her sassy mouth often got her in trouble with her mother, her grandparents, and even her teachers, as Kariss was never one to back down from an argument. But she was a good kid, with a good heart and an even better head on her shoulders, so most people simply brushed off her attitude as eccentricity. K.B. had to admit, she could be a strange child at times. But he figured that was because she had the makings of an artist of some sort, and artists were supposed to be strange people with attitudes.

"Well, have at it." He patted her shoulder, then picked up a stray baseball, strutting past the orange tree, his last orange tree, that stood tall in the middle of the yard. It was a tree that held its own against weather, against Man, against time, a tree that somehow, if by magic or the wonder of Mother Nature, never lost its beauty. K.B. felt both small and protected in the shade of the orange tree, felt all his worries and burdens lift from his shoulders at the sight of the bright green leaves and the smell of fresh, if not sour, fruit. A pair of wrens had nested deep among the branches, and he could hear the chipper cheeps of baby birds calling for lunch as he prepared to pitch.

"Get ready for the heat, Doodle!"

Satisfied and pleased that someone was finally willing to play with him, Colly stuck his tongue out at his older sister and lifted the bat to his shoulder. It was too big for him, too heavy, but he loved it and refused to use what he called the "baby bat" that his mother bought for Christian when he played in Little League a few years ago.

But it wasn't the fact that Christian's old bat was for babies that made Colly prefer the wooden bat he currently held in his hands. That bat, that heavy, wooden bat with all its nicks and scars, once belonged to his father, and that was all the boy needed to know.

"Come on, you big ole' smelly pitcher! You ain't got nothin' on me!"

K.B. pretended to spit out a mouthful of chewing tobacco, then drew back his arm, but waited to release the ball. "Hey Doodle, how 'bout we go to the park this weekend, just the two of us?"

"Kay! Throw the ball!"

"Wanna learn some history?"

"No!"

"Want me to pitch?"

"Yeah!"

"Then you gotta learn some history!"

"Kay!"

"Good boy." Satisfied, K.B. threw the baseball.

Colly prepared for the pitch, kept his eye on the ball, and swung hard.

The ball sailed into the outfield, flying past Kariss and scaring the cat so fiercely that he frantically tumbled off the hammock in a blur of orange fur and darted beneath the protection of a rusted, upside-down canoe.

"And it's a home run!" Colly cheered as he ran around the azalea shrubs that marked the bases. "And get outta the outfield, butthead!" he shouted at his sister as he passed, expertly dodging her book when she flung it at him.

He proudly pounced onto home plate, pumping his fists in victory. "Colly Standridge wins it for the team! He's the champ! He's the bestest baseball player ever! He's—"

His brother's sudden, angry shout shocked Colly into silence. Both he and K.B. turned to fourteen year-old Tony and twelve year-old Christian, who were shoving and wrestling one another against the car. Tony's arms and chest were covered with oil, and he was yelling at Christian for his clumsiness.

K.B. simply ignored them, rather than attempt to calm the situation. June was already on the back porch, so he would let her deal with her children. Instead, he looked back at Colly. "Boy, your brothers are crazy. And I'm gonna let you in on a little secret. Your sister's a bit of a nut as well."

"I know," Colly replied with a cheesy smile. "I'm the normal one. So *there!*" he shouted in his brothers' direction, then set the wooden bat against his shoulder. "Now try again, enemy pitcher!"

Chapter 3
GHOSTS OF TIGER TRAIL

Wide-eyed and captivated, Colly gazed up in wonder at the towering, terrifying Tyrannosaurus Rex that stood fierce and slightly hidden among the giant oak trees. Its claws reached out for him, giant jaws the size of go-karts wide open, ready for a tasty breakfast. The fact that it was made of concrete did nothing to still the boy's fascination. He walked up to the dinosaur, reached out and tentatively touched its leg, then spun around and raced back to his grandfather as though terrified that the T-Rex was chasing him.

"He ain't gonna hurt you, Doodle," K.B. chuckled as Colly hid behind his leg, clutching the cuffs of his jeans. "He's a good dinosaur."

"How do you know?"

"How do I know? 'Cuz we're good buddies. We go way back, me and Mr. T-Rex."

"Where'd he come from?"

"Oh, from Jurassic Park, I reckon."

"Why's he here?"

It was a good question. They were standing in the middle of Sugar Plantations, an old sugar mill from the 1800s that had been renovated into a twelve-acre plot of botanical gardens and community festivities—weddings, birthday parties, and even town-wide picnics. Sugar Plantations had absolutely nothing to do with the dinosaurs, which had been placed there some twenty years ago simply for the public's enjoyment, but rather with the very history of Florida, and that was why the old man wished to spend the day at the park with his grandson.

Instead of answering the question right away, K.B. led Colly over to the remains of the old sugar mill. He leaned against the fence that separated them from the ruins. Twenty-five years ago, anyone with a fancy for history could walk around the mill, toss coins in the giant metal kettles surrounded by chipped bricks or down the well and make a wish, crawl around in the underground walkways. Behind the kettles was an old mechanical wheel that led to giant rollers that once crushed huge stalks of sugar cane. When June was a child, K.B. remembered taking her through the mill, hoisting his daughter up on his shoulders so she could peer down into the rusted kettles that she had liked to call "cereal bowls for giants." Together, they had spent many hours crawling their way around the underground lair, pretending they had found a secret passageway that spread beneath the entire city or the portal to another world of elves and ogres.

Now, the weather and time-beaten structure was a safety hazard, and city officials made the decision to separate the public from the crumbling bricks and rusted metal. Instead of being able to explore the ruins personally, visitors were forced to settle with reading the signs that detailed the mill and the Battle of Dunlawton that resulted in its destruction.

Being divided by the fence didn't take away any of the wonder for K.B. Whereas Colly couldn't keep his eyes off the dinosaurs, K.B. couldn't take his off the remains of the plantation. It was history. It was magic.

It was his job to make sure it was never forgotten.

"Doodle," he said suddenly, turning Colly's head so he was looking at the mills, "you know anything about this place?"

"It has a cool T-Rex!"

"I mean about the history of this place."

"Like where T-Rex came from?"

K.B. scoffed. "Forget about the doggone dinosaurs for a minute, Doodle." He waved a bothered hand in the direction of the T-Rex. "Doodle, this is a very sacred place."

Colly frowned. "Sacred?"

"Special."

"Oh. How come?"

K.B. pointed to one of the few remaining towers of deteriorating concrete. "This here sugar mill plantation was once the site of a very important battle, the Seminoles versus the United States. You know who the Seminoles are?"

Colly knew the answer to this one. "Native Americans, like us. But we're Cherokee."

"That's right." It was that simple fact that kept K.B. looking young despite his sixty decades on earth. The good genes of his Cherokee ancestors were sculpted in every one of his grandkids—the shape of the eyes, the high cheekbones, the thick dark hair, and most important of all, what he called 'Indian Toes.'

Indian Toes were the Standridge family phenomenon—the three toes following the big toe all longer than their predecessor. Picking things up off the floor, opening a door, pinching the legs of one another, all could be accomplished with Indian Toes. K.B. attributed his long toes to his Cherokee ancestors, who he figured needed Indian Toes to get about in their daily life. It was an attribute they all shared, so that no matter how many differences divided them, Indian Toes held them together.

Just like their history.

K.B. continued with his history lesson, one that he actually wasn't making up. "You see, Doodle, all this here land used to belong to the Native Americans. The Choctaws, the Creek, all different tribes. The U.S. government called them all Seminoles, because they thought the Indians were all wild and savage and didn't have individual tribes." K.B. pushed himself off the fence and put a hand on Colly's shoulder, taking him for a walk on the dirt path that led all the way around the gardens.

"The year, oh, about eighteen-twenty-three, the government moved the Seminoles onto a reservation, to get them out of the way. But after a few years, they started having problems."

"Like what?" Colly ran a finger down the dark green leaf of a banana tree as he passed.

"Well, for one, the hunting weren't real good on the reservation, so the Seminoles had to go outside their property to get food. But also, they had runaway slaves on their reservation and the Seminoles refused to give them back to the government."

"Slavery is bad," Colly put in. They rounded a corner to find a giant triceratops standing between two pine trees. He raced over to it and crawled on top of the horns. K.B. followed, amused.

"Slavery *is* bad," he agreed, leaning against the dinosaur. "And those problems led to the government's decision to move all the Indians to Mississippi. But the Seminoles didn't want to go."

" 'Cuz they'd have to leave home."

"That's right." Happy that his grandson was actually listening, K.B. playfully ran a hand through Colly's thick hair. "Then Andrew Jackson, the president of the United States, told all the Native Americans that if they didn't leave, that he'd send the troops in to *make* them leave."

"Did he send them?" Colly hung upside down from the horns.

"Well, after that, a group of settlers attacked a small band of Seminoles, which led to small fights here and there, and all the Chiefs were removed from their positions by the government. Since the Seminoles refused to leave, the U.S. army decided to go to war."

"To kill all the Indians?" Colly's voice was incredulous. "But they were here first."

"It ain't fair, you're right. But that didn't stop anything. There were a lot of battles, and lots of people died on both sides. Then, on January seventeenth, the Battle of Dunlawton was fought, right on this here land during the Second Seminole War." K.B. lowered himself to the ground and picked up a handful of dirt, letting it trail between his fingers.

"Eventually, the Seminoles fled south, to the Everglades. They were experts of the land, and so they hid there from the army. Finally, the government decided that if the Seminoles stayed in South Florida, then there could be peace."

"Was there?"

"Eventually," K.B. answered. "There were some more battles, some more deaths, and even a Third Seminole War, but finally, there was a bit of peace." Peace may not have been the right word, but it was what K.B. hoped the world would one day find, one that Colly would best understand in his young age. "The sugar mill was burned down during the Battle of Dunlawton, and was rebuilt about ten years later. After the civil war, it was abandoned completely. And now, these twelve acres are all that's left."

Colly hopped down from the triceratops and picked up a handful of dirt, mimicking his grandfather. "Did anyone die here?"

K.B. nodded. "Oh, you bet. Some during the battle, others throughout all three wars. Doodle, do you know why I'm telling you all this?"

Colly wiped off his hands, smudging dirt down his clean white shirt. "So I can tell Kariss and Tony and Christian and Momma?"

"No, Doodle, they already know. And now you know, because our history is very important. I've told you because you always have to know where you came from, who has walked exactly where you're walking right now. It makes you smarter, wiser, and if you know where you came from, then you can keep your family's history and traditions alive."

Together, the two continued down the path until they came to an oak tree over one hundred years old. K.B. reached out and touched it reverently, running his fingers over the bark, gazing up with respect and honor at the wide branches that reached far across the sky.

"Doodle, this here oak tree saw all the wars, all the battles, all the deaths. It felt the heat of gunfire, heard men shouting, and dying. This is a sacred tree, and this is sacred land." He put a hand on Colly's shoulder as the boy touched the tree as well. "Now, I'm gonna tell you the really interesting part."

"Doodle, has your momma ever told you about the Ghosts of Tiger Trail?"

She hadn't, and Colly was instantly nervous. He lived on Tiger Trail, a dirt road less than a mile away from Sugar Plantations, and he didn't know anything about ghosts living there too. In fact, he wasn't so sure he even wanted to know anything about ghosts being near his house.

"Not to worry, Dood." K.B. laughed at the horrified expression on Colly's face. "They won't hurt you. You see, sometimes, late at night, when the wind blows just right and the full moon is out, the ghosts of the men who fought, the women and children who died in battle, come out from the earth."

"What...what do they do?"

"They live, Doodle, just like they did over a hundred years ago. Sometimes you hear horses stampeding through the trees, sometimes you hear children laughing. Sometimes you can even smell campfires, and deer meat cooking for their suppers."

"Are they...evil?"

"Evil? Of course not, Doodle! You been playing too many video games." K.B. picked up his grandson and sat him on one of the low limbs of the oak tree. "Doodle, the ghosts are our ancestors. Even if we ain't Seminole, we're all connected. If you ask your Mema, she'll tell you that we're all Florida Crackers, every last one of us, even the Indians. But the ghosts, they know who we are, and they're darn proud to have us on their land. But we have to respect them, and in order to respect them, we have to know their history."

"Oh." Colly now understood the point of the history lesson. "So when can I hear the ghosts?"

Looking up to the sky, where puffs of white floated across the sun, K.B. thought back to the last time he'd heard the soothing sound of hooves stamping the earth. "Oh, I reckon you'll hear them soon. Your momma, your sister, even your brothers heard them after they learned all about our history."

He couldn't wait. Normally, Colly would be terrified at the thought of ghosts wandering around his backyard. But after learning all about them, learning how they were forced from their land, killed because they refused to leave their homes, Colly could appreciate the fact that the ghosts of Tiger Trail were able to come back home after they died.

The Ghosts of Tiger Trail. He liked the sound of that.

"Papa?"

"Yes, Doodle?"

"You think the ghosts are afraid of the T-Rex?"

Instead of answering, K.B. burst into laughter, thinking that he probably should have given the history lesson *before* entering Sugar Plantations. Concrete dinosaurs were just too much a distraction for his imaginative grandson.

But K.B had to admit, they were pretty cool.

<hr />

Colly's time to see the ghosts came sooner than he expected.

June walked into her son's bedroom to find him perched on the edge of a chair next to the window, staring up at the night sky where a bright, full moon gazed back at him. His fresh, young face was illuminated in the white light, so sweet and innocent that June couldn't help but stare. She admired his child-like wonder, his imagination and belief in the magic of the world. It was an imagination she hoped he would never lose.

Leaned against the doorway, she wondered why her five year-old son was so enamored with the celestial sight. "Colly?"

Startled, Colly spun around and nearly fell off his chair. "Hi, Momma."

"Whatcha doing?"

"Lookin' for the ghosts."

June stifled a laugh. She knew her father had given her youngest child the same history lesson he gave the other three, and even June herself when she was a little girl, so she wasn't surprised that Colly was now, a week later, still searching for the ghosts. He didn't give up easily, and would keep a careful and determined eye on the yard until he saw exactly what he wished to see.

"Any luck?" she asked, kneeling down next to Colly and peering out the window. The night was still, windless. Nothing moved, nothing made a sound, the only light coming from the pearly moon that shone down through the trees.

It was the perfect night for ghosts.

June took Colly by the hand, her voice in a whisper. "Come on, let's go outside."

Together they stepped out into the warm night, barefoot as they stood upon the cool grass that tickled the bottoms of their feet. June lifted a finger to her lips, and silently they lowered themselves to the ground. Enthralled, as well as a little frightened, Colly sat on his mother's outstretched legs and gripped her hand, staring out into the darkness. The trees were illuminated in a swath of white light, the orange tree glowing in the middle of the yard. The leaves and branches were motionless; not even the crickets dared to chirp. High above, the full moon shimmered against the black sky.

Suddenly, in the midst of silence, the earth began to thunder. Colly's eyes snapped to the woods, his mouth parting in shock as he tightened his hold on June's hand and drew back against her. The thunder came closer, the ground beneath him quivering as he realized what he was hearing. A herd of horses, invisible yet immensely real, raced past him, hooves pounding the dirt and leaves trembling on their branches. His hair blew back from his face as they passed, a cold breeze meant only for him. An aroma reached Colly's nostrils, the smell of campfires and deer meat cooking over a fire.

June put an arm around her son, feeling his tense shoulders relax as he closed his eyes and took in the sounds and smells of history. She closed her eyes with him, for despite the magic before their ears, the backyard was full of only trees, overgrown grass, and small gardens. Yet all around them, footsteps padded across the ground, women and children laughed, horse hooves struck the earth, with the scent of smoked meat wafting through the air.

The Ghosts of Tiger Trail were alive.

Over the next year, Colly got to know the ghosts well. His fear of the supernatural gradually faded the more he sat out on the back porch in the dark of night, eyes closed as he experienced the culture of his ancestors, and eventually he could sit outside by himself without being afraid. Sometimes his grandparents sat with him, sometimes Kariss or June, and together they imagined what life must have been like hundreds of years ago. Colly pictured deer-hide moccasins and tepees decorated with bears and wolves, and could practically taste the smoked meats. Though he never directly interacted with his invisible new friends, Colly found comfort and fun with them, even burying a pair of new shoes as an offering to one of the children he heard playing with a dog as a Christmas gift.

"So he can run fast like me," he'd explained to his mother as she helped him bury the gift. "And then maybe we can be friends. And he can haunt Tony and Christian and make them scared and we can laugh at them."

The longer he sat with the ghosts, the more he learned about history, and about nature, from his grandfather and mother. And the more he learned, the more he wanted to experience what his ancestors experienced. He wanted to build a fire, sleep outside, tell time by looking at the sun, all things his Papa knew just how to do. He wanted to be just like his grandpa, and teach everyone he knew all the exciting things he would learn.

K.B. vowed that in the coming summer, he would make sure his grandson spent as many moments as possible outside, learning everything he could ever possibly want to know. Perhaps that way, he hoped, he would be leaving behind something valuable for his family, something for them to pass on, something that would create a legacy.

Chapter 4
ALIEN BOY

The four Standridge children raced around one another atop the towering, seven-story high sand dune that marked the site of what Kariss called Luna Island, her favorite island of the Halifax River. June, K.B., and Joyce, K.B.'s wife and June's mother, remained at the shore, unpacking a picnic lunch of sandwiches and cookies from their small speedboat. A perfect breeze, carried across the river by gentle, salted waves, cooled their hot necks as the sun smiled down from a cloudless sky. Occasionally another boat would appear, the driver and passengers offering a friendly wave as they passed.

K.B. enjoyed the marvel of the water, of the beautiful island seemingly untouched by man. It would be awhile before he, or anyone else for that matter, would be able to spend another day on the river, as all weather stations were reporting a series of serious and frightening hurricanes to hit the east coast one right after another in the upcoming weeks and months.

For that reason, he insisted that they spend the day out in the sun, coasting atop the waves of their own personal paradise. It was here that K.B. felt most at home when not in the glorious shade of his beloved orange tree, and it was here that he revealed the magic of nature to his grandchildren.

He had promised Colly that he would teach him all about nature over the summer, and that was exactly what he had done. Nearly every day since the end of the school year involved some kind of activity in which the boy learned valuable skills, right down to building a campfire using only two sticks. Colly had soaked up the information with an eagerness that K.B. admired, and wished could be spread to his two oldest grandsons so that the four men of the family could take a camping trip in the parks at Okefenokee or a canoe ride down the river at Juniper Springs. Tony and Christian weren't interested in such things, however, preferring to play video games or hang out at the mall instead.

Today, though, K.B. would settle for simply having fun on the water, enjoying what was left of the summer rather than worrying about the survival skills of his two eldest grandchildren.

"Time to call the kids down?" he asked, glancing over the lunch preparations. The women had set out a wide blue blanket and lined it with juice boxes, bottles of water, packages of chewy chocolate-chip cookies, pre-made peanut butter and jelly sandwiches, paper plates, and napkins held down in the wind by a rock.

"Just about," Joyce replied as she unwrapped the sandwiches and shooed away a rogue fly. "Good luck finding them rascals up there."

Before their grandfather could climb his way up the massive mound of sand and vegetation, dodging the sand spurs that threatened to attack his ankles as he followed the narrow trail carved by frequent travel, Kariss and her brothers made sure to cover every inch of the surface, exploring and playing. Tony and Christian insisted on playing the 'cool' way, which meant playing without actually looking like they were having fun, but they chased Kariss and Colly around the sand nonetheless.

Hiding behind a tree, Kariss sat back against the bark and looked out across the river, brushing sand off her dark red bikini. This was her favorite spot on the river, perhaps her most favorite spot anywhere, tucked away from the rest of the world and protected by the grandeur of the island. From that tree, she could see all the way across the river to what was commonly known as Disappearing Island, a patch of sand that appeared and disappeared with the tide. Sometimes, when the tide was just right and the sand mixed with just the right amount of water, an area of what Kariss called river mud would form, and she and her brothers could slip and slide from one side of the island to the next. Such an adventure typically resulted in being coated in filth from head to toe, but the river was right at their feet, ready to clean them off. They ate lunch at Disappearing Island occasionally, but today it was packed with weekend visitors, many of whom brought their dogs that ran around and barked at each other while others were camping out with coolers of beer. Radios blared so loudly that the breeze carried the rhythms and tunes across the water to Kariss' ears, and she was thankful for the peaceful atmosphere of her island.

Luna Island was, in her opinion, much better than Disappearing Island, the best that the Halifax River had to offer. She called it Luna Island because of the soaring sand dune that rose up toward the sky from a flat shore that circled the base of the dune. Kariss liked to imagine alien spaceships landing on that dune, being guided through space by the bright green leaves of mangrove trees and mass of tangled branches that engulfed the majority of the shoreline, where fiddler crabs dominated the landscape. From the top of the dune, she felt like she could see the whole world. She could see the boaters out for a day on the water, the fishermen wading in one of the many narrow, marshy channels off the main river, and even the tourists looking out from their balconies in the condos that lined the beach only a few miles away.

Digging her bare toes in the sand, Kariss frowned when her feet touched something strange and rubbery. She dug down a couple inches, flinching when a thorn from a rogue vine bit her finger and brought forth a drop of blood. With a grimace, she sucked on her injured finger and continued her search, finding two round objects the size of gumballs. One was bright red, the other dark purple. Curious, she observed them for a moment, lifting them up to the sun, then picked them up and ran out from her secret spot to find her brothers.

The only one she found was Colly, who was throwing handfuls of sand into the wind, then spitting and gagging when the breeze carried the grains right back into his face.

"Look what I found," she said as she approached, holding out the hand with the discovery while observing the thorn injury on her finger on the other.

Colly peered down at the object, wiping sand from his eyes and pulling his baby blue bathing suit that was half a size too big higher up onto his waist. "What is it?"

"Dunno." Kariss lifted one of the foreign orbs up into the light of the sun again, squinting curiously as she looked through the violent film. An idea struck her, making her forget the pain from the thorn. "Maybe...maybe it's from an alien spaceship! And the aliens left these little ball things behind to turn us all into aliens!"

Colly took a step back, searching around the wide stretches of white sand as though expecting evil aliens to jump out from behind the dunes. "How'd they do that?"

"Dunno," Kariss said again. "Maybe it's like a mutant juice inside that turns us into aliens. Or maybe it has to be buried, like it was when I found it, so it can grow into a plant and when we eat the plant we turn into aliens."

Curiosity got the better of the boy. Despite his worry, he stood at his sister's shoulder and gingerly poked the strange object. "Maybe you should put it back."

"Maybe." Kariss held the purple orb between her pointer finger and thumb, wondering at the rubbery touch. It was squishy, yet resistant. She squeezed a little harder, and suddenly, the rubber casing burst and a stream of thick purple liquid squirted out, splashing across Colly's bare chest.

Colly gasped and clawed at the purple goo, fighting to get it off but only spreading it around instead. His skin and fingers began to take on a purple glint. "Oh *no*!" he wailed, jumping up and down. "Kariss! Get it off! *Hurry*!"

"I'm *trying*!" Kariss wiped at the gooey liquid, succeeding only in coating herself in purple too. "It's not coming off! It's getting all hard!"

"Kariss!" Colly's eyes began to water. "I'm turning into an *alien*! I'm *mutating*! *Mommy*!"

With a loud sob, Colly took off for the path that led down the dune. He raced past K.B., who had finally reached the top, shouting for his mother. June turned around in time to catch her son as he threw himself in her arms, crying about mutating into an alien boy as he hugged his mom and accidentally transferred some of the purple stickiness to her own bathing suit.

Up on the enormous dune, Kariss gazed down at the purple that covered her fingers. She wondered if Colly was right, if he was mutating, because if he was then maybe she was too. If they were going to mutate, then at least they had each other, and hopefully their momma would still love them. She pondered over the idea of being an alien for a moment, wondering if it would be fun or frightening, and part of her welcomed the adventure. Sailing the skies, exploring the universes, having magical powers...yes, it could be a life worth considering.

Out of nowhere, Tony and Christian appeared, stopping at her side.

"What's all the fuss?" Tony asked, having heard his little brother's frantic cries. Kariss held up the second orb that was still in tact and handed it to her brother.

"I don't know what it is. We think it's from the aliens, and now me and Colly are covered with alien juice."

Tony took the object and laughed. "Relax, Kariss. It's just a paintball."

"A paintball?"

"Yeah, like the ones people put into paintball guns and have fights with."

"Oh...so Colly's not gonna mutate into an alien?"

From behind, K.B. snorted. "If that boy's gonna mutate into anything, it's gonna be a Bluto." He put an arm around his granddaughter. "Come on, Stinker, let's go clean you up and tell Doodle he's still a good ole' fashioned human being."

They did just that, calming Colly down after a good five minutes of hugs and comfort. Then they all sat down for a long lunch, cleaned up every bit of their trash, and left Luna Island behind for the last trip of the season.

Chapter 5
CANDY ARMPITS

Rain poured down outside, cascading to the earth in thick cold sheets from even thicker black clouds, pounding against the windows as a harsh and unforgiving wind blew through the trees and ripped away weak, feeble limbs. The angry, howling storm had been raging on for three hours, thunder ripping through the gales and lightning flashing in blinding white streaks across the black sky. Only a few dozen miles away, the hurricane named Charles that fueled the storm was making its way to the Standridge front door.

Tucked away in the comfort of his bedroom, Colly felt anything but safe. His brothers were in the room with him doing homework and his sister was in the living room putting together a puzzle of polar bears with their mom. He didn't understand how they could be so calm when it felt like the entire house was going to blow away with the wind. Even Latheena was content lying on her bed next to the couch, chewing on a plastic bone while the lights flickered and walls shuddered each time the wind came hurling through the night.

When a loud clap of thunder rattled his windows, Colly grabbed his favorite blue Braves blanket, wrapped it around his head and shoulders, and ran as fast as he could to the living room, winding speedily around the hallway and sprinting through the kitchen. He crawled into his mother's lap, pushing her hands away from the puzzle so she could hug him instead.

"It'll be over soon, sweetie," June soothed, wrapping her arms around her son tightly. "It's just a little rain."

"Nuh-uh. It's the whole ocean outside."

June stifled a chuckle at Colly's whimper, picking up a puzzle piece and connecting it to a corner edge. "You're fine, honey. Nothing to be scared of."

"Come on over here, Doodle," K.B. called from the couch, where he sat with Joyce Standridge, better known as Mema to the grandkids. Joyce, her gray hair tucked away in curlers, occupied herself with a pair of knitting needles while her husband entertained their grandson with magic tricks. "I got something to show you."

Cautiously, Colly crawled down from June's lap and hurried across the room, his quick footsteps keeping pace with the falling rain pitter-pattering on the roof. He nestled himself between his grandparents. "Is it a trick?"

K.B. grinned, having known the distraction would work. His grandson was easily sidetracked, and was a sucker for slight-of-hand. As Colly stared up at him with eyes filled with fear from the storm and excitement for the impending show, K.B. sneaked a hand in and out of his pocket.

"Did you know," he asked while holding up an arm above his head, "that if you scratch your armpit just right, candy will come out?"

Joyce scoffed, shaking her head in amusement while Colly gasped. "Really? What kind of candy?"

"Well, let's find out!" K.B. reached in his shirt, stretching out the thin white cotton as he scratched his armpit, a determined look spread across his wrinkled face. Then, with elation and surprise, he held out his hand and un-curled his fingers to reveal three caramels and a mini chocolate bar.

"*Whoa!*" Colly shrieked, forgetting all about the storm as he grabbed at the candy. "I wanna do that!"

"Then start scratching."

Colly yanked off his shirt, carelessly throwing it over his shoulder while lifting his arm. He scratched at his armpit, lightly at first, then harder when nothing came out. "Papa, it's not working!"

"Then you ain't doing it right." K.B. scratched his own armpit and produced another handful of sugary-sweet candy. "See there? Ain't nothing to it."

Determined to find candy under his arm, Colly set to scratching. June watched from the table, amused by her father's crazy antics, but also not doing a thing to stop them. After all, she'd fallen for every single trick as a child, so it was only fair that her kids did too.

She wondered at what age Colly would start questioning his grandfa-ther's wild stories. Tony and Christian had never been interested in fantasy, which meant that tricks were wasted on them and K.B. had stopped trying with the two long before they were old enough to know better. Kariss was still young enough to fall for some of her grandfather's playful gags, and al-though she was clever enough to figure out the truth, her imagination rarely let her do so. If given the choice, she would believe the made-up things rather than reality, hiding the truth in the corner of her mind for as long as her inner child allowed her to do so.

Colly, like his sister, had a mind made for dreams and imagination, a mind that frequently created fantasy worlds with lava monsters and pirates, dragons and mermaids. He would believe nearly anything that anyone told him, and when he had something set in his mind as fact, it was impossible to tell him otherwise. The best any of them could do was to play along.

"Papa!" Colly's frustrated shout was muffled by the thunder overhead. "Mine doesn't work! My armpit's outta candy! It's broken!"

"Okay, okay," K.B. said with a laugh when his wife sent him a warning glance. "Let me try." He reached over and gently scratched Colly under the arm. "Let's see what we got here." He pulled back his hand and uncurled his fingers.

"*Whoa!*" Colly yelled again, eyes widening at the sight of the cherry lollipop.

"Just takes practice, Doodle," K.B. informed his grandson.

Colly grabbed the lollipop and ran over to his mother. "Look! Papa got it out!" June simply chuckled and shook her head. Candy Armpits was an old trick, going all the way back to when June was a child. It was a game that even her two oldest boys once fell for, though it only took once for them to figure it out.

She knew what would happen next. Colly would spent all night scratching his armpit, trying to find candy, until he'd scratched himself raw, and she'd have to tell him the truth. Ultimately, she doubted Colly would believe her, which meant she would be taking over the scratching until her son was all candied out. But she didn't mind. June loved being a part of her son's wild imagination.

Like June as a child, Colly couldn't believe the discovery. Never would have he believed that candy came out of armpits before he saw it with his own two eyes. And if candy-filled armpits were possible, then maybe there was a secret way to get candy out of *everything*.

His mind drifted momentarily to a land of fantasy where candy was hidden behind the surfaces of his surroundings. He suddenly found himself in school, where candy was secretly stashed away everywhere he looked. The desks at school seemed to be made of hard plastic, but as his friends sat hunched over their chairs, bored while listening to the math teacher drone on and on about multiplication, Colly scratched a fingernail down his own desk, furtively glancing from side to side when a peel of taffy came off in his hand. He gingerly placed a small piece on his tongue, then savored the sweet strawberry flavor that hit his tastebuds. Curiously he regarded his pencil, poking the sharp lead tip, wondering what might be hiding inside. He quietly broke off the tip, then nearly shrieked in delight when he pulled a string of black licorice out from the wooden casing. No discovery could top this one. He would be the king of candy, and all of his friends would come running to him when they learned of the treats he could provide for them.

Snapping back from his dreamland, Colly yanked off the wrapper off the lollipop, but before he could enjoy the tasty cherry flavor, a loud, glass-rattling crash from outside had him leaping back onto June's lap. He stayed there until his heart stopped racing, hiding his head from the storm, clutching his blanket and wishing that it would all be over with as soon as possible. This was the scariest thing he'd ever experienced in his six years, and that included the threat of ghost horses and being turned into an alien.

Instead of his wish for the storm's end being granted, the hurricane only raged on. Kariss, now too distracted to finish the puzzle by the pounding rain, blinding lightning, and hard wind that shook the walls of their house, crawled down from her chair and sat down on the floor next to her cat, which had been brought inside and was unhappily lying in his carrier.

"It's just a storm, Kariss," June ran a hand through her daughter's hair. "Just some rain and some wind. Nothing to be scared about."

The words had no sooner left her mouth when an oddly familiar yet uncanny sound echoed in the distance, a sound like a siren or a horn, a sound that screamed of danger. June listened carefully as the noise made its way closer and closer.

"Dad?" she asked K.B., who had already exchanged a worried glance with Joyce. "They wouldn't be running any trains tonight...would they?"

K.B. didn't need to answer. June knew what was coming.

"Let's go! *Now!*" June scooped up Colly while K.B. grabbed Kariss, who had a tight hold on the cat carrier, from the floor. "Tony! Christian!" June burst into the boys' room and yanked them into the hallway, the safest place in the house. There was no time to explain, no time to be gentle—only time to hide.

"What's going on?" Tony asked as Joyce thrust a blanket into his arms. His heart started to pound as the walls shook to the crash of a siren-like wind. "Mom? What are you doing?"

June pushed her kids into the hall closet, surrounding them with blankets and pillows. Outside, the howling wind pushed harder against the house as the sound of the train—the sound of the tornado—slammed right on top of them.

Kariss wrapped her arms around a crying Colly, who buried his face in her shoulder. "It's okay," she whispered, looking down at her puffy orange cat as he wailed and fought against the walls of his carrier. Next to her, Christian rocked back and forth, his head hiding beneath a pillow.

"Don't be scared, Mommy's right here!" June cried over the wind and thunder. She kissed her kids on the cheeks, fighting back fearful tears. She tended not to handle herself well in situations of panic, but she had to hold herself together for them. She willed herself to be strong, silently ordering her hands to stop shaking as she secured her children in the closet.

"June, you get in there with them!" Joyce ordered her daughter, pushing her from behind, lifting her eyes to the ceiling when the roof shuddered from the raging wind. "You get in there!"

"Mom—"

"Don't you argue with your mother!" K.B. yelled, shoving towels and blankets and pillows all around his grandkids. His voice shook, but his face was fierce and brave. "You get in there with your kids!"

June tried to protest, or at the very least tell them she would make room for everyone, but just as she opened her mouth, K.B. slammed one side of the closet shut. Joyce huddled in the opening of the other side while K.B. pressed his back to the closet door, protecting his daughter and grandchildren.

The tornados ripped through the backyard, tearing heavy branches from thick oak trees and smashing them against the house. A window shattered somewhere in the back. Metal groaned outside, something far too close for comfort collapsing. And then the sound of that oncoming train roared through the front yard just as a second threat slammed the screen door against the frame in terrifying crashes. Colly screamed; Kariss squeezed her eyes shut; June did her best to cover all four children with her own body as K.B. and Joyce covered June with theirs.

There was nothing any of them could do but wait.

❦

It wasn't until late morning that the sky cleared and the sun dared to shine. Colly and Kariss were curled up on their mother's bed, where June had moved them only a few hours before. Tony and Christian were tucked away in their rooms, refusing to admit that the hurricane and subsequent tornados had scared them. In the living room, K.B., Joyce, and June had gathered, standing at the back door and looking out at the devastation.

Their houses stood on a lot of almost two acres, land passed down from one generation to the next, and it seemed like every bit of their yard was covered with hurricane debris. They stepped outside, carefully making their way around broken tree branches, roof shingles, shards of glass, and other mangled bits of cars, homes, and personal belongings that June silently and selfishly prayed belonged to her neighbors and not her own family.

It had been a long night. They remained in the hallway, the kids secured in the closet, until dawn broke and the adults could be sure that the worst was over. By some stroke of luck or miracle, the tornados hadn't hit either of the houses directly, but they had certainly left their mark.

That mark was in the backyard, a wide, grass-stripped dirt path that wound its way around and through the trees, between the two houses, and across the neighbor's driveway. Any tree that stood in its path was torn from the earth, thick, mangled roots now reaching up toward the sky. A second path tore its way across the front yard and through the woods, leaving behind a pathway of fallen trees.

June looked up. Only hours before, lush green treetops canopied the yard. Now, there was nothing but white fluffy clouds. Most of the small plants, including June and Joyce's herb-and-flower garden, were destroyed beyond recognition, beyond saving. The palm trees along the back fence were bent, some leaning dangerously low over power lines, and although many of the large oak trees were still firmly grounded, their branches littered the grass, lying in murky puddles layered with leaves and trash. In the distance, they could see the remnants of homes, some with their roofs completely missing, some with broken windows and walls, and some that no longer stood at all. Frazzled and shaken families were starting to emerge, sirens wailing in the distance to help those in need.

"I don't...I don't even know where to start," June whispered. "This is...a disaster."

K.B. scanned the yard, a pit of sadness churning in his stomach over the devastation of his pride and joy. The back of his throat burned with the threat of tears. He loved this yard, this land, and worked hard to make it beautiful. Now, after one powerful storm, it was gone, and would take months to bring it back.

Then, as he looked out at what was left of his family's heritage, he broke out into a wide grin. "No, not a disaster," he said as he walked further into the backyard. June and Joyce followed his hopeful gaze.

There, in the middle of the yard, stood the family orange tree, the last of the Standridge orange groves. Aside from a few oranges that had fallen to the ground, it looked perfectly untouched.

"It may be sour, but I don't care!" K.B. cried happily as he headed for the tree. "It's still there! The Standridge family tradition continues!"

Chapter 6
GADUGI DAY

The wonderful, mesmerizing aromas of the Standridge family's favorite holiday wafted throughout K.B. and Joyce's home, enchanting every breath with the promise of a bountiful feast. The long kitchen counter was decorated with the colorful sight of cranberry slices, creamed corn, large bowls of mashed potatoes and gravy. Next to the potatoes was June's homemade macaroni and cheese, a family favorite. A heaping plate of turkey, next to an equally heaping plate of ham, sat gloriously between a steaming green bean casserole and a bright orange sweet potato pie, topped with marshmallows. Three pies—pumpkin, blueberry, and key lime—decorated one end of the counter, cornbread and stuffing on the other. Joyce set out a bowl of black olives and a tray of deviled eggs, then poured four glasses of punch and three glasses of sweet tea.

The Thanksgiving Day feast was complete.

Eagerly grasping a plate and craning his neck to see the contents of the counter, Colly bounced up and down to the beat of his mother's scolding to be patient. The grandkids were always served first, so Tony and Christian made their way down the counter, Kariss following behind. The boys loaded up with turkey and mac n' cheese, while Kariss spooned a mountain of mashed potatoes onto her plate and topped it with an ocean of gravy.

June took her youngest son's plate. "Whatcha eating?"

"Turkey!" Colly pointed, still bouncing. "Mashed taters and gravy! No, gross!" he shouted when June attempted to spoon a serving of green bean casserole.

"Well, excuse me," June scoffed, instead plucking a slice of cornbread from the basket and slabbing on a heap of butter. He may not eat green beans, but Colly would scarf down butter by the spoonfuls.

"Doubled eggs!"

From the other end of the counter, Kariss giggled. "You mean *deviled* eggs."

Colly made a face. "That's what I *said*."

"Nuh-uh, you said—"

"Okay, okay, let's not start something," June cut in, adding a deviled egg to the plate. "Let's go sit down, Colly." She led him to the table.

"No!" Colly protested when she set his plate down. "I wanna sit next to Papa!"

"I know, I know, I forgot." June moved the plate, K.B. giving her a wink. Every year June attempted to sit her son next to his sister or brother, and every year Colly demanded to be placed next to his grandpa. It had become their own sort of tradition, June forgetting and Colly quick to remind her.

Content, Colly settled down in his seat and picked up a fork. The smells and sights of Thanksgiving were almost too much for him to bear, but he waited as patiently as possible for everyone to get their food and take their seats.

"Doodle, how about you say Grace?" K.B. requested.

"Kay…Dear God, thank you for this food, and for my olives, and for the turkey, and…" Colly thought for a second, then grinned widely. "Grace! Amen."

"Amen," Joyce and June echoed.

"Amen, Brother Ben, shot a rooster, killed a hen," Kariss put in.

"Amen," K.B. said, chuckling over the old phrase he'd been saying since he was a boy, and had subsequently taught his grandchildren. "Let's eat!"

They wasted no time in doing just that. Colly scooped up a mouthful of turkey, dipped it in gravy, and stuffed the food in his mouth.

"Chew, Doodle," K.B. instructed, watching as the boy spread butter on his slice of cornbread then licked the spoon he was using clean. The old man grimaced. He didn't understand how anyone could eat butter plain. Just thinking about it made his insides crawl and his arteries clog themselves.

"While we're eating," Joyce said from the other end of the table, "we should all say what we're thankful for."

"Blutos!" Colly immediately answered around a mouthful of mashed potatoes.

Kariss scoffed. "Well I could have guessed that. I'm thankful for my books and my kitty."

"Well I could have guessed that," Christian mocked from his seat next to his sister. He stabbed a green bean with his fork as though trying to kill it, since he hated vegetables. "I guess I'm thankful that winter break is coming up and there's no school for a month."

"And I'm thankful for the fact that the hurricanes this year didn't destroy our homes."

"Definitely," June agreed with her mother. It had taken them two full months to clean up their yard, a cleanup that resulted in a wall of debris six feet tall and forty feet long that lined the edge of their property, and every day was filled with fear that another hurricane would strike. "I'm thankful for my four wonderful kids, who I love more and more each and every day. Tony?" Tony, sitting next to his mother, waved her off as he chewed a large helping of turkey. "Fine, you'll go last. Dad?"

K.B. didn't have to think about it. "I'm thankful for Gadugi Day."

"What's that?" Colly wasted no time in asking.

"It's—" K.B. cut off his explanation when he looked over to see that Colly had covered the tips of all ten fingers with black olives and was pretending to be a snarly monster. "Doodle, what's the rule about playing with your food?" When June snorted at his question, K.B. glanced at Kariss only to see that she too had olive-tipped fingers, and was sheepishly staring at her plate.

"Oh, never mind. Go ahead and play." K.B. reached over and ran a hand through Colly's hair, then continued his lesson, part fact, part fantasy. "*Gadugi* is a Cherokee tradition, Doodle. It's a celebration of working together. Sometimes it just means helping out someone who needs it, like community service. *Gadu* means bread, actually, and so *gadugi* means putting the bread together and working hard for your food." He couldn't help but pause to laugh when Kariss and Colly popped the olives in their mouths one by one until all ten were squeezed into their cheeks. "The people believe that they must work together to survive, and the ones who are lazy don't get anything, no bread, no celebration, not a single thing, because they don't deserve it." That part was true, but what came next was all K.B.'s.

"So Gadugi Day is when the working together begins. And you know how we do that?"

"How?" Kariss prompted around a mouthful of olives.

"By planting a new garden. The day after a big feast, a new crop must be planted, and you kids are all old enough now to work together."

Kariss and Colly grinned, excited. Even June had to admit that Gadugi Day sounded like fun, especially since they hadn't had a chance to replace the gardens that were destroyed by the hurricane only a few months ago. But judging by the sigh Tony let out, she guessed that not everyone was thrilled by the idea of planting a garden.

"I know what I'm thankful for," Tony put in, leaning back in his chair and staring at the painting of a lake surrounded by marshlands and a cabin with a wispy trail of smoke rising from the chimney that hung on the wall. "I'm thankful that in a couple years I'll be out of school and can move out of this place to California or Hawaii."

"California or Hawaii?"

"Yeah." Tony glanced over at his grandmother. "So I can hang out at the beach. Work odd jobs when I need money and surf and hang out the rest of the time."

"So you want to be beach bum?" K.B. surmised.

"Pretty much." What he didn't say was that he would be free from all the stories and fantasies that his family insisted on putting inside his head. He wanted to live in the real world, not a made-up one, and more, he wanted to live in a world with as little responsibility as possible.

"I don't want to be a surfer," Christian said with a shake of his head. "I'm gonna live at home and work in a dollar store so I can get all the cool stuff in there. Then marry a really rich girl and move into a big house with servants."

"Good luck with that," June declared.

"I'm never getting married," Kariss put in, making a face. "Boys. Gross."

"Well, maybe one day you'll change you're mind." June smiled across the table. "And you two?" she asked to Kariss and Colly. "What do you want to be?"

"A writer."

"A professional baseball player!"

June nodded, interested yet conflicted. No matter what they dreamed of, one thing remained perfectly clear—her kids were growing up. And when they grew up, they would leave. Maybe they wouldn't go far, maybe they wouldn't even leave Barton County, but nevertheless, she would not be waking up to a houseful of children. That, she feared more than anything.

Of course, a mother couldn't hold on to her children forever, so June made the silent promise that this Thanksgiving she would be thankful simply for her children. For their presence, for their company, for every time they made her laugh.

She would be thankful that no matter what they wanted to be when they grew up, they were all good kids at heart, and wanted the best for one another.

The next morning, K.B. struck true to his word and celebrated Gadugi Day. Everyone, Tony and Christian included, prepared for a day of gardening. They wore work pants, boots, thick gloves, and hats to keep the sun out of their eyes.

For the first part of the morning, the men went to work clearing a rectangular patch of grass for the garden while the women tended to the vegetables waiting to be planted, pulling rogue weeds from the pots and arranging them by species. The sky was clear, the sun bright and warm as a light breeze made its way through the Standridge backyard—the perfect weather for Gadugi Day.

When the grass was cleared, K.B. stretched, pressed a hand to his aching back, and admired the work he had just done with Tony and Christian, and even Colly, who was spending his time running back and forth between the garden and the plants.

"Looks good, boys," K.B. complimented. "Let's get to planting!"

He set out the stakes that marked the lines of vegetables, one for each. They would be planting broccoli, carrots, collards, and spinach. All around the vegetable garden, K.B. was planning on planting an array of snapdragons and pansies—his favorite flowers—as decoration.

Instructing the kids where to set the plants after spreading out fresh soil, K.B. picked up a trowel and carefully lowered himself to his knees on one end of the garden, starting with the carrots. Joyce and June took their places at the other with the collards. He taught the four grandkids how to properly plant the vegetables, supervising them as they set out to do so.

"Easy," he said to Kariss, scooping away a handful of dirt. "You don't want to plant it too deep. Make it even with the ground." He showed her the difference.

"Oh." Kariss fixed the carrot plant. "I get it."

"You know," K.B. said as he helped, "this is how our ancestors used to eat, by planting all their vegetables and hunting all their meat. None of that easy stuff, going to the store and having it all right there for them to pick from. They had to do it the hard way. The real way."

"Cool." Kariss planted the entire row of vegetables by herself, then decided to take a break. She wandered over to the cooler and grabbed a can of Coke, taking a seat on the porch next to her mother. They sat quietly for a moment, enjoying the shade.

"Something on your mind?" June asked, already knowing the answer. Kariss never sat quietly for long unless she wanted to say something.

Kariss kept her eyes, thoughtful and slightly worried, on the garden. "Momma, do you really think I can be a writer someday?"

"Of course."

"And that Colly can be a professional baseball player?"

"Of course. Why?"

Kariss shrugged. " 'Cuz...most people say it won't ever happen 'cuz it's too hard to get a job like that."

"Who said that?"

"People."

"People like who?"

Kariss shrugged again. "Kids at school, my teacher. Tony."

June set down her glass of tea and moved closer to her daughter. She took Kariss' chin in her hand and moved her head so that she could see the young girl's face. In that youthful face she saw hope, hope masked by doubt. "Kariss, you can be anything you want to be. If you want to be a writer, then you be a writer, and don't you let anyone ever tell you it's not possible. You got me?"

"Gotcha."

The wide smile on her daughter's face warmed June from the inside out, but one small part of her darkened, the part that would soon be lecturing her eldest son on the importance of keeping his siblings' dreams and aspirations and feelings unharmed by words of disbelief and scorn. "And you tell Tony that he better believe in you too, otherwise I'm gonna hang him up by his toenails."

"Good!" Kariss laughed. It was a familiar threat of her mother's, one that none of them took seriously, yet knew that when spoken, June meant serious business.

At her daughter's rare laugh, June gave her a hug and rose to her feet. "Come on, future best-selling author, let's go help your professional baseball player in-the-making brother plant some collards."

"Kay."

Satisfied with the efforts being shown and the work being completed, K.B. rested on his haunches and grinned beneath the sun. This was what he loved most of all, even more than his last remaining orange tree—spending time with his family and teaching them about nature, about heritage, and about life.

The Standridge kids didn't have any other male role model to teach them such things. When their father died in a car accident, June was seven months pregnant with Colly, and the family had come close to tearing itself apart. June's refusal to speak of her deceased husband meant the children had only themselves and one another to turn to for support, and never being able to reminisce about their father with the one person who knew him best devastated them. K.B. and Joyce had, therefore, been the ones to answer all the questions, and help make sense of the tragedy. K.B. had feared for his daughter, terrified that her heart would never heal. For awhile the kids rarely spoke, their grades suffered in school, and June was helpless to fix things.

It was Colly's birth that brought them back together. Even as a newborn, he was the spitting image of his father, with thick black hair, big eyes, and that same pouty upper lip that was his dad's trademark. The moment June held Colly in her arms was the moment she smiled her first true smile since the death of her husband. It was the moment that she, as well as everyone else, began to heal.

But that healing process came with a price. June made the decision to return to her maiden name of Standridge, as well as the kids' names, and to the day had difficulty talking about the man she still loved. For that reason, she remained single, and for that reason, there was no man to help raise the kids other than K.B.

As a grandfather, he did the best he could, but he chose to stay out of the bigger matters to let June handle them on her own. She was a great mother and loved her children more than she had the words to express, and taught them to be the best kinds of people possible. K.B. pitched in when needed, but he preferred to bring a little magic into their lives more often than rules. It was important to remember what it felt like to be a child, something their wise-cracking and oftentimes goofy father had known well, and K.B. was determined to keep that spark alive, even if that meant merely tossing a baseball or going to the park.

The importance of magic and imagination was something K.B. learned later in life. He knew what it was like to grow up without a father, but he also knew something his grandkids didn't—what it was like to be a father in a boy's body. At only the innocent age of eleven, K.B. was left caring for his six younger siblings. Never having known his father and his mother being sick most of the time, there was rarely enough food and money to go around. All they had was their orange grove, and profiting off the fruit meant constant hard work and dedication to keeping the trees healthy.

As the eldest child, K.B. grew up quickly, deciding that the best thing for him to do was to quit school at eleven and find a job to feed and clothe his family. In his spare time he helped his uncle in the groves, where he found his only escape from the burdens of his world, and frequently took baskets of oranges home to his brothers and sisters. He learned how to be a father when he was still a child, and worse, he learned how it felt to be a father who lost a child when his youngest brother died in his arms of pneumonia. During his childhood, there was no room for imagination. There was no freedom to enjoy childish games. There was only responsibility.

K.B. didn't want that for his grandchildren. He didn't want them to know the painful cramps of an empty stomach, or the chill of the winter night without a blanket, or the bitter longing for a parent's hug. He wanted them to stay young as long as they could, to dream of things bigger than them, to believe in magic.

He thought about that as he walked around the garden, assisting when needed. June and Joyce had their vegetables under control, though Colly bragged about the great work and perfectly even rows being crafted solely by his own two hands. Kariss and the older boys were a different story.

"Papa!" Kariss complained, throwing down an empty plant container. "It don't look right!"

"It's crooked," Tony agreed. "How'd Mom and Mema get theirs so straight?"

"Many years of practice," K.B. answered. "But it don't matter what it looks like. What matters is that everything's planted, and soon we'll have a whole garden of fresh veggies to chomp on."

Christian grimaced. "Gross. Vegetables."

With a laugh, K.B. put an arm around his grandson. Together, the Standridge kin admired the garden they had planted as a team.

Gadugi Day was a success.

Chapter 7
Annual Sour Orange Derby

Rod stopped writing a few moments after Kariss stopped talking. He looked up to see her grinning over the antics taking place on the field. The pitcher was arguing with the umpire over which chunk of orange, of the many that scattered the field, had actually crossed one of the several white lines that marked out the points for each specific distance traveled.

Judging by her amused expression, as well as the chuckles coming from the crowd, Rod guessed that such an argument was a regular occurrence during the game, and this woman, with her grass-stained Team Colly T-shirt and her bright green eyes squinting despite the shade from the bill of her baseball cap, loved every minute of the chaos. He didn't quite understand the thrill, as the argument seemed rather trivial, but then again, nothing about the entire game made sense to him.

"How exactly does the point system work?"

Kariss pulled a small blue book out from her back pocket and handed it over to the reporter. "We had this printed up the third or fourth season." She waited a few moments while he flipped through it. He scanned the first few pages, which explained the rules, the teams, and the Derby founders. Flipping to the last couple pages, he found acknowledgements to all the people and companies who donated time or money to the event, and was slightly surprised by the high number. It seemed like the entire community, and even those surrounding it, supported the Derby.

"We have the same basic structure as a baseball team," Karris interrupted his reading, "but mainly just for the sake of having a team, since we don't really need anyone but a pitcher on the field and a couple of umps in the outfield for scoring. The field itself is marked, but I'll show you that later. The point is, you hit the orange when it's pitched to you."

Before replying, Rod watched a batter do just that. "Sounds simple enough."

Kariss turned her inquisitive eyes to the reporter, one brow slightly lifted. "Is it, Yankee?"

He felt he had, once again, struck a nerve. Being called a Yankee by the woman with a southern twang in her voice most likely meant that he was yet to be on her good side, and she was clearly still holding a bit of a grudge from his earlier comment. It was just as well, for he had no interest in her, or her game either. He was there simply because it was his job, not because he wanted to make friends.

"Is it not?"

"Tell me something, Mr. Jenkins." She lifted a brow. "Have *you* ever hit an orange with a baseball bat?"

He thought about the question, searching his memory. Hitting an orange with a baseball bat was something a child would do, and when he was younger, his days had been spent on the computer, learning the ins and outs of different programs, researching world events, whatever happened to catch his fancy at the time. Sports, video games, playing outside with friends, such things he had never done as a kid. Hitting an orange with a baseball bat had never been a thrill or even a passing interest, and even now, he couldn't imagine finding that inner child long enough to do such a thing. Yet it didn't surprise him in the least that Kariss found enjoyment in the game. She seemed suited for the fields covered with splattered oranges. Everyone there seemed suited for the game. He wasn't sure what that said about her, or about him for that matter.

"No...I can't say that I have."

"Well then," she settled back against the bleachers and pointed to the field, "take a lesson from the best."

"You can't just hit the orange," she began. "You hit it too hard and it bursts into tiny pieces, and you don't get any points. You hit it too soft, it don't go anywhere. You have to hit it just hard enough to get the chunks out into the field, but light enough so that it don't completely explode all over the place. It's harder than it sounds. Requires strategic thinking." She tapped her temple with a smirk. "Now, the further a chunk of orange flies, the more points you get."

"And how many points are possible?"

Kariss took the book from Rod and opened it to a diagram. "Five points from home plate to the pitcher's mound. Ten from the pitcher's mound to the edge of the infield. The outfield jumps up to twenty, but it goes up three points every foot from the edge of the outfield to the fence."

"Sounds simple enough."

Again, Kariss regarded the Yankee with steely green eyes. "No, not so simple at all," she replied. "Sure, you get the points, but only when a chunk of orange lands in that point zone. *But,* the size of the chunk also depends on how many additional points that hit earns. Points for chunk size are determined by length." She turned the page of the book and showed Rod another diagram.

Rod jotted down a few notes. "So...what happens if a batter hits the orange and it doesn't burst?"

Kariss grinned. "Jackpot."

"Meaning?"

"Meaning, if it doesn't go past the pitcher's mound, one hundred points. Anywhere in the outfield, one-fifty. But only if there are no cracks or breaks anywhere in the orange, which is harder than it sounds."

"Exciting," Rod commented dryly, getting a frown out of Kariss. "So how did all this get started? The game, the league, the point system?"

Kariss sat forward, watching her older brother Tony as he walked up to bat. He strutted up to home plate with a swagger perfected after many years of playful arrogance and propped the bat up on his shoulder, facing the crowd and placing the batting cap atop his head with a swift and smooth move that sent everyone in a round of loud, approving applause. It never failed to amaze her that throughout his childhood and during adulthood he had managed to maintain his thin, lanky frame and shaggy hair that their mother still, to the day, insisted he cut. In fact, June was known to make special phone calls to her son simply to remind him to make an appointment at the hair salon.

But regardless of his hairstyle, her brother was the perfect combination of Cherokee on their mother's side and Italian from their father's. Tall, handsome, with a sharp and accented bone structure that defied his real age, Kariss wasn't the least bit surprised that he never settled down with just one woman. Even as a teenager he'd enjoyed dating as many girls as possible, and not much of that had changed from one birthday to the next.

However, many years had passed since the first Sour Orange Derby that started in their backyard, and many things had changed for Kariss. She had a career now, a very soon-to-be husband despite her childhood claims of never marrying, her own home, and at twenty-nine, she was even starting to like sports. The one thing that hadn't changed was her love for the Standridge family tradition, and for her family as a whole.

Instead of answering the reporter right away, she watched as the pitcher picked up a sour orange and prepared to throw, inciting a round of playful taunts from the bleachers. But rather than cheering her brother on, Kariss kept her eyes on the aged wooden bat he held in his hands. She observed it propped up on his shoulder, watched it swing through the air, connect with the orange.

It was a great hit.

As he came off the field to a roar of a near-standing ovation, Tony scanned the
bleachers, pointing at his sister with the bat. "Yo Kariss! Get those skinny arms up here to the plate!"

Kariss waved at her older brother while the people sitting around her cheered in anticipation of her turn at bat. "Be right there!" She turned back to Rod. "Gotta go, Yank."

Kariss hopped down from the bleachers and jogged over to the field, ready and eager to bat. Her teammates slapped her on the back as she trotted through the dugout, put on a batting cap—purely a visual effect—and grabbed the wooden bat that only she, her brothers, and her mother were ever allowed to use. She was full of confidence as she walked up to home plate, eyeing the pitcher with a teasing glower. The pitcher, Erica Lane, a short, auburn-haired woman with a squeaky voice and cheery disposition Kariss had known for more than fifteen years, plucked up an orange from the ground.

"Prepare for a strike-out, Standridge!"

"Strike you right in that big, fat mouth!" Kariss yelled back. The crowd laughed at the common display of camaraderie, taking sides for and against the players, and yelling out mocking insults accordingly. "Let's see what you got, you big ole' smelly pitcher!"

Erica eyed the batter, pretending to be scrutinizing every move Kariss made, and tossed the orange. Immediately she ducked for cover. Kariss Standridge was a member of the SOD Squad, otherwise known as Sodders—the best of the best Sour Orange Derby players. The Sodders could hit any orange on the first pitch, and could decide on the spot how many points they wanted to score, and then score them. Most had been playing the Derby since the beginning, though a few were players who had simply caught on quickly or were taken under the wing of one of the founders. There were thirteen members of the SOD Squad, and they were always on the hunt for more.

As predicted, Kariss connected with the orange, the perfect hit. Not too hard, not too soft, with just enough force to launch the orange, without bursting it, into the one hundred fifty point zone. The crowd erupted into cheers and Kariss took a bow, laughing at her own boastfulness.

"You were saying, enemy pitcher?" Kariss haughtily mocked her friend. "Shall we go for two-out-of-two?"

"Like I have any choice?" As the rules stated, each batter had two hits, two chances to put some points up on the board. Erica picked up another orange and strategically tossed it to her opponent—harder than the last pitch, lower than the last pitch, with a little bit of a spin—in hopes that she would throw Kariss off her game.

Kariss had less than a second to comprehend and analyze the fake-out pitch, and it wasn't hard to do. She knew Erica's style, just as she knew that her team was so far ahead that there was little doubt they wouldn't win.

"Why not have a little fun?" she shouted as the orange came her way, and swung as hard as she possibly could.

Bits of orange chunks flew in all directions, juice splattering over Kariss and everyone sitting in lawn chairs behind the home-plate fence. Only one chunk of orange peel made it to the ten-point line, but neither Kariss nor the rest of Team Colly cared.

Sometimes, bursting an orange into a thousand tiny pieces was the best part of the game.

As she came off home plate, Rod watched as the man she had pointed out as one of her brothers, a man who looked exactly like an older, male version of Kariss, grabbed her up in a celebratory hug. Together, they ridiculed the other team before taking their place in the outfield. Rod kept his eyes on her, slightly amused by the fact that once she hit second base, she completely spaced out. Her thoughts went up to the clouds, a dreamy expression crossing her face as she imagined things he could only guess at. It wasn't until one of her teammates shouted at her to "look alive" that she turned her attention back to the batter.

After the inning was over, Kariss began to make her way back to Rod. As soon as she stepped out of the dugout, a small group of kids raced up to her, pens and paper in hand as they begged for an autograph. She signed without hesitation, and the children thanked her before racing up to Tony and Christian Standridge and begging for their signatures as well. A couple little girls timidly approached and asked to have their pictures taken with Kariss. Both had their hair in French braids, which told the reporter that the braid was another tradition that came along with the Sour Orange Derby. Rod watched it all with a hesitant smile. The woman was clearly a favorite, and her ability to shift from professional to storyteller to ballplayer to dreamer and back again was intriguing.

"You wanna go up to bat?" Kariss asked as she took a seat on the bleachers. She picked at bits of orange goop in her hair.

Rod could smell the bitter aroma of sour oranges, and the thought of getting his nice clothes covered with the stench was not the least bit appealing. "Go up to bat? I'm not on a team."

"Well, each team has two honorary positions." Kariss leaned back and kept her eyes on the game going on at the field next to her team's. She was eager to know which team she would be playing in the championship game. "When all this started getting going, there were always people who wanted to join in, and since we didn't want to always be turning people away, we came up with the honorary positions. For one entire game or only one play, it's all up to them, the person can join in without being obligated to join a team. Honorary players." She turned her head and eyed him for a moment. "You up for it, Yankee?"

"Oh…" The idea of taking part in a sports game was not one Rod had entertained prior to arriving in Barton County, and he certainly didn't wish to entertain it now. Watching was one thing, participating was a whole different issue. He adjusted his glasses, patted his slicked-back, gelled hair, and shook his head. "I'm not really the ball-playing type."

"And I am?" Kariss scoffed. "I spend the majority of my time inside, typing on a computer. Hell, I'm one of the laziest damn people you'll ever meet when it comes to this kind of physical activity. That woman over there," she pointed to a woman up to bat, "is a fashion designer. She hates getting all dirty and washes her hands 'bout forty times a day. That guy is an accountant. He didn't even know how to properly hold a bat until he joined the Derby. We ain't ballplayers either. We're Sour Orange Derby players."

"I didn't mean any offense by it." Rod held up a hand. "I only meant that it's probably best if I kept business and pleasure separate, for the sake of the article."

"I'd think that it'd be best to mix the two together, for the sake of the article. Get the feel of the game."

"Maybe later." Rod tapped his pen against the notepad in hand. "So, how—"

"Hey slugger, how about a snack?"

Rod glanced over as a man approached, tall and broad-shouldered with piercing brown eyes, strongly sculpted cheekbones and facial features, a day's worth of scruff, and short dark hair covered by a blue-and-orange baseball cap that read *Team Colly* across the front. His pants were torn at both knees, the soles of his shoes well worn, and his muscular physique suggesting a day job of hard, manual labor. In one hand he held two hot dogs, in the other a can of Coke.

"Refreshments for the champ," the man said as he handed over the food.

Kariss eagerly accepted. "My fiancé, Sam," she informed Rod before taking a bite. "He's on my team too."

"Really." Rod jotted down another note and made room for the man as he took a seat next to his fiancée. "So, how did you get started in the Derby?"

"Me?" Sam put a muscled arm around Kariss. "Oh, I blame this woman right here. When we met, she didn't give me a choice. I had to be on the team."

Kariss huffed sarcastically. "Hey, it's a family game, and you're a part of the family."

"A family where all the guys get bossed around."

"That's how it goes."

"Yeah, well, just you wait 'till the shoe is on the other foot."

"What makes you think you got any shoes to begin with?"

"You mean to tell me you'd make me walk around barefoot and get my pretty feet all scratched up? You women are damn crazy."

"Someone's gotta toughen you whiny boys up."

"Yeah, yeah." Sam playfully poked Kariss in the side. She laughed and squirmed in her seat, sloshing Coke over both herself and her fiancé.

Rod waited as the two engaged in a brief yet endearing tickling match, and while doing so, took the time to carefully observe them. The couple was happily in love, and cared for one another deeply. Though they were yet to be married, it was apparent that they were already joined as one, inseparable from each other and their family. He wondered how long they had been together, for along with their playful arguing they seemed completely comfortable with one another, and for a woman who insisted as a child that boys were gross and she was never getting married, she appeared entirely cheerful about her prospective husband. The reporter admired their relationship, never having had such a close and tender connection as the one displayed before him, and in his admiration he realized that there were, indeed, many layers to the Standridge family. He merely had to be open and willing enough to explore them.

"So how did the team get started?" Rod couldn't wait any longer to ask the question he'd been trying to get Kariss to answer all along.

After a moment, Kariss settled down and thought about it while Sam gathered up their garbage and headed down the bleachers to the trashcan. "You know, I'd really like to know first how you even heard about the Derby. I mean, as far as I knew, the Sour Orange Derby didn't go any farther than Barton County. You're out in New York. How'd you hear about us?"

"Word of mouth," Rod answered. "A friend of my boss has a cousin who has a friend who plays, or something along those lines. My boss thought it sounded interesting, looked it up, saw your website informing the players and basically all of Barton County and the surrounding areas about the game, and sent me here. The friend that plays and the cousin are thinking of starting up a game in Albany where he lives because they enjoy it so much. They've already talked to the city officials and everything, said they had your approval."

Kariss vaguely remembered someone planning such a thing in New York. "I always encourage new leagues. Spread the tradition, you know. People email us and talk about starting up their own leagues in their own cities all the time. Most end up back here next year. I've never heard of anyone actually going through with their plans to start up a new league."

"Nothing like playing with the original Sodders," Sam put in as he came back up the bleachers.

"I'm sure," Rod agreed. He didn't truly understand the thrill, but then, he didn't truly understand sports either. He'd been part of many debates with his paper's sports columnist about the uselessness of sports and the ridiculous amounts of money players were paid each year. "In any case, this league seems to be gaining some ground, and my boss wants our paper to be the first to tell the story of the Sour Orange Derby."

"Huh. I never would have thought it would get this much attention," Kariss replied around a mouthful of chips. She swallowed after a long moment of chewing. "But hey, that's cool...Still don't explain why you're here."

"Meaning what, exactly?"

"Meaning anyone can take one look at you and tell you're not a sports reporter. Fancy pants, button-down shirt, expensive shoes, perfectly manicured hands, not a suntan on you. Something tells me you're more likely to write about business affairs and bankruptcies rather than baseball games."

"...Very insightful."

"I told you, we ain't simple people. So why did your boss send you?"

"This article is a trial article for a possible promotion, so—"

"So if you do a good job, write a great article, you get a promotion, make lots of money, maybe get your own regular column. Well, for someone who is hoping for a promotion, you sure do a good job of not getting your story."

Rod frowned, unsure of where Kariss was going with her interrogation. "And how do I get my story?"

"How? By listening, of course. By asking the right questions. But more importantly, by thinking like a Standridge. Think you can do that?"

"I think so."

"Good."

Rod waited until she had taken a few gulps of soda. "So, how and where did all this begin?"

"How?" Kariss rested her head against Sam's shoulder. "Where? The Standridge

backyard, of course."

Chapter 8

THE HUNTRESS

Christian and Tony anxiously set up the target.

In the last light of the day, a chilly afternoon breeze worked its way inland from the choppy Atlantic Ocean only ten miles to the east. Before the sun could set, Tony dragged a large, orange construction cone onto the home-plate trashcan lid. Christian carefully balanced an empty water bottle upside-down on top of the cone, while Colly insisted from the background that his brothers hurry up so they could start the game. Then they ran back to the patio, where all the Standridge family members, minus Kariss, who was finishing her homework inside, were waiting.

K.B. held the BB gun that Christian got for his birthday from one of his uncles, having already loaded it while the boys were setting up the target. Joyce and June sat in the background, not wanting anything to do with the actual shooting, but interested in seeing how skilled the kids were.

"I'm betting Tony blows them all away."

"Not a chance, Ma. With all them video games Christian plays, some of that shooting ability must have worn off."

"Hey! What about me?"

"I'm sure you're a perfect shot too," June answered Colly with a laugh as the boy huffed and put his hands on his hips.

"Well, *duh.*"

"Alright, boys, let's see who the best shot is."

"Gonna be me," Christian bragged, taking the gun. It was his new BB gun, so he got the first turn. He stood on the edge of the concrete where it met the grass, pulled back the cuffs of his black jacket, and lifted the gun. It settled comfortably against his shoulder, and he felt like a real hunter. He aimed carefully, then squeezed the trigger. The BB didn't go anywhere near the water bottle, instead disappearing into the woods. His brothers snickered only to be shushed by their mother.

"My turn." Tony took the gun, aimed, and missed. The sound of leaves rustling as they were knocked to the ground met their ears as the BB traveled through the dense undergrowth.

"Ha! I'll do it! I'm a perfect shot!" Colly grabbed the BB gun from his brother, finding that it was heavier than he'd imagined it to be. He couldn't lift it high enough to get a good aim, the stock of the gun slipping from his shoulder, and naturally, he missed the target.

The boys took their turns one at a time, and when a half-hour had passed, the water bottle was still standing. Christian glared at the plastic container as though he believed that it still stood merely to mock him. Kariss came out of the house to find her brothers frustrated and slightly embarrassed. She wrapped a blanket with an American Indian design around her body and frowned when Christian stomped his foot.

"What's the deal?"

"Seems we ain't a hunting family," K.B. replied, amused as he leaned back in his chair. The boys could brag all day long about how great and strong they were, but obviously they couldn't back up their boasts.

"Huh." Kariss looked out at the target. "Doesn't seem so hard."

All eyes turned to Kariss. "Really," Tony replied sarcastically, holding out the gun. "Let's see what you got, hotshot."

Kariss hesitated. Never in her life had she ever held a BB gun, let alone shot one. Her firearm experience ended with water guns on the beach, and even then she rarely tried hard enough to actually hit her mark. Letting the blanket fall to the patio floor and bracing herself against the cold, she reached out and took the BB gun, lifting it to her shoulder as she'd seen people do in movies. It seemed like a natural fit.

Sucking in a deep breath, she peered through the scope, concentrating on the clear plastic. Her eyes zoned in on the target like a predator stalking its prey, and with a steady index finger, she pressed the trigger.

"You gotta be *kidding* me!" Tony shouted in disgust and Christian let out a frustrated yell when a loud pop sounded and the water bottle toppled to the ground.

Kariss lowered the gun and grinned. She didn't know how she did it, but somehow, she made the first hit.

"How'd you do that?" Colly asked, wondering if his big sister could give him shooting lessons.

"Beginner's luck. Bet you can't do it again," Christian challenged, determined not to let his younger sister show him up, especially using his own birthday present. "I'll set it up again." He ran over to the target and placed the water bottle, which now had a hole in its center, back on top of the cone. "Do it again," he commanded as he came back to his sister's side.

Kariss let out a deep breath and lifted the gun back up to her shoulder. She aimed, trained her eye on the target, and fired. The bottle tumbled to the ground to the sound of Tony and Christian's amazed shouts of disbelief and jealousy.

"What?" Christian yelled, stomping a foot. "Come *on*! She's a *girl*!"

"Yes!" K.B. cheered, lifting his hands as though he had just won a great victory. "The South shall rise again!"

"How do you figure, Dad?"

"How do I figure? I figure we just witnessed a miracle here! Our little Stinker here, who would rather spend all her time inside typing away on the computer, has just shown herself to be a natural-born soldier! Who'd a ever thought it?"

"How'd you do that?" Colly asked again, excited rather than jealous that his big sister was a good shot. Maybe she could teach him how to be one too.

"I'm...I'm not sure," Kariss answered. "I just did it."

"I'll tell you how," K.B. cut in. "There's only one explanation. Boys, your sister here is a huntress."

"A what?" Tony and Christian asked in unison.

"A huntress, in an old life." K.B. took the BB gun. "In Stinker's past life, she lived with our ancestors, and was one of the greatest female warriors the world had ever known."

"Really?" Kariss grinned again and squared her shoulders. "Cool."

"No way," Christian disagreed. "You're too lazy to be a hunter. Even Papa thinks you're lazy."

"In this life, maybe, but that's because she gets to rest after an old life of hard work," K.B. countered, holding up a hand. "You boys should feel lucky to have a sister who has huntress blood pumping through her veins. You never know when you'll need her to save your butts. Especially since you're all lousy shots."

"Oh, Dad," June said from behind, a smile on her face. "You and your stories."

K.B. lifted a brow. "Stories? This is the truth, Curly, and you better believe it. I can even prove it."

"How?"

"Like this." K.B. handed the BB gun back to Kariss and pointed across the yard. "Stinker, take a shot at that birdfeeder over there."

Kariss followed the direction of his finger. "Way over there? On the tree? I can barely see that thing."

"Try it anyway."

"Fine." In the dim light of the lowering sun, Kariss peered across the yard at a blue feeder hanging from a limb of an oak tree and took the shot.

"See?" K.B. crossed his arms proudly when the birdfeeder fell to the ground and put a hand on his granddaughter's shoulder. Kariss stared across the yard at the fallen feeder in amazement. "Like I said, a huntress."

"A huntress who owes me a new birdfeeder," June said, smirking back at her daughter when Kariss stuck her tongue out at her mother.

"What was I?"

"You?" K.B. pulled Colly up onto his lap. "You, Doodle, were an ancient gladiator. You spent your days fighting tigers and battling your enemies in the Coliseum in Ancient Rome. You were a warrior, just like your sister. And one day, when your time here on earth is up, you'll get to return to your old life with all the new knowledge and experience you learned and be the best gladiator the world has ever known."

"Awesome," Colly breathed.

Tony crossed his arms. "Okay then, what was I?"

"You were a turkey!"   Everyone laughed at Colly's outburst, even Tony.

"No, Doodle, Stretch weren't a turkey." K.B. ruffled Colly's hair.

"Was too!" Colly shouted with a grin. "Turkey, turkey, turkey!" He pranced around his big brother, poking him in the stomach. "Gobble, gobble! And you're a opossum!" He pointed at Christian. "Me and Kariss are warriors! We eat you for breakfast! Get 'em!"

Each picking up a stick, Colly and Kariss chased their brothers around the yard. The four giggled and rolled around on the grass, Tony mockingly squealing when Colly pretended to catch and tie him up. On the patio, the adults watched joyfully, laughing at the fantastic display of sibling companionship.

June's eyes narrowed as she watched Kariss. The girl raced around the yard with more speed and agility than June had known was possible from her. Her long hair flowed across her back, thick brown tresses being picked up in the wind as she ran up to Colly, and together they hatched a plan as warriors to hunt their older brothers. The fact that she was brandishing a long, pointed stick only enhanced her fierce image.

"You know," June observed, "she really does look like a huntress."

K.B. held out his hands with a grin. "Hey?" he asked innocently. "Would I lie?"

Chapter 9
ACORN CITY

Only a few days after their grandfather declared his sister a huntress, Colly sat hidden behind an oak tree, clutching a large bucket filled to the brim with acorns, waiting for the perfect moment to prove his worth as an ancient gladiator. While he waited, he ran his hands through the acorns, loving the sound they made when they rustled up against one another. Acorn season was his favorite. He had six more bucketfuls in the garage, collected throughout the past two years, saved for just the right occasion.

Leaning against the hard bark, shifting to find a comfortable position, Colly lifted his eyes to the treetops and watched the birds fly from one tree to the next and the squirrels leap from branch to branch, chipper and energetic in the early afternoon air. They didn't seem to mind the chilly breeze, but Colly did. He hadn't put up a single fight when his mother insisted that he wear a jacket outside, and usually, he hated jackets and sweaters. They made it harder to play baseball.

While he waited, the boy carefully planned his attack. He was supposed to be at his friend Jess's house, but had to stay home when Jess's mom called to say he was sick, so the people who thought he was gone for the day were sure to be surprised. Only Kariss knew of his plan, and since she promised not to say anything, she was safe from attack. Besides, Colly liked his big sister a little more than his big brothers because she played baseball with him more often and liked to make up crazy stories like their Papa, so Colly didn't mind having one less victim. He decided that he would throw an entire handful first, then, once his victim was caught off-guard, he would throw acorn rockets everywhere he saw skin. Everywhere but the face, since that was June's rule. The face was off-limits, and Colly could understand why. He wouldn't want to be hit in the eye with one of his acorn bullets either.

"Watcha doing, there, Doodle?"

Colly jumped, startled by the interruption, then moved so that his body was guarding the bucket. He was waiting for Tony to come home from the movies, but didn't want to admit that to his grandfather for fear of being told to go back inside. "Nothin'."

With a grin, K.B. held out a handful of acorns. "Want some more ammo?"

Colly relaxed and K.B. tossed them into the bucket. His grandpa carefully lowered himself down onto the ground next to the boy. They sat quietly for a moment, enjoying the warm breeze, the bright sun, the smell of the Confederate Jasmine that Joyce had planted all around the house a few months ago. Lost in thought, Colly peered up at the clouds, while K.B. watched a trio of squirrels chase one another around the thick branches of the oak tree and thought about the upcoming event that was sure to bring excitement into his grandson's life.

"So, Doodle, you looking forward to your first big game?"

"Yeah."

"Gonna hit a bunch of home runs?"

"Yeah."

"How about we go for ice cream after the big game?"

"Kay."

"Well, that certainly sounded like you're excited," K.B. commented dryly. Colly's Little League started in a month, and his grandson, while looking forward to his first game, refused to admit to the nerves that everyone could read on his face and hear in his voice. "Don't worry, Doodle, you'll do fine. We'll practice near every day and make sure you're an expert pitcher and hitter. How's that sound?"

"Good."

"Good, it's a plan."

The idea of practicing almost every day sounded like fun to the boy, but the thought of playing in a real game with real players who really wanted to win made his stomach churn. He'd never been a part of a team before. When he played with his siblings or his Papa, he could do whatever he wanted, make up his own rules and then break them, but now he would have to follow the orders of a coach, and Colly worried that he would do something, or possibly everything, wrong.

"Papa?" Colly asked suddenly, picking up an acorn and hoping to change the subject. "Where do acorns come from?"

"Acorn City, of course."

"Acorn City?"

"Yeah! Ain't you ever heard of Acorn City before?" When Colly shook his head, his thick brown hair falling across his eyes, K.B. pointed up toward the treetops. "Well, you see, Doodle, up there is a place called Acorn City. It's this huge, sprawling city up there in the branches with little acorn stores tucked away in all them little nooks and crannies. Some stores sell itty-bitty acorns, some sell big fat ones, some have the bright green ones with the orange circle around the top, all different stores for whatever kind of acorn you could possibly want. Acorn City is where all the squirrels and chipmunks go to get their acorn breakfasts, lunches, and dinners, and where they get all their acorns for the winter."

"Oh." Colly kept his eyes on the squirrels and imagined them shopping. "Then how come all the acorns are down on the ground?"

"Well, those are the rejects," K.B. answered, running a hand through his jet-black hair. He may have been in his sixties, but he was yet to lose his hair, and he thanked his Cherokee ancestors for the good genes.

"You see, Doodle, every day Acorn City gets a brand new batch of acorns to put on their shelves. And every day, the squirrels and chipmunks go through and decide which ones they want, and so at the end of the day, all the acorns they didn't want get dumped onto the ground, to make more oak trees so they can have more acorns."

"Oh," Colly said again. "I get it."

Satisfied with the explanation, Colly went back to his daydreaming, pondering what it was like for the animals to go shopping and run their own stores. He wondered how they paid for their acorns. Did they have coins and bills like people? Or maybe they paid with special leaves and tree bark.

It wasn't until he heard the slam of a car door that he snapped to attention and crouched down against the tree. He let his gladiator instincts kick in, feeling the blood of a warrior pulsing through his veins. He listened to the footsteps on the grass as they walked away from the driveway, across the yard, toward the front door.

K.B. watched gleefully as Tony rounded the corner and passed the tree, and was bombarded by the child bearing two handfuls of acorns, with another bucketful resting at his feet. With a grin, he sat back and watched the playful fight as older and younger brother engaged in the first acorn battle of the season.

The next morning, K.B. took his family to visit his youngest sister in Brooker, a small town in Florida named after a member of the Standridge kin. His sister, a joyful, bright-eyed woman in her early fifties with a passion for cooking and the skills to match, had been begging her big brother to make an appearance for more than six months, and now K.B. was finally taking her up on her offer.

The Standridge family, minus Tony and Christian, who had decided to spend the day with mutual friends at an amusement park, loaded themselves into K.B. and Joyce's minivan and drove three hours to Brooker. When they arrived, stepping out of the van onto twelve acres of farmland, Hester Standridge appeared in the doorway of her old, two-story brick house, filling the frame. Originally from the hills of Alabama, with a thick southern accent to prove her home state, she was a large woman with auburn hair streaked with gray that, despite being tied back with a white scarf, seemed to burst into a hundred tiny curls around her plump cheeks. Grinning black eyes narrowed in delight as she laughed at the sight of her family. She hadn't grown up with her brother, but instead had been sent to live with a relative in Alabama along with the second-youngest Standridge daughter when illness had struck the family. Now, as an adult, she worked hard to keep her siblings close.

"Big brother, you better hug my neck!" she shouted across the yard, wiping her hands on the apron adorned with sunflowers tied around her waist. She tucked a wooden spoon into one of the apron's pockets and rushed across the grass, grabbing K.B. into a tight hug before turning to the others. When Colly hugged the woman he barely knew, he could only think that she smelled like fried okra, collard greens, and vanilla ice cream, and the mix of aromas made him hungry.

"Oh, I know that look," Hester said as she ran a hand through Colly's hair. "You get on up in the house and grab you a bite to eat. You too, Miss Kariss."

The kids followed her orders and ran up to the house, passing the chicken coop off to the side of the yard and jumping up the rickety steps of the front porch. They raced through the door, stopping in place when they saw the grand display of food.

Two long buffet tables were set up in the alcove just off the kitchen, lined with a feast that easily trumped any Thanksgiving meal that K.B. and Joyce could ever cook up. Steaming bowls of mashed potatoes, macaroni and cheese, corn on the cob, baked beans, sweet potato pie, and collard greens began the line-up, all of it homemade. Huge plates of roast beef and meatloaf sat on either side of a crock-pot full of meatballs. Freshly churned butter rested next to an overfilled basket of cornbread, and that was where Colly headed first. He slathered a heaping mound of butter on his plate while Kariss began her meal with potatoes and white rice covered with brown gravy, and a fried chicken breast on the side. Colly, discovering that he couldn't reach, pointed to the bowl of macaroni and cheese and Kariss spooned a generous helping onto her brother's plate.

They turned around to the second buffet table and marveled at the desserts. Homemade vanilla ice cream was chilling in an ice bucket with chocolate syrup and sprinkles waiting to be poured on top. Fresh-baked cookies, one platter of chocolate chip and another of macadamia nuts, were in the center of the table, next to another platter of brownies and what looked to Kariss like blueberry pie.

The two kids were awestruck by the sight of so much food, but what they didn't realize was that for Hester and everyone who knew her, such an event was commonplace in her home. Hester loved to cook, and had three successful cookbooks and a well-known catering company to show for her talents as a gourmet chef. She specialized in southern cooking, but could whip up nearly any cuisine that was asked of her. Her house was always filled with mouth-watering aromas and long buffet tables packed with food, and was open to any and all of her neighbors, friends, and family. They stopped by regularly and ate like royalty, and Hester loved being the one to fill their stomachs. She grew most of her own fruits and vegetables and raised the majority of the meats she cooked, from chickens to cows to pigs, and felt that her guests respected her more for it.

After loading what room was left on their plates with an array of desserts, Colly and Kariss took their seats at the dining room table, where sat five others, all enjoying their food. They spent some time digging into their meal before chatting with their aunt's guests.

"Who are you?" Colly asked the person to his right, a boy in his late teens with scraggly blonde hair, lazy brown eyes, and a morose expression across his face. His skin was tanned and weather-worn despite his young age, and he wore jeans torn at the knees and a blue flannel shirt. A straw hat frayed at the edges topped his head.

"Dewey," Clondike 'Dewey' Standridge answered around a mouthful of potatoes, not lifting his eyes from the food before him.

"My name's Collin Adam Standridge!" Colly proudly announced. "My momma calls me Colly. So does everyone else, except Papa. He calls me Doodle. Do you live here?"

"Sure do."

"Are you Auntie Hester's son?"

"Nope."

"Then how come you live here?"

"Just do."

The truth was that Dewey Standridge came to live with Hester after a car accident when he was seven, a crash that killed both his parents and left him with a long, jagged scar down the right side of his face and a left shoulder with a permanent tendency to pop out of place when moved just the wrong way. He'd been living with his Aunt Hester for twelve years, learning the ropes of the farm, helping out with business matters, and was preparing himself to take over when she decided to retire. He didn't like to talk about his past. In fact, he didn't like to talk at all.

But Colly wasn't finished with his interrogation. "Are you my uncle?"

"He's your cousin," June answered as she entered the house. "How you doing, Dewey?"

"Alright." He still didn't look up from his plate, but jumped when Hester approached from behind and flicked him in the ear. "Come on, Aunt Hester!"

"You have some manners, boy," she ordered, pointing a finger at her nephew. "What have I told you 'bout wearing hats at the table?"

"Forgot, ma'am," Dewey muttered, dragging the straw hat off his head and setting it on the floor next to his chair.

"Kariss? Did you say hi to your cousin? You two haven't seen each other in about five years," June asked from the buffet table.

Kariss, who had been ignoring everyone as she ate, glanced up at her cousin. "Hey," she said to appease her mother, momentarily wondering about the scar on his face. "I thought your name was Clondike."

"Go by Dewey."

"Oh. Why?"

" 'Cuz my name's Clondike."

"Oh."

Bored by the talk of names, Colly shifted the conversation back to what he thought was interesting. "Auntie Hester? Do you got any sour orange trees?"

"Sour orange trees?" Hester repeated as she looked out the window at her farm. "Can't say that I do, Mr. Colly. But you know what we do got? We got a big apple orchard right out there in the backyard, next to the vegetable garden and goat pen."

"Goats?" Kariss perked up at the idea. "Momma?"

"Go ahead."

Kariss jumped up from her chair and abandoned her meal as she ran out into the backyard. Colly followed, not sure where she was going but not wanting to be left out of the fun. Dewey trailed behind them at Hester's request.

Approaching the goat pen, which was a large patch of grass surrounded by a wooden fence that ended at a small building with one window and two doors, Kariss squatted down and held out a hand, encouraging the pygmy goats to come her way.

"Hey, buddy," she said to the fat black goat that trodded over. The animal sniffed her fingers, searching for a treat. "Ain't you a cutie."

"Name's Paco," Dewey said, leaning against the fence and chewing on a piece of straw, his eyes shaded by the brim of his hat. When he saw the girl reaching in to pet, he picked up a bag of feed in hopes of distracting the goats. "He bites." He barely got the words out of his mouth when Paco tired of sniffing Kariss' fingers and nipped one of them instead. She drew back her hand with a sharp cry of pain.

"Told ya so." He dumped half the bag of feed into a bucket to keep Paco from biting again, and the rest of the hungry goats made their way across the pen to investigate.

Kariss gave her cousin a nasty look as she rubbed her finger. At her side, Colly peered over her shoulder and grimaced at the drop of blood. Suddenly, neither one wanted anything to do with the goats.

"Wanna see the apples instead?" the boy asked his sister, grabbing Kariss by her uninjured hand and yanking her to her feet. Together they walked over to the apple orchard. Kariss imagined that the rows and rows of apple trees resembled what her grandfather had once witnessed with his orange groves—tall trees with brilliant green leaves that created a shady canopy, sweet-smelling fruit that hung from thin branches, a tranquil and colorful oasis of nature away from the busy bustling of society. Kariss could certainly get used to this kind of life.

"I want one!" Colly shouted, plucking an apple from one of the trees. He bit into the fruit. "Hey! It ain't even sour!"

Kariss chuckled as her little brother devoured the apple. She was guessing that the only reason why he was so eager to eat a piece of fruit was because it came from the orchard and not the grocery store, and he wanted to be able to brag that he gets his fruit from his auntie's farm. Otherwise he would have turned his nose up at the very thought of chowing down on an apple.

When he picked another one, Dewey put his hands in his pockets and narrowed his dark eyes. "Don't eat too many," he ordered, his deep and commanding voice not doing a thing to deter the boy. "Get a stomachache after all that food you just ate."

"Nuh-uh, *Clondike*," Colly responded, taking a big bite and knowing that his cousin didn't like being called by his real name. "I can eat anything I want and not get sick." He finished the second apple in less than five minutes and picked one up from the ground. "Kariss? Is there an Apple City? Like Acorn City?"

Before replying, Kariss sat down on the grass and took a moment to observe the farm. It looked like any other farm she'd seen on television or movies, with horses running around a corral and stables being attended to by one of the men she'd seen sitting at her aunt's table. A cornfield took up most of the back acres and vegetable gardens protected from wild animals by high fences lined the right edge of the property. The smell of goat and cow manure wafted in the direction of the orchard, and the sound of hammers banging in the distance prompted her to glance over at the house, where she saw a few men fixing the shingles on the roof. From her point of view, more than just the roof needed patching. The house's white paint was peeling from every corner, shutters were hanging by threads on the windows, some of which were cracked, and there were several holes in the deck that wrapped around the entire perimeter. But the house's outer appearance didn't seem to matter, because the warmth that radiated from within, as well as the spectacular food, made up for the shabby exterior.

When Colly repeated the question, Kariss snapped back to attention and caught the apple when he tossed it at her. "I don't think so, Colly. Acorn City is special. Apples just fall from the trees."

"Oh. Boring." Colly started chomping on his third apple.

"Gonna make yourself sick," Dewey said from behind.

With a frown, Kariss turned around to face her cousin. "You always so grumpy?"

"More like practical."

"Whatever." Kariss knew all about Clondike 'Dewey' Standridge. She felt sorry for him for losing his parents and knew that their deaths likely affected him every day of his life, but every time she ever met him he was sullen, moody, and not at all fun to be around. He was an enormous contrast to her Aunt Hester, who was one of the happiest and nicest people she had ever met, and even at nineteen he acted like an old man who had lived a hard, grueling life and now found enjoyment only in grumbling to everyone he met. She'd never seen him smile, let alone laugh, and rarely heard him speak an entire sentence, just a few words here and there, which confused her because she knew that he went to church every Sunday and believe deeply in the religious teachings, and she'd always thought that religious people were supposed to be nice, especially to their family.

"Hey, Colly, look at that." Disregarding her cousin, Kariss pointed to a cluster of oak trees behind the orchard. "Betcha Acorn City's over there."

"Cool!"

The two headed over to the trees, Dewey trudging behind only because Hester had ordered him to watch them as they explored the farm. As expected, acorns were scattered across the ground, some eaten and discarded, others plump and ripe. Colly began collecting them into a pile at the base of the tallest tree, half an apple bit between his teeth as he used both hands for the job.

"You might want to stand back," Kariss said to Dewey, hiding a grin at his confused frown and furrowed brow.

Dewey didn't like the mischievous glint in his cousins' eyes, and he definitely didn't trust them. Being family didn't matter, for he didn't trust any kid, and although Kariss wasn't all that much younger than him, she was young enough to easily get herself into trouble.

Despite himself, he was curious to know Colly's plans with the acorns. "Why?"

"You just might want to." When Dewey merely shrugged, Kariss lifted a brow. "Well, I warned ya."

When he'd gathered about sixty acorns, Colly sat back with a hand to his stomach. "I have a bellyache," he told Kariss with a grimace, throwing the apple in his mouth into the grass. "Too many apples."

Dewey scoffed. "Told ya so."

With insult and irritation, Colly and Kariss exchanged a knowing glance before grabbing up a handful of acorns and throwing them at their moody cousin. Dewey ducked and covered his face with a shout when the acorns stung his flesh.

"Quit it!" he yelled at his cousins, not sure if he should be furious and retaliate or simply walk, or in this case run, away.

"No mercy for the grouch!" Colly cried as he bombarded Dewey just like he had done to Tony the day before. His young, high-pitched voice carried throughout the orchard and into the house. "The gladiator and the huntress are gonna take you down, enemy warrior!"

"Prepare for the heat!" Kariss shouted, throwing acorn after acorn in tune with Colly as he heaved handfuls at his older cousin. "Hey Colly, why don't you use him for target practice? Get some pitching practice in before your first Little League game!"

"Yeah!" Excited by the idea, the boy did just that. "Take this, Clondike bar!"

To get away from the stinging acorns, Dewey hid behind an oak tree. Before his cousins could catch up with him, his eye caught sight of a small pile of acorns that had fallen from the tree, acorns not yet discovered by Colly and Kariss.

"What the hell," he muttered, stooping to pick up two handfuls, then stepped out from behind the tree.

"Come and get—*hey*!" Colly shrieked when Dewey released six acorns, hitting the boy squarely in the chest. "*Run*! He's got *ammo*! *Help*!" He raced over to his sister and did his best to hide behind her.

"Take *this*!" With a laugh, Kariss aimed and got the perfect shot for Dewey's forehead. She wasn't supposed to aim for the head according to her mother's rules, but she figured her cousin deserved it. The hat toppled off his head, but he left it lying on the ground as he ran after Kariss and Colly.

Hearing her great-nephew's screams, Hester walked out onto the back porch with K.B. and the others and stopped short when she saw the three racing around the oak trees, and caught the smile spread across Dewey's usually-surly face.

"Well, would you look at that," she commented, crossing her arms and leaning against the railing. The wooden spoon in her hand dripped red sauce. "I ain't seen that there boy smile in…well I don't think I ever saw him smile." The sight amazed her, and she captured the moment in her mind, etching it permanently in her memories—his eyes lit up with amusement, his rugged face gleaming with a wide grin, and a deep, hearty laugh escaping his lips, a sound Hester never thought she'd live to hear.

K.B. grinned at the sight of his grandchildren chasing Dewey around with handfuls of acorns. In the nineteen years he'd known the boy, he'd never seen him put forth such energy into anything other than his work on the farm, and it was refreshing to know that Dewey was able to let loose and have fun. "That'd be the power of the Standridge kids."

"Must be, big brother," Hester agreed, loving the sight of the boy who lived through the tragic death of his parents laughing and momentarily forgetting about his sullen attitude. "Now, how 'bout we let them kids have their playtime and we grab a bite to eat?"

"Sounds good to me." June shook her head at her kids, amazed by their ability to put a smile on Dewey's face. But then, she figured, her kids could put a smile on anyone's face. And she absolutely loved that about them.

Chapter 10
LUCKY DIME

Kids in Little League uniforms roamed about the ballpark that would later become the site of the Annual Sour Orange Derby. Some eagerly awaited their team's upcoming game by meeting with their friends and bragging animatedly about how great they were going to play, others tiredly gathered for team meetings after a long nine innings while their parents lugged their gear to the car. The director of the League, a large, frizzy-hair woman who consistently dressed in light blue tracksuits, made her way throughout the crowd. She held a basket filled with raffle tickets, grumpily trying to convince everyone who passed to spend five dollars in hopes of winning a gift card to the restaurant of their choice. A few of the older kids who had outgrown Little League were tossing a football on the large stretch of grass behind the fields, occasionally cheering on their little brothers or sisters, and those too young to be on the field were enjoying themselves on the playground in front of the ballpark.

A couple groups of teenagers were heading to and from the Rec center adjacent to the fields to play a game of basketball, while some of the adults took a walk around the lake less than a half-mile from the baseball games, taking their time as they stopped to watch the turtles or to point out one of the many anhinga nests tucked away in the canopies of Cyprus trees. In a couple of months, that lake and the surrounding area would be alive with the festivities of an annual celebration complete with carnival rides and local vendors setting up booths. For now, it was a peaceful place filled with children's laughter and the sound of baseball bats connecting with their targets.

Back at the fields, the concession stand was packed with hungry spectators, a grill set up out back with burgers and hot dogs sizzling, almost ready to be served. Occasionally the shout of an umpire was heard and the boisterous cheers of proud parents and family members filled the park.

It was a great day to play baseball, but eight year-old Colly refused to leave the backseat of his mother's van. He had gotten only so far as to unbuckle his seatbelt when the nerves hit him, and now he sat with his arms crossed and his head hung low, determined not to budge from his safe spot in the seat.

This was his first Little League game. Sure, he'd played baseball a thousand times before in his backyard, and his Papa said he was getting pretty good, but he had never played on a team before, or even on a real field. He knew *how* to play on a real field, especially since he'd been watching every baseball game possible for as long as he could remember, but that didn't mean he couldn't be scared. After all, studying the sport and all the professional players ever since he learned to read didn't mean he actually knew how to be a professional himself.

"Collin, you've been looking forward to playing all year," June soothed her timid son, ruffling his hair. "Don't you even want to try?"

"No. What if I mess up?"

"What if you hit a home run?"

Colly shook his head. He'd never hit a home run. He was too small. All the other kids on the team were huge; some even looked like fifth and sixth-graders. There was no way he could run as fast as them, or throw as far, or hit as hard. They would all laugh at him, and then he'd be so embarrassed that he'd never want to play baseball again. Not even with Papa.

"I wanna go home."

June sighed and stepped out of the van. She'd been trying to get her son to the field for fifteen minutes now, and he was about to be late for his first game. Not even K.B. could talk him out of his nerves.

"Collin Adam Standridge, you—"

"Mom?" Kariss approached the van, tying back her long brown hair to cool off her neck from the heat. "Mind if I give it a shot?"

"Go for it." June gave up and walked a few feet away, watching the kids on the playground but listening closely as her daughter attempted the impossible.

Kariss hopped in the van next to her little brother, chewing on a piece of watermelon bubblegum. She sat there for a moment, simply looking over at him, observing Colly as she blew a bubble. She thought he looked just like their Papa, with dark brown hair, even darker brown eyes, and a small mouth full of big teeth. She didn't remember much of her father anymore, but she suspected Colly looked like him too.

The bubble popped, sending a sheet of red gum down her chin. Kariss picked it off nonchalantly. "So, you gonna play or what?"

"No."

"Why not?"

" 'Cuz."

" 'Cuz why?"

" 'Cuz I'm not as good as them."

"Oh." Kariss nodded, pretending to think about her brother's predicament. "Well, maybe what you need is a little Luck."

That got his attention. "Luck?"

"Yeah. Ain't you ever heard of Luck?"

Colly dared to move, even if only a little, as he shifted and peered up at his sister. "How do I get Luck?"

Hiding a grin, Kariss reached around to her brother's ear, an old magic trick, and pulled back a shiny dime imprinted with the year 1992. "Well, well. Look what I found."

"Whoa! From inside my head?" Colly scratched at his ear, wondering where the dime came from as he felt for a hole or a slit like the one in his bank shaped like Albert the Alligator, mascot of his favorite football team, the Florida Gators.

"Not just inside your head," Kariss replied, holding up the dime. "This dime is special. This dime came from your Luck."

"My Luck? Where's that?"

"It's inside you. Sometimes it just gets scared and hides, and you have to go find it."

"Where's it hide?"

"Oh, sometimes in your head, sometimes in your belly," Kariss poked her brother

and got a giggle out of him as he squirmed away, "and sometimes it just floats all around until it gathers up the courage to come out and help. You just gotta find it and give it something to do, so it can prove just how lucky it can be. See this?" She pointed to her ring, a silver band shaped in a triangle with a turquoise bear claw set in the middle, a ring she hadn't taken off in over four years, refusing to part with what she believed was a true and powerful symbol of her heritage that would guide her throughout her life. "This is my Luck. I needed it a long time ago when some kids at school were being very…cruel…mean to me," she corrected at her brother's confused expression, "and it kept me safe. And this is your Luck." She leaned over and tucked the dime into Colly's sock. "Keep it safe, and it will bring you lots of Luck. Special Luck."

Colly patted his sock, feeling the cool dime against his skin. "Even with baseball?"

"*Especially* with baseball. This is a Lucky Baseball dime." Kariss smiled and patted his shoulder.

"Wow," Colly breathed, still rubbing his ear. It amazed him, learning that he had special Luck inside of him. He wondered what other people's Luck looked like. Maybe, when he got home, he could find Tony and Christian's Luck and give it to them. He imagined himself searching through his brothers' minds, picking through their thoughts and secrets. He could find their Luck. Maybe they had special baseball Luck too, and once they had it, they would want to play ball with him.

Outside the van, June stared in astonishment as Colly leaped out, excitedly grabbed his bat and glove, and raced to join the rest of his team. Soon he was in the dugout, being greeted by both the coach and his friends, and his mother turned to her daughter, who was still chomping hard on her gum while staring off into space.

"How on earth did you do that?"

Kariss shrugged and popped a few bubbles, much to June's annoyance. "Lucky dime. Special Baseball Luck."

"And when did you learn that?" June put her hand on her hips. Special Luck that hid inside a person until it was most needed was her grandfather's trick.

"Middle school, when all those kids who claimed to be my friends made fun of me for not wearing expensive clothes." She crawled out of the van and shut the door. "I'm gonna go get a hot dog."

"Okay." June watched her daughter until she made it to the concession stand, remembering how hard that year had been. Kariss had never been like most kids her age, and grew up understanding the value of a dollar, something her brothers knew as well, having grown up with the need to carefully pinch pennies whenever possible. She had never pressed June for new clothes when she had old ones that worked just as well, and never cared what others thought of her.

But her seventh grade year, she'd been forced to face her fellow peers, who taunted her daily about her wardrobe choice that, they teased, was full of outdated junk that normal people threw away, and were particularly harsh about the one maroon jacket, her only jacket, that she wore during the winter months because they knew Kariss didn't have anything else. Soon their daily taunts turned into nasty rumors that haunted her well into high school, and some bullying even became physical. Kariss had held her head high during that year, but she came home every day unable to speak, and it wasn't until K.B. bestowed upon his granddaughter her Special Luck that she found the confidence to ignore their words and discover her own.

It made sense, then, that Kariss would continue the cycle of Special Luck, and find her brother's in his greatest time of need.

With a smile of approval, June then did a quick head count of her other three children—Colly in the dugout, Tony tossing the football with his friends, and Christian sitting with his grandparents on the top row of the bleachers. Satisfied with everyone's whereabouts, she joined her parents and son and waited for the game to begin.

Colly's team took the field first, her son heading to second base, his favorite position. His nerves seemed to have been soothed, though he did occasionally glance down at the shoe with the lucky dime, much to Kariss' satisfaction.

By the third out, Colly had made two catches and three misses—not bad for his first time out on the field. The ball had sailed over his glove on two occasions, rolling right between his legs on the third, and although he reacted with a look of disappointment that revealed his embarrassment, his friends and family in the stands only cheered him on. Their encouragements were nice for the boy, but ultimately it wasn't the field position that had Colly, as well as June and the other Standridges, anxious—it was going up to bat.

He was fifth on the line-up, and he chewed on his fingernails as he watched the first few players take their turns. They were certainly bigger than him, and three had been in Little League since they were old enough to play T-ball. When they hit the ball, the mere sound of the crack of the bat sent the crowd into a frenzy of approval, which only made his nerves worse. By the time it was his turn there were two outs and runners on first and third.

As he headed for home plate, desperately trying to ignore the sounds of the crowd all around him, Colly silently wished he was allowed to bat with his Daddy's old bat, the one he used at home. Though he'd never met his father, and wasn't even born yet when he died, Colly felt a special connection when he played ball with the special bat, like his Daddy was helping him swing, helping him learn to hit the ball at just the right second and send it straight into the outfield. But, his coach had explained that there were rules for that sort of thing, and that the heavy wooden bat was against those rules, so Colly had no choice but to give in.

With each step he felt the dime press against his skin, and he remembered Kariss' words. His Luck was inside him, and the dime was his Special Luck for baseball. It didn't matter how big the other boys were or how fast they could throw the ball, because he had something they didn't have—Special Baseball Luck. Plus, his Papa was there cheering him on, and if anyone knew anything about baseball, it was Papa.

Colly dug into the clay a little and set his feet, eyeing the pitcher. He took in a deep breath, kept his eye on the ball like Papa had taught him, and missed.

"Strike one!"

"You'll get 'em next time, Colly!" June called out, clapping her hands while Kariss and Christian shouted out similar encouragements to their brother.

Colly shook it off and pretended not to see the pitcher smiling. He waited for the second pitch. When the ball was released, he tried to imagine it was getting bigger and bigger, coming right for the bat and all he had to do was swing at just the right second.

"Strike two!"

Instantly nervous again, Colly stepped back from the plate, head hung dejectedly, terrified that he was going to strike out his very first time up to bat. And not only strike out, but get the third out and let his team down. Everyone would be mad at him, and no one would want him to come back and play next Saturday because he wasn't good enough to be on the team. And if he couldn't hit the ball, how was he supposed to become a professional baseball player? Professional baseball players had to be good hitters, and just because he could throw and sometimes catch didn't mean that would make up for a bad batting average.

"Get ready for the heat! That pitcher ain't got nothing on you, Dood!" K.B. shouted, recognizing the look on the boy's face as desperation and sadness, and Kariss followed up his cheer with a cheer of her own.

"You got what they don't have, Colly!" When he glanced over his shoulder, she winked knowingly.

Colly nodded. "Come on, lucky dime, time to start giving me some Luck," he whispered, and stepped back up to the plate. He swallowed hard as the pitcher wound up, then released the ball. Watching it carefully, everything else that surrounded him completely disappeared as the ball sailed toward the bat. Colly swung just when he thought the time was right—and connected with the ball.

He didn't bother to see where the baseball was going. As soon as he heard the crack of the bat against the ball, Colly took off for first base. If anything, he was a fast runner, and he knew he was safe the moment his foot hit the white square. Thrilled over reaching first base his very first time at bat, he jumped a celebratory jump, and then realized that the runner on third had run home, all thanks to his hit, and now everyone was cheering. People he didn't even know were shouting his name and congratulating his great RBI, and his teammate's great run home.

Kariss was right. He had a Lucky Baseball Dime.

⌐◪◩¬

"Colly Standridge steps up to the plate. It's his team's last chance to win! Two outs, runners on first and third! *Can he do it?*" Colly hit the ball that K.B. threw hard. The ball sailed across the yard, over the top of the orange tree, and into the dirt driveway. "And it's a home run! Colly saves the team! Who'd a ever thunk he could do it!" The boy ran around the backyard, pouncing on each of the makeshift bases. "He must have some kind of luck, that Colly Standridge!"

He landed on home plate, panting from his run, but after a quick drink of water was ready to go again. "Let's see what you got now, enemy pitcher!"

K.B. wiped the sweat from his brow. "Not another one, Doodle. I gotta take a rest."

His grandfather's break didn't stop Colly's game. He continued to play, narrating his every move, as K.B. made his way to the patio, where sat June and Joyce.

"Can you believe that boy's still going on about his hit? It's been near a week since that game." He laughed as he plopped himself down onto a plastic chair, leaning back and soaking up the sun.

"He's proud," June replied as she poured her father a glass of sweet tea, which he gratefully accepted. "He loves the game, that's for sure."

"So do I. Just wish I had the energy to play more." K.B. gulped down nearly half the glass of tea. There was a time when he could have spent all day, heat or cold, rain or shine, tossing the football or pitching a fastball, and feel good as new by the time he went to bed. Now, fifteen minutes under the sun wiped him out for the day, something that deeply disappointed him. Playing with his grandkids was his greatest enjoyment.

June caught the sad expression on her father's face as she took a seat next to him, tucking her curly hair behind her ears. Her almond-shaped brown eyes, a shape accented by the sharp angles of her nose, scanned the backyard that was so full of memories. "Remember when all the kids wanted to play with us?" she asked, taking a sip of tea and watching her youngest child run around the yard, needing no one but himself to play the game. Occasionally he ran laps around the lone orange tree in the middle of the yard. The tree stood over ten feet high, but Colly's energy seemed larger, reached higher.

"Those were the days," K.B. agreed.

"We're lucky if they even hug our necks anymore," Joyce put in, rubbing K.B.'s shoulders. "Our family's growing up."

June nodded. "Yep. Tony goes out on dates now, if hanging out at the mall is considered a date. Christian's on the basketball team, pretty good, too. They're even talking about getting jobs this summer, odd jobs like mowing the neighbors' yards. They want to save up for a car. Can you believe it?"

"I can." Joyce stole a quick glance over at the two, who were giving the dog, Latheena, a bath. Latheena, getting fatter and fatter by the month because of all the scrap food the kids fed her, was thoroughly enjoying being pampered. She barked happily and nipped at the water, spinning in circles and nearly tackling Christian in the process.

"Ten bucks says the mutt rolls in the mud as soon as they're done," K.B. challenged.

"You're on," June and Joyce said at the same time.

"You know," June said as she tossed a rogue baseball to her son, "all the kids are growing up to be good people. Tony can be a bit of a goof-off, but he knows when to buckle down. Christian is a little distant now and then but he's always right there when you need him. And they're smart, too. Tony's actually thinking about what college he wants to go to." That shocked her more than anything, considering that her son once wanted to be a beach bum. "And then there's Kariss. That girl's in a league of her own."

"She's a good girl," Joyce put in.

"Oh, she's great," June quickly said. "I just meant that she's...she's something else. She continually surprises me. You think she's the most serious kid in the world, then she starts talking about flying dragons and wondering whether the purple bird she saw this morning was real, or if it was a dream and she forgot it was a dream."

"Nothing wrong with a little imagination," K.B. said under his breath.

"Not at all. She's gonna be a writer, that's for sure," June agreed, and continued. "Then you think she doesn't care about anyone in the world, and suddenly she pulls the Special Luck trick."

"Stole my trick," K.B. murmured.

Joyce laughed and playfully swatted her husband's leg. "What are you complaining about? It looks like we have someone to carry on the family tradition."

"Family tradition of craziness." The three looked behind them to see Kariss walking out the back door. She sat down on the ground and called her cat over into her lap. "What are we talking about?"

"Adult stuff," June answered.

"Ah, boring stuff," Kariss corrected, standing back up. "I'm going back inside."

"Wait a doggone minute there, Stinker." K.B. reached for his granddaughter as she passed. "It's a beautiful day. Enjoy the outdoors. Enjoy the smells. Enjoy the fresh air. Enjoy the oranges."

Kariss frowned. "They're sour."

"That's why you would enjoy them."

Everyone but Kariss laughed. Instead, she crossed her arms and lifted a brow. "Sticks and stones may break my bones, but sour oranges I can throw at you."

With that, she turned on her heel and flounced back indoors, satisfied with having the last word.

"She's quick, I'll be the first to admit to that."

"Got a mouth on her, too," June answered to her father.

With another laugh, K.B. turned his eyes back to Colly, who had switched gears from baseball to golf. He wasn't a very accurate shot, and the only club he had was an old putter, but that didn't stop him.

"Fore!" Colly shouted, pointing in the direction the ball would go like a baseball batter before hitting a home run. He reached the putter back and slammed the golf ball as hard as he could.

The ball ricocheted off a rock and bounced across the yard, but before Colly could retrieve it, a big bundle of wet black fur raced across the grass. Latheena barked excitedly as she reached the ball, grabbing it up and proceeding to roll over in the dirt as she played with her new toy. Tony and Christian ran after her, shouting angrily.

K.B. held out a hand. "Y'all owe me ten bucks."

Chapter 11
GUMDROP TREES

Fall had come, a light breeze flowing in through the open window as the Standridge family gathered around the dinner table, a rare event as the kids typically ate at the counter while June took care of things around the house. The actual dinner table was usually reserved for holidays and other special occasions. Tonight, June had decided to take advantage of the fact that both Tony and Christian were home for dinner, since lately they seemed to prefer hanging out with friends, and had cooked the family favorite—lasagna and garlic bread. Just to make sure the kids had their daily dose of healthy food, June had tossed in a side of green beans, much to the boys' disgust.

A lamp decorated with palm trees hung over the table, casting an orange glow throughout the alcove as tiny, sun-colored flecks of light glittered against the white tile of the kitchen and dining room floor. The light green, slightly worn curtains were drawn for the night, but the noisy chirps of frogs and crickets calling for rain after months of drought still met their ears as they settled down in their seats, K.B. at one end, Tony at the other. In the corner was a fake palm tree strung with festive white lights, and a few feet away from the table, June stood at the stove and heaped generous lasagna portions onto blue glass plates.

"No!" Colly shouted anxiously as his mother made his plate, bouncing in his chair. "It's touching! Don't let it touch!"

June looked down at the plate, then huffed, exasperated. They went through this every night, and every night, she forgot to make sure that none of the different food items were touching one another. After seven years, she figured she wouldn't need to be reminded by her frantic son that when foods touched they rubbed off all their taste onto one another and nothing was left but grossness, but it seemed like such a trivial matter that June just couldn't seem to remember until it was too late.

"Jeez, Collin, relax." She set the plate down in front of Kariss, who had no qualms about her green beans touching the sauce, and carefully made up another one for her son. "Better?"

"Yes." Satisfied, Colly wasted no time in digging in. He loved his lasagna.

Once everyone was served, June sat at the head of the table, across from K.B., who sat at the other end. Immediately Christian and K.B. started a discussion about basketball, while Joyce asked Colly about his next Little League game. Tony simply ate, and June knew he was hoping to clear his plate as soon as possible so he could excuse himself and escape to his room to call a girl he had a crush on. But it didn't bother her, for she was enjoying the fact that they were all together.

"Hey Mom?" Kariss asked suddenly, wiping her mouth with a napkin. "Can we plant some trees in the backyard?"

June looked out the window at the wide open, grassy places in the yard before replying. "I'm not sure it's the right season for planting, but we can give it a shot. Where in the backyard?"

"Anywhere."

"What kind of trees?"

"Any kind."

Confused, June set down her fork. "So you don't care where or what kind, you just want trees?"

"Yeah."

"Why?"

"Why not?"

"Okay." By this time, their conversation had piqued the interest of the others. "Sure. We can go to the nursery this weekend."

Colly raised his hand excitedly. "I want a sour orange tree!"

At that, K.B. proudly slapped a hand on his grandson's shoulder. "That's right, Doodle! Bring on the sour oranges!"

"You can't plant sour orange trees," Tony cut in with a scoff. "It's impossible."

"Nuh-*uhhh*." Colly made a face at his brother. "Nothing's impossible, right Papa?"

K.B. nodded. "That's right, Doodle. Nothing's impossible."

Tony sighed, tired of all the make-believe that he constantly had to listen to. "Papa, you can't just *plant* a sour—" One stern look from his grandfather had him shutting his mouth and staring down at his plate.

Wide-eyed, Colly sought his mother for reassurance. "Can I?"

"Of course," Kariss answered for June. "In fact, that's what we'll do. After all, what's better than sour orange trees?"

True to her word, June took Kariss to the nursery, though they were forced to postpone their trip for a month since none of the local nurseries had any of the orange trees they wanted. They weren't in season, and the landscapers they spoke to had little hope about them surviving if planted now, but her daughter was determined. Kariss had made her mother call every week until finally, one nursery got in a brand new stock of trees of multiple varieties, and now it was time to shop.

They went first thing in the morning and spent two hours deciding which would look best in their yard against the backdrop of palm trees and azalea shrubs and came home with eight trees of all different sizes. As soon as they were unloaded from the back of the truck, Kariss began planning out where they would be planted.

K.B. and Joyce were sitting on their front porch drinking steaming cups of coffee and reading the newspaper when they saw their granddaughter walking around the backyard with a clipboard and pencil. Curious, they made their way over, Joyce carrying a pitcher of tea and a stack of plastic cups, speculating that whatever Kariss was up to, it was going to take some physical labor.

Joyce was right. Kariss had mapped out the trees' new destinations, and June had recruited her two oldest boys to do the digging. Colly stood idly by and watched.

"I think they'll be big as Papa's orange tree some day," Kariss said as Tony planted the first tree, the smallest of the bunch. "Maybe even bigger."

"Are they sour orange trees?"

"Yeah, right," Tony scoffed in Colly's direction, packing dirt around the base of the tree trunk. "Eight sour orange trees, just like you ordered."

"Are they?"

June, who was dragging the long garden hose through the yard from its place at the side of the house, turned around to address Colly's question. "Actually, yes, Colly. They are sour orange trees." A glare at Tony had him shutting his mouth and taking hold of the second tree. "They're going to take awhile to grow, though, so be patient. You too, Kariss."

"I know." Kariss sipped her tea and kept her eyes on the trees as they were planted into the ground. She took the hose from her mother when Christian turned it on and watered the first tree. "I can't wait. Our own Standridge family orange grove, just like it used to be."

The next two months destroyed Kariss and Colly's dreams of growing their own orange grove. In a strange twist of weather, a storm passed through every week, bringing with it flooding rain, torrential winds, and temperatures that seemed to be in a constant state of unrest—cold, wet nights accompanied hot, muggy afternoons. Tree tops lost their fresh green leaves in the gales. Endless puddles harbored mosquito eggs and drowned the roots of plants, and budding fruits never got the chance to ripen as they were blown to the ground to rot.

By the end of the second month, when the rains and winds gradually ceased and the skies cleared, the earth finally drying, there was little left in which to take pride. Kariss faced her trees sadly, taking in the sight of the wilted and leafless branches, the pale bark, the rotten fruit, and all in all, the dead orange trees. She had big dreams for those trees, big aspirations, hoping to start her own grove and feel the connection to nature that her grandfather had known so well as a child. She had imagined going into the Christmas season with twinkling lights on her trees, shining brightly in the night. Now those dreams were shattered, and she was left wondering if Tony was right and she dreamed too big.

Colly walked out of the house, searching for his big sister. She had been sad lately, so sad that she didn't want to play baseball with him or write any short stories or do any of the things she usually enjoyed, and he was determined to be the one to cheer her up. As he made his way across the yard, he thought of what his Papa would do. Maybe he could make a snowman out of sour oranges and say he was the guardian of the dead trees. Or maybe they could cut up the trees and use them for mulch like their momma put in the gardens and then the orange trees could still be a part of their yard.

He found his sister sitting behind the Standridge family orange tree. She had a long blade of grass in her hands, and was tearing it into tiny shreds.

"How come your trees died but Papa's orange tree didn't?" he asked, taking a seat next to her and leaning his head against her shoulder.

Kariss peered up at the orange tree. The storms hadn't touched it. It still stood in all its towering glory, branches and shimmering green leaves arching the tree into a perfectly rounded shape, bright orange fruit boldly gleaming beneath the sun.

"Because it's magic," she answered, honestly believing that her grandfather's tree was protected by forces that were beyond her ability to see, hear, or even comprehend. Tony may have been right when he said that fantasy wasn't real, but if it wasn't, then how was the miracle of the orange tree possible? *Something* kept that tree alive for so many years, surviving so many storms. If not magic, then what? She desperately wanted to believe in magic. She needed to believe that there was the possibility of enchantment and supernatural forces. Because if there weren't, then what was the meaning of life? What was her purpose, or anyone's purpose, if not to discover the unknown?

K.B. watched Kariss and Colly from his kitchen window. Once, his entire yard had been filled with orange trees. Even as a kid, he remembered walking around the groves, picking oranges, making sure all the heat lamps worked while his uncle and the other workers treated sick trees. He'd climbed plenty of trees in his day, eaten his share of the fruit, found secret hiding places and built forts during his teenage years when he needed an escape from the reality of his life at home. There was no feeling that could ever match the one when he found himself lost in the trees, tucked away from the everyday noises of society, warmed by the rays of the summer sun, surrounded at every turn by bright green leaves and bundles of oranges hanging from thin branches.

When the frost killed the groves, he was heartbroken. And as each surviving tree died in the following winters, what was left of that fraction dedicated to the groves broke off piece by piece until all that was left was one tree, and one piece of his orange-grove heart.

Now his grandchildren were heartbroken over the loss of their own orange trees and their own dreams of raising a grove, just as he had been. K.B. still had one tree left, one tree that stood the test of time, that endured, that brought a smile of pride and love to his face whenever he gazed upon it. The children deserved the same.

He had a plan.

⊰⊱

The first light of dawn broke through a deep cobalt sky, lighting the treetops and casting its beams across dew-dropped grass. Morning's mist was slowly lifting, creating a cloud of mystery around the Standridge land. The rays slipped their way through the curtains of June's house as K.B. silently entered. He woke Kariss first, then Colly, whispering to both that something magical had happened outside.

Tired yet already fascinated, his grandchildren dragged themselves out of bed, dressed in thick, warm robes, and followed him to the back porch.

"What happened, Papa?" Kariss rubbed her eyes and wrapped her robe tighter around her waist.

"Stinker, Doodle, do you know what happens to an orange tree when it dies?" K.B.'s voice was quiet, mysterious.

"What?" Colly peered through the window out at the dead trees in the backyard.

Before answering, K.B. ushered the kids through the porch door, starting their way across the wet grass. "Well, I'll show you, but first, you have to promise me something."

"What?" Colly asked again.

K.B. stopped them at his thriving orange tree. He knelt down, taking in the sight of their young, eager faces in the early morning light. Somewhere behind him, a nest of cardinals had begun to chirp, singing the arrival of dawn.

"You see," he began, his voice still quiet, "when an orange tree dies, it turns into something magical. But not everyone can see it. Only the most special people in the world, the ones who believe in magic, can see it, and the orange trees choose which people to show their secret to." He smiled as their sleepy eyes widened hopefully. "That means, if you can see their secret, then you have to keep it a secret, too. Promise?"

"Promise!" Kariss and Colly said in unison. "But why does it have to be kept a secret?" Kariss prompted.

"Because," K.B. tucked a loose strand of hair behind her ear, "it's magic, and magic is meant only for the people who believe in it."

Kariss understood. Not everyone believed in magic, like her older brothers, but she certainly did. She, like Colly, needed magic. And those who didn't believe just didn't understand the thrill and beauty of magical forces. They couldn't appreciate the things that didn't make sense. "So what happens to the orange trees when they die?"

"They turn into snowmen?"

"...What?"

Colly shrugged. "It could happen."

"Well, Doodle, there's no snowmen out there, but let's go see what we can find."

K.B. put an arm around his grandchildren and, together, the three of them witnessed the magic of the orange trees in an explosion of color that painted a dazzling rainbow just before their eyes.

As the fiery sun shimmered its way through wispy clouds, a magnificent glow radiated around the eight bare, lifeless trees that had been planted in hopes of continuing the family tradition. Only now, the trees weren't bare, and they certainly weren't lifeless. Something colorful was covering the branches, something round and tear-shaped, something with a sweet and alluring smell. Kariss and Colly creeped forward, curious and astonished, watching the rays of oranges and purples and reds and greens shimmer against the grass, across their hands as they held them out in the rising sun.

"What are they?" Cautiously, Colly reached out with a lone finger and touched the tree, yanking back his hand when his finger felt the strange, squishy substance.

Kariss touched as well, leaning over and breathing in the sugary smell. "They're...gumdrops," she answered, turning to her grandfather. "Candy?"

"Not just any candy," K.B. said as he plucked a round, blue gumdrop from the tree. "Orange tree candy." He held the gumdrop up in the light. "This is what happens when an orange tree dies. It magically turns into a Gumdrop Tree, and it grows gumdrops for an entire week before the tree finally dies away." Bravely, Colly took the blue gumdrop his grandfather held and popped it in his mouth.

"But why?"

K.B. shrugged. "No one knows why. I think it's because the orange trees know that we love them so much, that when they die, they want to give us a treat for being so loving."

Kariss peered at the trees suspiciously. They certainly *looked* authentic, all eight trees sprouting dozens upon dozens upon dozens of perfectly shaped, colorful bits of candy, covering the dead branches the way bright green leaves had before the storms came. They smelled wonderful, just like the oranges on her Papa's tree, and she had no idea how they got on her trees. Then again, she wondered, why would gumdrops grow on a dead orange tree? It didn't make any sense, and her teenage mind was fighting skepticism and imagination. Candy didn't grow on trees, just like it didn't get scratched out of armpits. The only solution that made sense was that their grandfather had put them there himself, but that was a lot of work for one old man so early in the morning.

Or maybe Papa is right, she mused. Maybe orange trees really were magic. How else did his tree survive so many years? Survive frosts and freak snowstorms and hurricanes? And if they were magic, then maybe they really did appreciate all that their people did to care for them. Who was she to second-guess Mother Nature?

With a wide smile, Kariss stared at the trees, rainbow-splattered with candy. They were beautiful, a magical secret that she and Colly could enjoy for a whole week. Deciding that she would savor every bit of the magic, she grasped a handful of gumdrops and ate them all at once. Colly pointed at a particularly large gumdrop too far out of reach, and she eagerly retrieved the candy for him.

As the two laughed together, running from tree to tree, smelling and eating, and best of all, falling in love all over again with their dreams, K.B. felt only joy. His grandkids were happy, and that was all that mattered.

When the sun had risen and the dawn turned to morning, Kariss and Colly were still with the trees. By the time June had woken and stepped outside, wondering where her two youngest had run off to, they were gorged on gumdrops, entirely elated.

For the next week, every morning for seven mornings, K.B. snuck outside just before dawn to cover the dead orange trees with gumdrops. And every morning for seven mornings, Kariss and Colly raced outside to taste the candy and enjoy the sights and smells, counting down the days until the magic would end.

Chapter 12

Annual Sour Orange Derby

With perfect timing, Kariss reached into her pocket and pulled out a small, thin box, tossing it over to Rod. He caught it and looked down to see that he was holding a box of gumdrops.

"Fresh from the grove," she said with a grin and a wink.

Rod held up the candy and, despite himself, was amused. Briefly, he wondered if she had planned to tell that story and pull out the gumdrops at just the right moment for effect, or if it just happened to work out that way. He was leaning toward effect rather than an all-too-perfect coincidence. "So the game started after you planted more sour orange trees?" he asked, unsure what the point of the story was.

Kariss scoffed and leaned over to tie her shoe. "We didn't plant sour orange trees."

"Then what did you plant?"

Rather than answering, Kariss paused, leaned back, and whispered something to her fiancé, who had been staring off into the distance at another game. He nodded in agreement. She pulled back her head and stared at Sam, seeming to speak to him silently through her eyes.

Then she stood up. "Mr. Yankee, I've decided not to answer any more of your questions until you play an inning of the Derby."

With that, she hopped down the bleachers and headed for the field, where her team was preparing to take the field. There was an air of smugness in her step. Rod looked helplessly at Sam, but the other man merely shrugged and adjusted his cap.

"She always gets the last word," Sam informed the reporter. "Always, so don't bother trying to ask any more questions. And she's always true to her word. She won't talk until you play. Guaranteed." Then he left for the field as well, not looking back.

Rod remained sitting, an inward battle creating a pit of anxiety in his gut. He was not an athlete. He was a reporter, and a stereotypical one at that. Wide-rimmed glasses, gangly frame, prying eyes, button-down shirt complete with a pocket-protector, Rod knew he had no business being on that field.

Growing up, he'd never had any sports skills, and had gotten used to being picked last during the gym class kickball game. Everyone knew him as the spazz on the field, the guy who never made a catch, who couldn't run fast enough to keep up with the rest of the team. It wasn't like he ever bothered making an effort. Even from a young age, he'd thought of football and baseball and basketball as useless ways to pass the time. Not to mention dangerous ways.

The bottom line was that sports made him nervous. Even the very *idea* of hitting a baseball or trying to throw a football caused his palms to sweat. In fact, the moment his boss had asked him to cover the event, Rod's breath went short at the thought of having to attempt to understand a sporting event well enough to ask intelligent questions. Over the years, his fear of sports eventually turned into scorn for the entire athletic department.

In his opinion, sports were an unnecessary part of life, and that was why he chose to report on greedy CEOs being jailed for embezzling money from the corporation or the latest threat against the economy. He didn't quite understand why his boss had even asked him to cover the Sour Orange Derby in the first place, as their paper had a perfectly capable sports reporter, but he guessed it was because his editor was simply looking for a fluff piece to take up space on the front page that the readers would enjoy. But the way the story was going, Rod had the feeling that this story was more than fluff, and if he could get Kariss to answer the one question he'd been asking since the very beginning, he could get to the heart of the event.

Regardless, the bottom line was that he wanted to get the story and get out, and not take any personal play time for himself that involved putting even one foot on that field.

Leaning forward with his elbows on his knees, Rod watched the inning begin, somewhat indifferent about the entire game. A few players from the opposing team, Team Apple—an obvious play on the term 'apples and oranges'—took their turns at bat, each scoring a decent amount of points. From what he could surmise, this was the next-to-last inning, which meant he didn't have much time left to get the information he needed the most.

A buzzer sounded from another field. Rod turned his head to see that the game between Team Hard Hitters and Team Citrus had come to an end, with Team Citrus parading off the field victorious by a sixty-five point lead. Seeing his chance, Rod rose from the bleachers and headed for the young man who appeared to be the center of attention from the winning team. Judging by the amount of people who knew his name, congratulated him on his many great hits, and asked numerous questions about the happenings of his life off the field, he guessed the man was most likely the captain and star player, as well as another favorite of the Derby.

"Hi, Rod Jenkins," he introduced himself to the man, holding out a hand.

The man, Jess Smith, took a swig of water and congratulated a few of his friends before replying. "Rod Jenkins?" he repeated, stealing a quick glance over at Kariss, who was laughing with a friend in the dugout. Momentarily, he wondered what they were talking about, as it was typically hard to get anything more than a chuckle out of the woman. "So you're the fancy New York reporter?"

Rod wasn't sure if the six-foot-three captain was mocking him or just being friendly. "Yes. I was wondering if you had time to answer a couple questions."

Jess shrugged, his bright blue eyes accenting his youthful face as he searched for a place to talk. "Sure. Why not?" He led Rod to a less crowded area about twenty feet away where they could stand beneath the shade of an oak tree. "Okay. Whatcha wanna know?"

Rod quickly read over his notes. "Well, let's get the basics. How old are you?"

"Twenty-three."

"What is your position with your team, Team Citrus?"

"Me?" Jess lifted his head proudly. "I'm the captain. I used to play with Team Colly back when there was only one team, but eventually we got more people and I started up Team Citrus. I've been a part of the Derby pretty much since the beginning."

"The beginning," Rod repeated. "Let's start with the beginning. How did the Sour Orange Derby begin?"

At the question, Jess held up his hands with a hesitant smile. "Hey, man, that's a question you should be asking Kariss Standridge."

"Oh, I have. We're still discussing it. I was hoping to get different viewpoints on the story."

"There's only one viewpoint on how the Derby began," Jess answered, pushing back his shoulder-length blonde hair and taking another gulp of water. "And that viewpoint ain't mine, but good job trying to trick me into talking."

Rod shook his head. "I wasn't—"

"Tell you what, Yankee," Jess interrupted, "you tell Kariss to tell me that it's okay for me to talk, and I'll tell you anything you want to know. Otherwise, I ain't saying a word."

He walked off before Rod could reply, and Rod found himself wondering how many more times that day people would turn their backs on him. Frustrated, he spun around on his heel, and out of the corner of his eye saw Kariss staring at him suspiciously from the dugout. Obviously, she had told the Derby players that he was coming, and obviously, he would get nowhere with them. If he wanted his story, he would have to charm Kariss Standridge, and he hadn't gotten off to the best start. It seemed that charming her was next to impossible. He knew how people were when they didn't want to talk to a reporter, how defensive and distant they could be, and when those walls were put up, it was a gamble as to whether or not they would ever be willing to reveal intimate details about themselves and their private lives.

Resigning to that fact, Rod went back to his seat on the bleachers and watched the game, trying to make sense of it but only half-trying at that. While he waited for the game to end, he read over his notes, mentally writing his article and realizing that without the origin of the Derby, he had absolutely nothing. Without the origin, the Sour Orange Derby was just a game, and not one that made a whole lot of sense.

Rod nervously adjusted himself in his seat when he discovered that Sam was walking his way, presumably sent by Kariss to convince him to play. He wasn't sure he wanted to say no to the man, considering the fact that Sam packed more muscle than Rod could ever even begin to imagine having for himself.

"Kariss says you're up."

"Up?"

Sam gestured to the field, where the game appeared to be on hold. "To bat. And before you say no, consider that you won't get anything out of her, or anyone else for that matter, until you play."

Rod eyed the field. It seemed that everyone was making it a point *not* to look his way, instead staring at their hands, the sky, the oranges, anything else, and being at the center of their discreet attention made him incredibly uncomfortable. "Why is it so important to her?"

Shrugging, Sam propped an arm up against the railing. "Simple. You can't love the game until you've been a part of it. Trust me, I know. Before I stepped out on that field, I didn't get it, and I even knew how and why all this got started. Truth be told, I thought it was kind of lame. Now, I can't imagine life without the Sour Orange Derby. I can't explain it. It's like...it's like you get to be a kid again, and all the other kids are your friends, your family." He smiled, thinking about the first time he played, remembering his skepticism over the sport, his willingness to take a turn at bat only because he knew how important it was to the woman he loved, and his immediate passion for the game. His words, though, had no effect on the reporter. In fact, he didn't react at all.

"You not gonna say anything?" Sam asked with a frown.

Rod looked the man over. "Just waiting for you to call me a Yankee."

"Me?" Sam laughed and slapped the man on the shoulder. "Why would I do that? I'm a Yankee, too."

Rod had to admit that he was shocked. "You?"

"It's true," Sam confessed with a nod. "Kariss and her family converted me about eight years ago, pretty much since we've been together. Must have been all that bluegrass her grandfather had me listen to over the years, Old Dixie and such. Or maybe it was the cornbread and grits," he mused.

"So that would make you...a Southern Yankee?" Rod guessed.

Sam shook his head with a grin. "More like...A southern rebel with unfortunate Yankee tendencies." He laughed, pleased when Rod laughed with him. "Well, that's what K.B. says about me, anyway. So...how 'bout it?"

Rod cleared his throat. "I really do appreciate the offer, but I'm just here for the story of the Sour Orange Derby."

Sam patted the reporter on the arm. "You don't get the story of the Sour Orange Derby until you get the story of the Standridge family. *That* is your story, because the Derby isn't just a game to them. This whole thing was created by Kariss and K.B. as a way to heal, and if you want to find out why they needed to heal, and why this means so much to them, then you have to do things their way. Think about it."

She didn't know how her fiancé did it, but Rod Jenkins of New York City was taking his place at home plate. Kariss leaned against the fence, arms crossed, while Sam quickly explained the rules to Team Colly's newest honorary player. Simply stated, honorary players got a minimum of two hits, but as many more as needed in order to score at least five points.

Rod sucked in a nervous breath as he prepared to bat. The last thing he wanted to do today was take part in a sports activity, especially one that wasn't even a real sport. And even more than that, he didn't understand why it was so important to Kariss that he play. The only reason he had reluctantly agreed to bat was because Sam's comment sparked his curiosity. He wanted to know why the Standridge family needed to heal, and why that healing process led to the Annual Sour Orange Derby. He wanted to know for his article, but also because he was starting to get invested in the story personally.

Sam may have been right, he considered, that the Derby would just be a game to him until he picked up a bat and experienced the thrill for himself.

The pitcher held a large, perfectly round orange in her hands, waiting for him to signal that he was ready, kicking her feet in the clay impatiently. With a sigh, Rod lifted the bat to his shoulders. It was a strange, foreign move, something he hadn't done since being forced to play softball in eighth grade, and that was at least twenty years ago.

Fighting back his nerves, as well as his bitter memories of being taunted by the bigger, more experienced ballplayers in his class, the reporter gave the signal that he was ready—a single nod in the pitcher's direction.

The pitch was slow, and the orange seemed to grow twenty times in size as it made its way to home plate. Rod fought to remember all the things any coach had ever told him about how to hit a ball, and when he judged the time to be right, squeezed his eyes shut and swung.

Whether by miracle or marvel, the bat swung true.

Rod opened his eyes just as a dozen chunks of orange peel burst before him, juice spraying across his cheeks, splattering his glasses. Behind him, the crowd screamed with support and satisfaction and shouted out their guesses for how many points he just scored. All Rod could do was stare in amazement at the mess on the field, the mess he'd just helped create. For a moment, time seemed to freeze as he felt something deep inside. It wasn't panic, it wasn't nerves—it was something completely different, something alien.

It was fun. Hitting that orange, getting covered in the smell of sour fruit, was actually fun.

Kariss and Sam ran up from the edge of the dugout, slapping him on the back as they pointed to the field, where the umpires were counting up the score.

"Nice job there, Yankee," Kariss commented.

"I only scored three points."

"So? That's three more points than you would have scored just sitting on the bleachers. And you still got another hit, so go score some more."

It took him eight embarrassing strikes in a row, but he finally managed to hit the second orange and earn another three points for Team Colly. Kariss led Rod off the field as a female member of Team Colly took her place at home plate.

Ten minutes later, they were sitting on a bench in the dugout while the thin, blonde-haired woman in her early fifties who had just walked up to bat was attended to by a paramedic. She wasn't seriously injured, merely temporarily blinded by the chunk of orange peel that had struck her in the eye upon bursting, as well as the juice that was currently stinging her retina.

"And they say fruit is good for you," the woman joked as the paramedic rinsed out her eye.

"Happens every year," Kariss informed the reporter. "Someone always refuses to wear a pair of sunglasses or a pair of our safety glasses, and gets a little more juice than they asked for."

"Is she going to be okay?"

"Ah," Kariss waved a hand, "she'll be fine. Like I said, happens every year. Just tease her like the rest of us and we can get on with the game."

The team was doing just that. "Boo hoo!" an older man taunted from the bench. He grabbed his eye and feigned injury. "It hurts! Oh, it hurts!"

"The pain!" Another man joined in, encouraging laughter from the rest of the players. "I can't handle the pain! I'm such a girly-girl! I'm blind! Fix me up, doc! Hurry!"

"Boo hoo!" the two cried together, faking tears.

Soon everyone was mocking the woman, Kariss included. After a few minutes, Rod couldn't help but laugh. They sounded like obnoxious children, absolutely ridiculous, and were thoroughly enjoying their juvenile behavior. Even the injured woman was laughing as her eye was being flushed with water.

"Suck it up, pansy!" Kariss shouted, nudging Rod in encouragement. He resisted, preferring to simply listen to the insults. "Even the hoity-toity Yankee reporter ain't hurt yet, and he ain't ever even played the Derby before!"

"That's because I'm not a wimp!" Rod shocked himself by replying with the energized jibe that had all the players laughing and hollering out more taunts. He felt his cheeks flush, but he beamed with enthusiasm when the other men jokingly shoved him and the injured woman pointed at him with a smirk and promised her revenge.

"By the way," Kariss said to Rod with a grin as the paramedic finished and the game resumed, "that woman is my mother."

The horrified look that crossed the reporter's face caused everyone in the dugout to burst into laughter as he paled and stammered out an apology.

"Don't worry about it," June Standridge assured the man, rubbing her eye. "Just get on the field and make Team Colly proud."

From her place in the outfield, Kariss kept her eye on the reporter rather than the batters, since it wasn't like she had a pop fly or grounder to watch out for. She felt the attitude that had surfaced earlier begin to fade as she watched him loosen up and actually grin as more batters took their swings.

She couldn't be mad at anyone who played in the Derby. After all, she didn't really care how many points Rod scored, or how long it took him to get the story, or even how obnoxious he was in the beginning. What mattered most to her was that another person had fallen in love with the Sour Orange Derby. He hadn't yet said it, but she could tell by the look in his eyes—the look of shock at actually having connected with the orange, the look of pride in having scored, and the look of pure enjoyment in simply being on the field, part of a team—that Rod Jenkins was hooked for life.

When the next inning began, Kariss took a seat next to Rod in the dugout, who stole a glance up at the old man sitting on the top row of the bleachers. K.B.'s attention was on Team Colly and the last inning, but he knew he was being watched. K.B. didn't miss a thing. He may have been old, but that wasn't something he let slow him down. If anything, his seventy-plus years on earth had taught him just the right amount of wisdom, and now it was a rare event that someone kept their eye on him without his knowledge, and even rarer that some young scalawag came along and challenged the old man to a duel of intelligence, strength, and character.

The arrival of one Rod Jenkins was the first such scalawag he'd seen in well over ten years, as everyone in Barton County knew that K.B. Standridge was not a man to be tested, for he was well-versed in the art of debate, and even more well-practiced in the life experiences that test a person's heart and mind. They were experiences that in his old age he knew made him stronger, but the Annual Sour Orange Derby made K.B. feel young again, and he cherished the reminders of youth and all its glories. Watching the bustle of the game, he felt the enthusiasm and energy of a teenager pulsing through his old veins. There was nothing better than holding a mustard and relish-loaded hot dog in one hand, an ice-cold Coke in the other, listening to the crack of a baseball bat as it connected to the ball, or in this case an orange, and cheering on his favorite team while friends and family gathered together for a day of carefree yet momentous fun.

Life just didn't get any better.

"He really loves this game, doesn't he?"

Kariss looked fondly up at her Papa. She thought it was both amusing and charming that he was pretending not to see them staring, but at the same time, was straining to listen intently to their every word.

"He really does," she answered softly. "I mean, the Sour Orange Derby is the new Standridge family tradition, and he helped created it. When Papa was a kid, the Standridge legacy was the family orange groves. Our family, way before I was born, of course, owned hundreds of acres of land, all filled with orange trees. Papa grew up with those trees, running around the groves, picking fruit. He says that was his favorite place to be as a kid, sitting in the middle of the orange groves, smelling the oranges and staring at the rows and rows of trees." Her eyes took on the same faraway glint that Rod had noticed when she took the field, the same one she spoke of Colly having as a child.

"When the groves died off, Papa says it was like a part of his heart died with them. The Standridge family was known for those groves. In fact, it was the promise of orange groves that brought my family together in the very beginning."

Rod suddenly found himself on the edge of his seat, interest piqued. "How so?"

"Our family goes back to the Civil War," Kariss began, hands gesturing wildly as though to enhance the tale. She leaned back against the dugout wall and her eyes glazed over. It was a look that anyone who knew her would be recognizable as her mind having drifted off into a dream world where great stories were being created. And this was the story she loved most in the world, more than candy armpits or trees that grow gumdrops or any tale of fiction and fantasy that she could ever possibly create herself.

This was a story of history and fate, and she was living proof of its magic.

⁂

It was a long, exhausting night along the wooded mountains of Virginia. The black of the sky was clouded with smoke from the hundreds of muskets fired earlier that afternoon, a haze of bitter reminders of a country torn in half as it turned against itself. The Confederate and the Union armies had decided on a peace offering after a bloody day of fighting, agreeing that no man would lift a weapon until the sun hit the horizon. They had all witnessed enough death in the light of the sun, so much so that even in the dark of night, the bloody images of war would creep into their nightmares.

To ensure that the peace was kept, each troop had sent one man to guard the picket line. On the Rebel side sat William White. On the Yankee side, Ronello Calvin Standridge. Both knew the other was there, but had no desire to talk, fight, or even acknowledge one another's presence.

Leaning against a tree, William White, an idealistic soldier in his mid-twenties with a pale complexion and black hair that matched his piercing eyes, opened his canister of chewing tobacco and took a few moments to relax. For once, despite the smell of gunfire and rotting bodies that tinged the air, the world around him was quiet, only the calming sounds of nature surrounding his spot of isolation. He missed that. Back home, where he and his family lived miles away from the bustle of city life, every day was filled with such tranquility, a tranquility that disappeared the second he signed up for war. Now, if he tried hard enough, he could pretend that he was alone, that the Yankee soldier camped out only a few feet away was just another bump in the road, a lifeless shrub, and that the rest of the world was hidden away from all the hate and misery that ran wild on it today. It was a world away from war, away from blood and bullets, a world he could call his own.

He'd thought he was protecting his land, his heritage, but now, after months of endless fighting that never seemed to result in any progress or resolution, he realized that neither side fought for such a thing. The only thing they fought for was pride, to prove that their way of life, their beliefs, were right, were better, and William was willing to give up his self-righteousness if it meant having the chance to see home again. It didn't feel right, shooting at men who never harmed him, fighting to defeat the people of his own country, and he had come to realize that neither side was right or better, because they both had succumbed to murdering their own brothers. He knew the war was supposed to bring an end to the country's problems, but what saddened him was that he also knew that all the war did was divide it in half. No matter who won, their country was destined for a permanent division between the north and the south.

William wanted peace, and could only hope that one day the world would find such a thing.

"Hey Rebel, got any chewing tobacco?"

William opened his eyes and glanced to his left toward the enemy camp. Peering through the darkness, he made out the figure of the Yankee soldier sitting just across the invisible boundary line, a musket resting across his lanky, outstretched legs. The soldier, like William, was young, thin and scarred from battle, dark hair framing a tired and dirt-smudged face. Deciding to be friendly, too tired to fight, he shrugged and offered the canister, their own sort of individual peace offering.

Ronello Calvin Standridge, known to friends and family as R.C., packed the tobacco in his mouth and turned his eyes up to the smoke drifting across the sky. He watched the wisps of gray swirl around and eventually disappear into the night, mingling and becoming one with the haze that churned in the breezeless air. "War should be over soon," he commented, willing to talk to an enemy if it would make the hours pass by faster.

William huffed. "So they always say." He'd been hearing that phrase from the very beginning.

The Union soldier was quiet for a moment, glancing back at his troop. He could vaguely see the tents and fires in the distance. At camp the soldiers were practicing drills, cooking, and most importantly, relaxing from battle. Part of him longed to be with them, to have just one night of conversation and company with the soldiers who had become his closest friends without the threat of an ambush, while the other part savored the solitude of his post. "We lost a lot of men today," he tried again, sighing heavily. "Doesn't seem worth it."

"It ain't," William agreed. "Our friends and family dying every day, some killed by their own brothers. And for what?"

"For the war. For our beliefs."

"Beliefs?" William scoffed quietly. "We've forgotten what we believe in."

They fell silent, letting the statement sink in, each thinking that there was some

truth to the Rebel's words, until William let out a heavy sigh. "I might be sounding like my baby sister, but I'd give anything to go back on home."

Thinking back to his own home, R.C. didn't see the thrill. His home was a tiny, rundown brick house in Vermont with broken shutters, no yard, and a father who would rather drink than work. Every cent he earned went to that house and that man, who threw it all away on booze and gambling. His mother was a basket-case of a woman who spent the majority of her time crying, sleeping, and ordering him to do the chores or fix whatever was broken. No, R.C. had signed up for the war to get away from home, not to dream of the day he'd return.

"What's so great about home in the south?"

William ignored the demeaning tone. "Well...it weren't so great for awhile. My daddy died a few years ago, and my momma...she didn't handle it so well, being left to raise me and my little sister all by herself. It was rough for awhile, 'til she decided to turn the patch of orange trees out back that my daddy planted into four acres of orange groves." And beautiful groves they became. His mother certainly had a knack for nature and a mind for business.

"We decided that when I get back home, I'll take over the family business. Help raise my sister, let Momma have her days off again. We got some of the best farming grounds around, endless sunshine and fertile soil." He reached over and took back the tobacco canister when R.C. held it out. "Someday I'll get back there. This damn war ain't gonna kill me. I promised my momma and baby sister that I'd come home, and that's what I plan on doing."

In the distance, a group of men laughing echoed trough the trees from the Rebel camp, but neither soldier paid them any mind. "Oranges, huh?" R.C. rubbed his aching neck. A bunch of fruit certainly didn't sound appealing. "Our specialty is syrup back home. Tapping the trees and making maple syrup and the like...That's about it back home. What's so great about these oranges of yours?"

"They ain't just any oranges," William replied as he held up a hand. "These oranges are like magic, not like anything you ever saw before. Walking through the groves, you get completely lost in an entirely different world. The sun shines through the leaves, the smell of oranges surrounds you. You can't see anything but orange and green, can't hear anything other than the wind passing through the branches. It's like your own personal heaven. Like finding peace, away from all this blood and hate and war. Ain't nothing better."

As the Rebel soldier talked, R.C. found himself closing his eyes and picturing the orange groves. He imagined a tranquility he had never known, strolling around orange trees, bare feet crunching over grass and fallen leaves, losing himself in peace, forgetting about the problems and worries of his everyday life.

The orange groves sounded like a place that could be called home. Just picturing the sight he had never seen made all the sounds and images of hate and war that were spread all around him in the night completely disappear.

Suddenly, he feared the night's end. Daybreak meant the truce was over, and William and R.C. would find themselves on opposite sides of enemy lines with no offer of truce to be made.

<hr />

The shrill yet happy shriek of a child snapped Kariss out of her daydream. It took her a moment to realize that she had been talking the entire time, and she was only made aware of that fact by sneaking a peek at Rod's notebook to see her family history written down on the page.

Kariss cleared her throat and stayed focused. "In the morning, the truce was over, and the two enemy friends were forced to fight one another. At the end of the battle, they didn't know what happened to one another, if they were killed, if they lived, and so they parted ways. Before the war ended, William White was discharged after getting what he later called a 'violent cold' after months of sleeping on hard grounds without blankets in the dead of winter. He went on home after developing diphtheria, lung fever, and rheumatic heart disease. He took over the orange grove business from his momma, letting her retire in peace, even though he was never as healthy as he once was. Then," Kariss leaned forward, her voice energetic, "four years after the war ended, William stepped out on his front porch to see none other than Ronello Calvin Standridge standing in his front yard."

"No way," Rod found himself saying. The idea of two battling soldiers befriending one another on enemy lines, let alone finding each other four years later, fascinated him.

"Way," Kariss confirmed, then continued her story. "It turns out that R.C. had been searching for the White farm ever since the war ended. He never forgot the orange groves, the life of peace and beauty that the groves promised, and he longed for groves of his own. So he packed his things and found his way to Florida, to William White's front yard. But the story doesn't end there." She held up a finger and grinned.

"The best part of the story comes later. William and R.C. became best friends, as could be predicted. But what neither of them ever expected by such a friendship, a friendship that eventually became a partnership as they each played a hand in the orange grove business, was that they would become family."

"That's right," Kariss said to Rod's inquisitive frown, "R.C. Standridge married June White, William White's baby sister, who my own momma is named after."

"And the rest?" She held out her arms to encompass the entire scene around them. "The rest is history."

"That it is," Kariss agreed with a nod. She tucked a loose strand of hair behind her

ear, and Rod noted the silver ring on her right hand with a turquoise bear claw in the center, the ring she had described in her earlier story as her source of luck and courage. "But what you have to understand is that the orange groves became the family tradition, something passed down from generation to generation, first from the Whites and then to the Standridge kin. The groves were passed down to my Papa. When all the trees died, it meant that suddenly, Papa didn't have anything to pass down to his own kids and grandkids."

"So he searched for a new tradition," Rod realized, putting the pieces together. K.B.'s tricks weren't just for amusement; they were to make sure he had something to leave behind. "Was the Derby an immediate tradition?"

"Oh," Kariss laughed, "Papa and Colly were determined to be sure of that."

Chapter 13

THE SOUR ORANGE DERBY

Colly was thrilled.

His brothers were both out at friends' houses, probably even staying the night since it was the weekend and they had already finished their homework. His mom and sister were out shopping, something he despised ever having to do. Shopping was the one time he could really make his mom angry, because rather than cooperate and try on the clothes he liked, he grumbled and complained about how bored he was and how everything in the store was ugly whenever June suggested a shirt or pair of pants. To avoid a long day of irritation, June had left her son in the care of his grandfather so she and Kariss could shop for school clothes and groceries in peace. Only about an hour after they left, his Mema was picked up by her cousin, and together they went out to lunch.

He had his Papa all to himself.

After an hour of begging, he finally convinced his grandfather to turn off the TV and go outside to play some baseball. To Colly, there was no such thing as lazy Saturday mornings and quiet afternoons. As far as he was concerned, there was no reason to be inside watching TV when there was a perfectly sunny backyard to run around in. After all, the three baseball games that were scheduled for that day had already ended, with two of his favorite teams winning, and although he was stuffed from four hot dogs and half a bag of Blutos, he was ready to practice his pitching and hitting. If he could learn to pitch really well, then his Little League coach promised he could try pitching in a real game. And if he could hit really well, then maybe he could hit a home run like the coach's son did just a few games ago. He'd been practicing almost every day, and with the help of his Lucky Dime, he was turning into an awesome player, getting stronger, faster, smarter about the ins and outs of baseball.

"Okay, Doodle, let's get this game going." K.B yawned and stretched his arms. His grandson was getting to be just a little too active for him to keep up with, though he would never admit it aloud.

Colly reached for his basket of baseballs, drawing his hand back in panic when he discovered that it was empty. "They're gone! Someone stole my baseballs! Papa, *do* something!"

K.B. scanned the yard. "Relax, Doodle. They must be out here somewhere. Doesn't your momma teach you to pick up after yourself?"

"*Yes*," Colly answered grumpily, and K.B. had to hide a grin at his childish reaction. "Now we can't play. *Man!*" Angry, he flopped down on the grass with crossed arms.

"Well, now, don't throw a hissy fit." K.B. continued to look around and didn't see anything but grass that hadn't been mowed in two weeks, effectively hiding the missing baseballs. Giving up the search, his gaze rested on his beloved orange tree. An idea popped into his head, one that could promise to be the beginning of another wonderful Standridge family tradition.

"How 'bout this, Doodle?" He plucked an orange off the tree, perfectly round and ripe. "How 'bout we play the Annual Sour Orange Derby?"

Colly scrunched up his face in confusion. "The what?"

"The what?" K.B. repeated in mock surprise. "You really mean to tell me you never heard of the Annual Sour Orange Derby?"

"No. What is it?"

"Well! It's only the most exciting game to play with fruit ever invented!" The old man picked a few more round, ripe oranges. "It was invented by the ancient people. Your people, from your old life as an ancient gladiator. You see, they didn't have anything to do back then except build big monuments and make gladiators fight in the Coliseum, so they invented the Sour Orange Derby. Luckily, your Papa knows all about it."

"Cool!" Colly was so excited that he didn't care how Papa knew about it, or even who the ancient people were, for that matter. All he cared about was that he had a new game to play. "Hey, Papa? So when I die and get to be a gladiator again, I can play the Sour Orange Derby with my past life friends?"

"Sure can, and you'll be the most awesome player ever."

"Cool! Let's play!"

The pair headed for the fake field in the yard. Colly took his position at home plate, lifting the heavy wooden bat, his favorite bat, resting it on his bony shoulders. Recently, all the Standridge kids, including Kariss, who rarely attempted to hit a ball, carved their names into the wood. Seeing his brothers' and sister's name next to his made him feel like an extra-strong batter.

"What do I do?"

K.B. held up the orange. "You hit it, just like you hit a baseball. The goal, though, is to get a chunk of orange past that fence." He pointed to the metal fence behind him that was overgrown with vines, separating his property from a large batch of woods. "One point for each chunk over the fence, five if you hit the whole orange over without busting it. A little split with some juice coming out is okay as long as the orange is in one piece. We'll count up the points at the end of the game, and whoever has the most, wins."

"What if I can't hit the orange right and never get any points?"

"What are you talking 'bout, boy? You're an ancient gladiator from Rome, where the whole thing began! The Annual Sour Orange Derby is in your blood! You're a natural!"

"Cool!" Colly lifted the bat. "Let the Annual Sour Orange Derby begin!"

When the first blast of sour orange juice splashed across his face, Colly fell in love. By the end of the game, he smelled horrible, desperately needed a shower, was sticky from head to toe, and had never been happier. June came home to find her son lying on his back in the tall grass, squealing with laughter as Latheena raced around the yard, picking up stray orange peels and tossing them in the air as she played fetch with herself. The boy reeked of sourness, and it took June a good twenty minutes to coax him into the tub, succeeding only after promising him a bowl of ice cream and a game of the Annual Sour Orange Derby next weekend.

They did just that, though it was only the three of them—Colly, June, and K.B.—that gathered in the backyard for an hour of orange-filled entertainment. Colly and K.B., however, played the Annual Sour Orange Derby twice a month for the next year, sometimes alone, sometimes with Tony and Christian, and sometimes even with Kariss and June, while Joyce was content with documenting the games by taking as many pictures as possible.

The Sour Orange Derby had become a tradition.

Chapter 14

CHICKEN DOOKIE

It took them the entire year since the creation of the new family game, an entire year in which school dragged on, Christmas came with all its bright lights and exciting presents, summer vacation arrived much to the anticipation of frazzled minds. But despite the chaos and the distractions of everyday life, Colly and K.B. had finally done it. Every member of the Standridge family was standing in the backyard, baseball caps donned, sneakers tied tight, ready to play the Annual Sour Orange Derby. It was the first time since the creation of the game that everyone was going to play together, and getting them to do so certainly hadn't been easy. Bribery and begging played a major part in the gathering.

K.B. quickly explained the rules. "One point for getting a chunk of orange over the fence. Not *through* the fence, but *over* it. But if you get the entire orange over without bursting it, then you get five points."

"Piece of cake," Tony muttered, picking up the wooden bat.

"It's self-pitch," K.B. continued, tossing Tony a sour orange. "No strikes or outs. We each have a pile of oranges, same number," he gestured to the piles behind him, "and we hit one at a time until all the oranges are gone. The player with the most points at the end of the game wins the Derby."

"Piece of cake," Tony said again, preparing himself at the metal trashcan lid that designated home plate. Only this time, he turned around and faced the chain-link fence rather than batting with his back to it. He shook his head to clear his brown eyes of the curly, chin-length hair that his mother had been bugging him to cut for the past three months. At this point, he wasn't sure which he liked more, the thick tresses that gave him an aura of sensuality that all the girls loved, or the fact that not cutting his hair was seen as an annoying act of rebellion by his mother. Either way, he figured, it still worked out for him, so there was no reason to take a trip to the salon. And now that he was looking at community colleges, he was likely going to move out within the next year or so, which meant he wouldn't have to worry about what his mother thought about his personal appearance anymore.

Tony tossed up the orange, watched it come back down, and swung hard.

"Haha!" Colly yelled from the sidelines when the orange burst, the chunks landing within two feet of home plate. "No points!"

Christian took his turn. After seven self-pitches, he still hadn't hit the orange. His cheeks reddened slightly and he grit his teeth in concentration as Colly continued to laugh.

"That's what you get for never playing with us! It's 'cuz you're not a natural gladiator Derby player just like me! That's what you *get!*"

"Shut up, Colly."

"Make me, meanie!"

"I will if you don't cut it out!"

"Both of you cut it out."

"Fine, *Momma.*" Colly stuck his tongue out at his mother, who only shook her head. Arguing with Colly during a sporting event was pointless. Her son may have been a sweetheart during any other time of the day, but he went into a competitive zone when playing a game that turned him into a feisty, as well as mouthy, opponent.

Obnoxious as he was, though, no one could be mad at him. It was all but impossible to be mad at Colly. At nine years old, he was a bundle of energy and passion, always on-the-go and ready for the next game to play. A big smile was practically permanently stretched across his face, a toothy grin that stretched to his wide, innocent eyes. He reminded June of a puppy—always happy, always excited to meet new people and go new places, always full of bouncy energy that shook his entire body—and no one could ever be mad at a puppy.

Besides, he was so happy that his brothers and sister were finally playing in the Sour Orange Derby together that he couldn't contain himself.

"My turn!" After Christian finally hit an orange, earning one point, and Kariss walked away from her turn with two points, Colly jumped up from his seat on the grass and raced to home plate.

"No, Latheena, it's my turn!" he cried as the dog raced right along side him, barking excitedly and wrestling Colly for the bat. At sixty-five pounds, a combination of muscle and fat, she was a worthy adversary. "Bad doggy!"

"Latheena, come," June ordered, and the dog immediately dropped the bat and flounced over, taking a huffy seat next to her owner.

Satisfied that he was the center of attention, Colly picked up an orange in one hand and gripped the bat in the other. In his mind, he imagined that he was about to bat in his first professional baseball game. He stepped up to the plate, adjusted his batting cap, eyed the nonexistent enemy pitcher, and prepared for the first throw. All around him, screaming fans shouted his name, holding up big foam fingers and wearing jerseys with his number. The tall spotlights illuminated the field in the night, highlighting the perfect place for him to hit the ball, right between the outfielders.

Colly tossed up the orange and swung lightly, but just hard enough to make the best hit of the game so far. The orange sailed over the fence, only the slightest bit of juice escaping from a tiny crack across the bottom of the fruit.

"Five points! In your *face!*"

"Collin," June warned, already exasperated. Her son was not the most gracious winner. While many people were sour losers, her son was what she thought of as a sour winner. "Be nice."

Colly playfully scrunched his face into an expression of grumpiness and snobbery in his mother's direction before taking a seat next to Latheena. June took her turn, then Tony rose for his second chance at batting.

"Wait!" Colly ordered, holding up a hand, "it's Papa's turn."

"No, I'm just a spectator," K.B. replied from his green lawn chair, which was placed next to Joyce. "Today it's just y'all playing."

"Why?"

"Because I want to watch y'all play. Besides, Doodle, I'm the oldest, so I get to choose if I want to play or if I want to watch."

"Why?"

"Because it's more fun that way."

"But why?"

K.B. didn't have the heart to tell his grandson that he simply couldn't find the energy for sports anymore. Each day was growing longer and longer and each night he couldn't get to bed fast enough, but at least today he had the satisfaction of sitting in the sun watching his family come together for the sake of the Sour Orange Derby. The Derby kept him young, so no matter what his body was telling him, no matter the pains in his chest or the doubts in his mind, K.B. felt like a little boy on his first trip to Disney World, and nothing could keep him down. Not old age, not the doctor's orders, not even life itself.

"Because I said so, that's why."

"But you *always* play the Annual Sour Orange Derby."

K.B. forced a smile. "And today I get to watch the Annual Sour Orange Derby, something I've never done before. And since I'm watching, I can decide what we need to do to make the Derby better for next time."

That answer satisfied the boy. Colly gave his older brother permission to bat and Tony continued his way to home plate. He scored two points, Christian scoring zero, and Kariss beating them both with three.

"Piece of cake," Colly mocked his brother as he took the bat from Kariss. He looked over his shoulder at his siblings, thoroughly enjoying the fact that they were covered in orange juice. He hoped that now they understood the thrill of the Derby and would want to play with him again, over and over and over until there were no more oranges left on the tree until next season. They would play so much, he guessed, that his mom would have to buy more oranges from the store, and somehow they would make them sour, or at least pretend that they were, so they could play even more.

Colly tossed up his second orange and slammed the bat into it. The orange slit down the middle, but didn't completely break into two separate halves as it sailed over the fence. Five more points for the champion Derby player, and Colly wiped the orange gunk from his eyes as he cheered.

"Over the fence! Five points for me!" Colly never beat his siblings at anything, so his high score filled him with joy. "How many points do I have now, Papa?"

"Ten, Doodle."

"Am I winning?"

Although Colly already knew the answer, K.B. told him anyway. "Yes, you are."

"Ha! I'm winning!"

"Yeah, yeah, we know," Christian complained. "Get off home plate."

"You're just jealous 'cuz the Sour Orange Derby is in my blood and you just got opossum blood so all you can do is play dead when you're chicken!"

"Shut up, Colly."

"Why? 'Cuz you said so?"

"No, 'cuz it's my turn. I want to take another shot at this," June replied for her son, rising to her feet.

Colly flicked orange goo at his brother and put his hands on his hips, lifting his chin high in the air. K.B. recognized the stance. His grandson was about to break into song. *"Weeeell, excuse me while I linger, but I have chicken dookie on my finger!"*

The kids exchanged confused glances, June covering her face with a hand as she snorted.

"Um...what?" Kariss asked, wondering why her mother found the song so amusing.

"Weeeell, excuse me while I linger, but I have chicken dookie on my finger!" Colly jumped around, dancing to the beat of the song as he edged his way closer to Christian. *"Weeeell, excuse me while I linger, but I have chicken dookie on my finger! And I gotta get it off!"* He leaned over and wiped a finger down Christian's cheek, leaving behind a trail of sour orange gunk.

"Gross!" Christian wiped at his face while Kariss and Tony burst into laughter.

June lifted a brow at her father, who was staring sheepishly down at the score sheet. "Well, that one's new."

K.B. shrugged, an expression of pride crossing his face. "Just came up with it yesterday. Boy learned it quick."

"Of course he did. It's disgusting."

"It's a family song."

June, Joyce, and K.B. shared a laugh, then sat back and watched the three older kids as they engaged in a retaliation match against the youngest, Tony holding Colly down while the others doused him with sour orange juice.

It was just another day in the Standridge family backyard.

Chapter 15
CHERRY RED LIPSTICK

Later that night, the Standridge kids sat up at the counter after having showered to rid themselves of the sour orange stench, three picking through their food and the fourth almost finished. The boys made faces at the green beans, Colly attempting to hide them in his biscuit and Tony mashing them into his potatoes, irritated by the fact that even as a high school graduate with plans to enter college next semester, his mother was still making him eat his vegetables. Every time their mother turned away, Christian slipped a few beans onto his sister's plate, who accepted without complaint. She loved green beans, and had no problem covering for her brother.

In fact, it was a common nightly ritual. The kids did anything possible to hide the vegetables they didn't want to eat, and over the years had come up with some creative ideas. Sometimes the boys ate out the middle of a piece of chicken and filled the center with corn. Sometimes they hid tiny plastic containers in their laps and dropped in peas one by one until none were left. Many times they argued over who got to give Kariss their vegetables, since she only had the stomach for her own serving and one other, leaving two of the boys on their own to figure out another way. More than once, Christian came to the table with his shirt tucked in to his pants, and when his mother wasn't looking, would sneak his veggies into his shirt and head to the bathroom as soon as dinner was over to flush them down the toilet. Colly loved this idea, but hadn't yet quite figured out how to hide the food without squishing them all over his stomach in the process.

Most importantly, though, was that they never ratted on one another. In fact, they often helped each other. Tonight, Tony did just that, reaching over and hollowing out the two halves of Colly's biscuit and smushing the beans further into the bread, making room for more.

By the time June returned from the garage, where she had been switching over a load of laundry, most of the green beans were gone. She didn't bother asking if they wanted more; she knew better by now.

"Colly, eat your biscuit, then you can be excused," she said as she passed through the kitchen, not waiting behind to see the look on her son's face when he realized he would have to now eat what he had been desperately trying to hide. When she heard a snicker coming from the counter, she called out to her oldest son, "And Tony! Eat those potatoes!"

"And they think they can outsmart me," she said to herself as she dropped the basket of laundry on her bedroom floor. She knew all their tricks, but didn't put a stop to them. She enjoyed seeing what new scams they could come up with, and enjoyed even more getting the chance to bust them. It was becoming her own family tradition.

"*Man*," Colly whined, poking his green bean-filled biscuit. "I don't *wanna* eat it. Kariss? My bestest sissy ever?"

"Not me." Kariss waved a hand and shook her head. "I'm stuffed."

"Thanks a lot, *Christian*," Colly spat out at his brother. His attention was briefly interrupted when the phone rang, but he decided to ignore the call instead of rushing to answer it like he usually did. He concentrated on his plate and the pile of mushed green beans, trying to figure out how he could eat them without tasting a bit. "Maybe...maybe they're magic beans. And if I eat them I'll grow strong like Popeye. Then I can have skinny girlfriend that I have to save from a fat, smelly bad guy, and I'll live in a garbage can."

His older brothers stared at him. "You're weird," Tony said, then forced himself to eat his green-bean potatoes.

Suddenly, June rushed through the kitchen, snatching her purse from the dining room table. The look on her face was one of panic and anguish, and she was fighting back tears as she fumbled for her car keys. "Tony, you're in charge!" she called over her shoulder as she bolted for the door, slamming it shut behind her.

The kids exchanged worried glances, but it didn't take long for their unasked questions to be answered. Only moments after their mother had run out the door, red and blue lights flashed outside, an ambulance's siren cutting into the night.

<hr/>

It was a week before K.B. was allowed to come home, one week before the doctors thought his heart was strong enough, one week before he could finally stop taking the medication that made him so woozy that he barely knew what was going on around him.

That week had been difficult. K.B. didn't even remember how it began. One minute he was sitting in front of the television, enjoying a piece of his wife's delicious apple pie while he watched a video of college football highlights that his grandkids bought him for his birthday, and the next he was waking up in a hospital bed. He had flashes of what he guessed were memories, those in-and-out moments that would haunt him for the rest of his life.

His heart had stopped. Completely stopped. No amount of medical technology could save him. His doctor, a tall, stoic man named Everett Albright, who would forever be in K.B.'s prayers, had taken a drastic action, the only action left that could bring K.B. back to life.

Under the harsh lights of the emergency room, with the steady and frightening mechanical beep that signified the loss of a patient blaring in the background, Doctor Albright had cut open K.B.'s chest from navel to sternum and taken the old man's heart in his hands, manually pumping the life-force back into his body. Timed with the beating of his own heart, Doctor Albright didn't stop pumping until suddenly, by miracle or luck or the grace of some higher guardian power, K.B. came back to life.

Placed under the careful watch of the nurses in the ICU, K.B. slept his way through several days, during which a pacemaker was inserted into his chest to aid in the beating of his heart. After a week of stress and tension, as Dr. Albright struggled to stop his patient's body from rejecting the new device, the old man was finally allowed to rest in a room outside of critical care.

Now K.B. was home, alive and well. He was weak and tired, but nevertheless, alive.

Slowly and gently, he lowered himself onto his bed, grateful for the feel of his own sheets and his own soft pillows. With the help of June and Joyce, who each stood on one side, K.B. laid back and sighed with content. The morning light shimmered in through the crystal-clear window, casting a ray of comfort across the bedroom. On the walls hung memorabilia from his days in the Navy, commemorations of his Cherokee heritage such as dreamcatchers and photographs of his great-grandparents dressed in ceremonial regalia, and pictures of his children and grandchildren.

It was good to be home.

"How 'bout some boiled peanuts for the old man, Curly?" he joked to his daughter, affectionately using her childhood nickname based off of her wild and curly blonde hair, as she and Joyce helped him settle into bed.

"Yeah, right, Dad," June answered tiredly. "That's just what you need. A big steaming bowl of clogged arteries. " She straightened, stretching her aching back. It had been a long, nervous, tearful, and tiring week, and she was feeling every last minute. Losing a parent was something a child would always have to face, but she wasn't ready—not yet. The fear and hurt of her father's potential death had ruled her emotions every day, even when Dr. Albright had given him a clean bill of health and approved his discharge.

K.B. thanked his daughter as she pulled the comforter up to his waist and adjusted a pillow behind his back so he could sit up against the headboard. He settled himself, making sure not to tire himself out with quick and sharp movements, then caught sight of the two heads peering timidly around the corner.

"Y'all can come on in." K.B. waved in his grandkids. Kariss and Colly entered the room gingerly, afraid that walking too fast might further injure their Papa.

"Be careful," June warned as Colly sat on the edge of the bed, tucking his feet under him. "Y'all can't stay long. Papa needs his rest."

"Ah, they're fine. Let 'em stay. It's good to see their faces."

Both Kariss and Colly were now on the bed, staring at the bright red wound, about an inch wide, that ran up the center of K.B.'s stomach from his naval to his heart. Colly had never seen anything like it before. Although Kariss had seen plenty of scars in movies, films used in health class to discourage behavior such as drinking and driving, and even on her best friend's face after a bad car accident the beginning of their eighth grade school year, she still had to hold back a grimace. K.B. followed their eyes, tracing a finger down the edge of his new scar.

"You know what your Mema did to me?" he asked,   pointing to Joyce. "She got mad at me and drew on me with her cherry red lipstick. Drew all the way up my belly, pressed down so hard that it won't come off no matter how hard I scrub it, she was so mad."

Colly laughed. "Why'd you do that, Mema?"

Joyce put a hand on K.B.'s shoulder. "That's what happens when he doesn't take out the trash. I warned him twice, but he just wouldn't listen.

That's what he gets." Her response was enough to get another laugh from Colly, but June and K.B. could hear the sadness in her voice, the fear at what nearly happened just over a week ago.

There were many things Kariss was willing to believe, but on this one, her fifteen year-old mind knew better. "Does it hurt?" she asked softly, her eyes narrowed thoughtfully.

K.B. ran a hand through her dark, thick brown hair. "Not anymore."

"Do you have to go back to the doctor?"

"Hope not."

"Did you really die?"

"Collin!" June snapped, her voice breaking as she reprimanded her young son. Both she and Joyce cringed at the question, but K.B. didn't seem to mind.

"I sure did, Doodle," he answered truthfully. Some things he would make up, but not this. This was not another trick. This was real life, and Colly needed to know about that just as much as he needed magic. "And you want to know what happened?"

"Mema made you *eat* the lipstick?"

Kariss huffed while K.B. shook his head, his expression serious and a bit nostalgic. "No, Doodle. I saw heaven."

"Dad," June warned, not being one for religious talk. "Don't—"

"Hey, my grandson asked a question, and I'm answering it. I ain't gonna lie to him about what I saw."

June knew that tone of voice and held up her hands in defeat, sitting on the end of the bed and waiting for what her father would say next.

K.B. continued, eyes staring off into space as though seeing what he remembered right before him in the golden light of the morning sun. "It was quite a sight, Doodle, let me tell ya. So beautiful, so full of light and colors. I felt so happy, not worried or scared about anything. It was like I didn't have anything bad to worry about, and all I had to do was sit back and relax, and I liked relaxing. But you know what? Heaven wasn't the best part."

"It wasn't?" Colly edged himself closer.

"No, it wasn't. Best of all, was that I got to see my momma."

"Great-grandma?" Kariss asked. None of the grandkids ever had the chance to meet their great-grandma before she died, and had only pictures and stories to remember her by.

"That's right." K.B. nodded. His mother died more than twenty years ago from cancer. She had been sick for a long time, and there were times when he didn't think he could remember far back enough when she wasn't ill. Eventually, her body failed, and the strength she fought so hard to maintain for her family dwindled into a peaceful sleep. While K.B. mourned for her death, a part of him celebrated the fact that she was in a place away from pain, from medication, from suffering.

"And Doodle, she was beautiful. She hugged me, gave me a big kiss, and told me how much she missed me. She said she's been watching over me all this time, making sure I was safe and happy." He wasn't the only one getting choked up at the thought. Joyce lowered her head to wipe the tears from her eyes, remembering how kind and gentle his mother was. Her own mother had been a mean, unpredictable woman who would rather throw things than calmly settle a dispute, and Joyce had found love and harmony in the company of Evelyn Standridge, K.B.'s mother.

Still able to feel the warm touch of his mother's hug, K.B. continued his story. "Then Doodle, then she told me that even though she wished I could stay, that I had to come on back home."

Colly, his big brown eyes wide and fascinated, leaned forward. "Why?"

"Why? Because I still had some young 'uns to take care of who needed me."

"Like me?"

"And me?" Kariss put in.

K.B. opened his arms. "Like the both of you, and Tony and Christian, and your Mema, and of course, your momma." He put an arm around his daughter, who was desperately trying not to cry, and gathered the rest in his arms. "She said that no matter what happens, I have to take care of y'all and make sure you're always happy. And you know what, Doodle? She said the Sour Orange Derby is the best thing that ever happened to the Standridge family." He tightened his hold on his family, and they hugged silently, each thinking of what could have happened.

Everyone but Colly, who was enthralled by the sight, averted their eyes from the cherry red scar.

Chapter 16
Annual Sour Orange Derby

The game came to an end, Team Colly winning by sixty points. Kariss and Sam came walking out from the dugout arm-in-arm to the exploding cheers of celebration from the crowd. All the players congratulated one another, even those from the opposing team, with proud shouts of victory and triumphant high-fives. Everyone looked exhausted and sticky, yet exhilaration radiated through their tired grins. On the field, the green St. Augustine grass was littered with scattered bits of oranges. In the heat of the early afternoon sun, the oranges baked and released a bitter aroma that matched the smell of the Derby players.

"So I guess that's a day, then?" Rod assumed as they returned to their place on the bleachers, worried that he wasn't going to get the rest of his story.

"A day?" Kariss repeated incredulously. "We still have the championship, Yank."

"Championship?"

"Yeah," Sam put in, taking a seat next to the reporter. "Team Colly versus Team Citrus, for the championship game."

"We always win," Kariss informed Rod, smugly putting her hands on her hips.

Rod could guess why that was. "Because you're the founders?"

Kariss huffed. "No, because we're the best," she answered. "They don't give us any favors because we're the first. We earn it."

Rod held up his hands. "I meant no offense." He waited to continue until Kariss had gulped down half a can of Coke. In those couple moments, he observed the woman. She was covered in sour oranges, and smelled just like she looked. Her long hair was coated with chunks of fruit, the slimy residue dripping down her cheeks and arms and legs. But she didn't seem to care, or even notice, for that matter. Her eyes glittered with exhilaration, and she seemed unable to keep her hands still as she watched the people in the crowd. Some were refueling at the concession stand, some were sharing conversations with the Derby players, while others led their kids out onto the field to try hitting a few oranges.

"Championship starts in twenty minutes," Sam took over the conversation while his fiancée rested. "We use this time to relax, hang out with friends. Some of the players take their kids out, or other people's kids, and teach them how to play." He pointed to the field he had just come from, where a group of children had gathered, eagerly awaiting their chance to hit a sour orange. Two little boys wrestled over a shiny blue bat, while a group of girls debated whether or not they wanted to get their clothes dirty with sour orange juice. At home plate stood a scrawny six year-old boy who missed thirteen pitches in a row. Finally, after his father moved closer and closer until he was a mere two feet away, the bat connected with the orange and the boy cheered as his dad swept him up in a victory hug. Behind home plate was a line of kids shifting from foot to foot as they impatiently awaited their turn at bat. A cluster of parents and spectators watched from the other side of the fence, pressing their faces up against the metal links. "You got twenty minutes," Kariss informed him, her attention on the kids. "You got any pressing questions, ask them now, because we're up to bat first."

Quickly, Rod scanned his notes. He knew exactly what he wanted to ask, and hoped he would get the answer in the designated time. "Okay, so I've met your mother, seen your grandfather and your two older brothers." He gestured in their direction. "When do I get to meet Colly?"

The reaction wasn't one that he expected.

The relaxed expression on her face tightening into one of unease, Kariss slowly turned her head and simply stared at Rod mouth slightly parted, the energy starting to drain from her face. She clutched her hands together, swallowing hard. She'd known that eventually, as the reporter dug deeper and deeper into the Sour Orange Derby, she would have to talk about Colly, but even now, more than twelve years later, the memories still stabbed deep into her heart. Next to her, Sam lowered his head, sucking in a deep breath.

Kariss looked away when her eyes started to tear. "You really didn't do your research, did you, Yankee?" she asked, refusing to look at him, instead focusing her gaze on the field.

Rod frowned, nervously scratching his chin. "I'm sorry, I don't understand."

Kariss sighed, and when she spoke, her voice never rose above a whisper. "We thought...we thought he just had a sore throat...We were wrong."

A tear slipped down Kariss' cheek. She rested her head against Sam's shoulder as he slipped an arm around her waist. Rod let out a deep breath, removing his glasses and pinching the bridge of his nose. He didn't need to press the question to know that whatever happened involved the death of one of her brothers. The grief spread across her face told a story that spanned more than a decade of coping with the loss of a little boy who was loved and cherished beyond words. It was a love and cherishment that could only be witnessed in the eyes of a sister, a brother, a mother, a grandfather, who still remembered exactly what the boy looked like, the exact sound of his voice.

Though the championship game wasn't to begin for another fifteen minutes, Kariss nodded at her fiancé, who understood the gesture and rose, leaning over to kiss her on the cheek before trotting over to the field.

Kariss wiped her eyes. "The cancer...it spread too fast." Her tired voice was raspy, and when she sighed, it was the sigh of a sister who still grieved for the loss of her little brother. "There was nothing we could do. Nothing... except sit back and watch Mother Nature at her worst." She shook her head sadly, then, with a sudden renewed energy, jumped to her feet.

"I have some things to take care of before the game starts," she informed him. "I won't be back until it's over, so...do whatever you want until I get back."

With that, she jumped down the bleachers and jogged to the field. Rod stared after her, amazed that someone who so obviously still mourned the death of a loved one could find such enthusiasm, and he was troubled by the turn his story was taking. He hadn't been expecting the fact that something so light-hearted and fun could be founded on such a tragedy, and though he hated to admit it, even to himself, there was some truth to Kariss' accusation of not doing his research.

Prior to arriving in Barton County he'd merely skimmed the Sour Orange Derby website, briefly scanning the announcements and latest news concerning the founders, and had only looked at two or three of the photographs from the games of previous years. The Derby simply hadn't interested him, and his conceit had prevented him from believing that the game could ever be a complex network of history, hard work, and people willing to keep the memory of the deceased alive for as many years as possible. Kariss was right—this wasn't a simple story about simple people. This was something much, much more.

"Her energy comes from her heart," an old, rusty voice, twanged with a southern accent, said from behind. Rod glanced over his shoulder to see the man Kariss had pointed out as her grandfather slowly and carefully lowering himself to the seat next to him. K.B. gestured to his granddaughter. "Her and my Doodle were connected like that…at the heart."

Rod took a moment to observe the old man. He honestly couldn't tell his age. Lines shaped by age and experience were engraved deep in his leathery face, surrounding dark brown eyes that stared straight down into his core. They were eyes both haunting and hopeful, old with a spark of youth that flashed from their centers. Dark hair lined with silver framed his face, and tanned, strong arms traced down from even stronger shoulders. Two blue, faded symbols of the U.S. Navy were tattooed on either forearm.

"K.B. Standridge," Rod confirmed, a little nervous as he shook the man's hand. For his age, Rod was amazed at how good he looked, but despite K.B.'s healthy aura, the reporter could also tell that he was old, and feeling his many years on earth. "Those sour oranges must be keeping you young."

K.B. laughed whole-heartedly. "Must be, Yankee," he agreed, then pointed to the field. "Quite a game, isn't it?"

Rod followed K.B.'s eyes. The championship game was being set up, the time and first inning already marked on the scoreboard. "It's unlike anything I've ever seen before," he agreed earnestly. "You've created something big here."

"Oh, I didn't do all this," K.B. informed the man with a shake of his head. "This was all Kariss. I may have created the Sour Orange Derby and got it started in the beginning, but she's the one who took it to this level." He smiled sadly, eyes heavy with old age and many years of memories. "And I always thought it would be Doodle who carried on the family tradition." He spoke his grandson's nickname with affection. "Stinker over there, Kariss, was always a dreamer like Doodle, but she was much more independent. I figured once she was old enough, she'd set out on her own, set the world on fire or something, and Stretch and Bubba, Tony and Christian to you, couldn't wait to get out of this here town. But Doodle…just always thought he'd be the one to stick around."

Rod wrote down the quote. "Do you think that any of this, the Sour Orange Derby, the relationships among your family, would be as they are today, if...um..."

"If Doodle hadn't of passed away?"

Rod nodded. "I didn't...I didn't want to assume...but I did wonder..."

"I understand." K.B. thought about his question. "Hard to say," he admitted. "But I can tell you this. There ain't nothing better than the Standridge kids. All of 'em. They got more heart than anyone you'll ever meet."

Chapter 17

MONKEYS ON FLAGPOLES

"Told you you're not faster than me!"

Colly leaned over with his hands on his knees to catch his breath. It was the first time he'd ever lost a race to his best friend, Nick, and he wasn't the least bit happy about it. He hated to lose. Nothing was worse than losing, especially when he lost to one of his friends, surrounded by the kids on the playground who loved to see the champion defeated. Nick and their other friend, Jess, prepared to race one another to determine who was the fastest of them all.

"You only won 'cuz I'm sick," Colly argued, truly believing that was the case. He'd been home sick for the past three days, and only after his doctor's appointment yesterday had his mother finally let him go back to school. His cold started a week ago when he woke up with a sore throat, but it didn't go away when he took the gross grape medicine that he always had to take when he was sick. He hated that medicine, but not as much as losing.

When he went to the doctor, sitting in a cold exam room with diagrams of the body hung on the walls, he had to go through a series of tests, his least favorite of which included a big cotton-tipped applicator being put down his throat to get a sample of whatever was wrong with him. He didn't have a fever, though, and so the doctor said that, for now, Colly could go back to school, and the boy was thrilled. He loved being home, playing with his Papa, but he also loved being at school, hanging out with his friends, racing one another, playing tag, teasing the girls during P.E.

He was still a little tired, but was determined not to let that ruin his racing status. He was the champ, the fastest ten year-old at his school, and no one was going to take that title away from him.

"I demand a rematch!"

"No way!" Nick shook his head, his shaggy brunette hair falling across his hazel eyes. "You're a slow-poke."

"Oh yeah?" With teasing arrogance, Colly ran a hand through his thick hair in a way that he often saw Tony do when he was trying to impress girls. "Well I'm better looking."

"Well I'm smarter."

"Well I'm funnier."

"Well I'm funner."

"Well I'm a better singer."

Both Nick and Jess laughed. They knew all too well what Colly's singing sounded like, a bizarre, gargling cross between a goose's honk and squealing car breaks. He loved to break into opera, and not very good opera at all as his voice had a tendency to get very high-pitched and even more off-tune, but at the very least, it was entertaining.

"So sing a song," Jess challenged, crossing his arms and grinning from ear-to-ear. He glanced around, hoping there were some girls around so that his friend would be embarrassed. "Bet you won't do it. Bet you're too chicken."

"Wanna bet?" Papa had just taught him a new song just a few days ago, when he was home sick. It had only taken him forty-five minutes to memorize the words, and another five to learn the dance.

Colly walked a couple feet in front of his friends so that he would have an audience. He loved being the star of the show. Clearing his throat, and wincing slightly at the twinge of pain, he prepared himself to sing and dance.

"*Weeeelllll…a monkey wrapped his tail around the flagpole, and showed his butthole, to the world!*" Colly jumped and spun himself around so that his back was to his friends. "*Papa monkey thought the flagpole looked like fun, so he climbed on up, and shook his buns!*" At his friends' enormous laughter, Colly shook his rear to the beat of the song. "*And at the end of the day, the legends always say, the Standridge monkeys all, partied on top of the flagpole!*"

Colly concluded his performance with one giant leap backwards as his friends, both Nick and Carson as well as a few of the boys who had gathered around to watch, crowded around him and begged to be taught the song so they could show their other friends and siblings.

"Okay, okay, I'll show you." Satisfied that he was the center of attention, Colly began to repeat the words, but a sudden wave of fatigue had him hesitating and taking a step back.

"What's wrong?" Nick asked, immediately concerned by the strange look on his friend's face.

"Nothing." Colly shook his head. "Just tired."

Colly tried to shake it off, pretending he was fine. His throat hurt a little more now, but he figured it was because he'd just shouted the song across the entire playground, and he was probably sleepy because he was still sick.

"Whoa, gross, dude!" Jess suddenly cried out, pointing to Colly's face. "Your nose is bleeding!"

Colly lifted a hand to his nose, feeling the warm, sticky substance dripping down his chin. When he pulled his hand back, his fingers were bright red with blood.

"Guess I should go to the nurse," he mumbled, and headed off the playground.

K.B. picked his grandson up from school at the nurse's request. A regular nosebleed wasn't something she always worried about, but combined with a sore throat and slight fever, she had decided it would be best to give the young student the rest of the day off. June was at work, unable to leave as she had spent the past three days at home with her son, so she sent her father to make sure Colly was taken care of, and tried to push the worry to the back of her mind and focus on the mound of paperwork on her desk.

At home, Colly turned on the television and happily settled down to watch an old baseball game tape. One day, he'd be there, on that field, practicing his pitching on the sidelines and smelling the fresh cut grass of the outfield. Hopefully he wouldn't be playing for that team—he wanted to be an Atlanta Brave—but playing on that field anyway. He would be in the batter's box, taking his practice swings to hit the perfect home run. Then he would be pitching, striking the batters out one by one, the huge crowd cheering his name. Little kids would use his autographed picture as good luck charms, and his baseball jersey number would be the most famous number in the country. He couldn't wait for the day.

From behind, holding a steaming bowl of chicken noodle soup, K.B. observed his grandson as he animatedly watched the game. He smiled every time Colly cheered, every time he reenacted a hit or catch. When Colly was watching a game, everything around him seemed to disappear. K.B. admired that about the boy.

"Here, Doodle, eat some soup."

"Papa," Colly complained, pushing the soup away. Soup was boring and gross and no fun at all. "How 'bout some hot dogs!"

"How 'bout some soup." K.B. put the soup back in front of the boy with a stern look fixed across his old, wrinkled face.

"Papa!"

"Eat it, or go take a nap."

There was nothing Colly hated more than naptime, except losing, though there were times he'd rather lose than take a nap. At least by losing he was still doing something active rather than wasting time by being asleep.

He resigned with a grimace and picked up the spoon. Satisfied, K.B. lowered himself to the couch, knowing that the moment he left the room would be the moment Colly threw down the spoon and began hunting for junk food. If he searched hard enough he would find the unopened bag of Blutos in the cupboard by the refrigerator, and K.B. knew of his grandson's ability to sniff out a bag of chips. It was like a sixth sense with the boy, and so for that reason, he had to keep his eyes on Colly at all times.

Colly sipped the broth, his eyes trained on television. By the fifth inning, he was finally finished. "Now can I have a hot dog?"

K.B. picked up the empty bowl. "If you're still hungry, you can have some more soup, or some crackers. Stop asking for hot dogs."

"Mema would give me one. So would Momma."

"Don't go on lying now."

"*Man!*" Colly leaned back and pouted. "You're grumpy today. Meanie." In his own way of rebelling, he turned up the volume of the television so that all he could hear was the sound of the game.

Rather than ordering his grandson to lower the volume, K.B. stood and headed to the kitchen, where he leaned against the counter, closing his eyes in silent worry. Colly didn't look well. His normally tanned complexion was pale, his bright eyes tired, his nose scabbed with blood.

This was no sore throat.

But what it could be, what he prayed it wasn't, was so much worse that K.B. refused to admit that it was a possibility. Instead, he went back to the living room, sat down on the couch, and handed his grandson a hot dog loaded with ketchup.

June walked in the door later that afternoon to find her son passed out on the recliner, empty soda cans and a half-eaten bag of Blutos spread across the coffee table, stuffed from his afternoon of fun and food.

"Dad? You let him eat all this?" she gestured to the soda, the bread-crumbs, and the remains of a hot dog. "If he's sick, you know better than to let him eat junk."

"I know. He had some soup first." K.B. started to clean up the mess. A sudden stitch of pain in his back had him straightening and pressing a hand against his spine. He grinned sheepishly at his daughter. "Your old man's getting old."

June shook her head and waved off the comment with a tense hand. "Old, my butt. You're an overgrown child. It's no wonder Colly's head is all up in the clouds." She laughed and helped her father clean, wiping up a spill on the gray-tiled floor. When K.B. didn't return the laugh, she sent a curious glance his way. "Dad? You okay?"

"Fine, Curly." There was no need to express his concerns at the moment. "Let's get the boy to bed."

<hr>

June got the call two hours later.

The three eldest Standridge siblings were gathered in the living room, staring down at the floor, unable to speak, barely able to breathe. A basketball game was playing on the television in the background, completely ignored by the boys, and Kariss' book laid abandoned on the coffee table. June had locked herself in the bedroom with Colly, who was sleeping soundly on her bed, unaware of the situation. None of the kids had eaten dinner, let alone finished their homework or completed their daily chores. Though they were hungry, eating just didn't seem important, or even possible, at the moment.

K.B. and Joyce rushed over at Tony's call. Kariss grabbed her grand-mother in a tight hug the second she walked through the door, unable to contain her tears. The boys were quiet, not looking up at their grandparents. The entire room was somber, right down to the dim lighting and dark shadows cast upon the walls. K.B.'s stomach churned as he studied his grandchildren, their faces strained with anxiety, hands balled into tight fists as they rocked back and forth on the couch.

"Momma won't come out of her room," Kariss quietly told her grandparents, her own face buried in Joyce's shoulder. "She won't even talk to us. She won't say anything at all."

"Did y'all eat anything tonight?"

"...No. We didn't want to ask Momma to make anything, and besides..."

"Who can eat now anyway?" Tony finished for his sister.

"I'll go to your mother." K.B. gave Kariss a quick hug and headed for June's room, squeezing Tony and Christian's shoulders as he passed.

The door was locked. He knocked lightly.

"Curly? Can I come in?" There was no answer, but on the other side of the door he could hear the distinct and heartrending sound of weeping. "June?"

Though it was locked, K.B. knew how to open the door. He had, after all, built the house with his own two hands more than twenty years ago, had made nearly all of the repairs throughout those years, and he knew every inch of it by heart, all the tricks, all the quirks, all the charms.

It took only a slight jiggle of the handle while lifting the door and K.B. was in. The sight that met his eyes was heartbreaking.

Colly was asleep, curled up in a ball beneath the light green comforter. Lying next to him was his mother, her arms wrapped tightly around her sleeping son, one hand gently brushing his hair. In the other hand, a wad of tissues was tightly clutched. June's eyes were squeezed shut, but tears still managed to escape. The small, yellow flower-shaped lamp on her bedside table provided the only light in the room.

K.B. sat on the edge of the bed. "June..." There were no words for his daughter, no words to bring any amount of comfort, no words to make anything better. He sighed heavily. "June...I'm sorry." He rubbed her back. "Please, talk to me."

After a few moments, June lifted her head a bit and wiped her eyes. "It's not a sore throat," she whispered, gazing down at her son's sleeping face. "It's...it's...*cancer.*" Just saying the word made her nauseous, and she was nearly sick to her stomach as she clasped her hair with both hands and hid her face behind her palms. She couldn't say anything more as the reality continued to set in, and although there was a part of her that desperately wished to be an adult about the situation and take control, to get a grip on herself, the other part, the bigger and stronger part, was ransacked with painful sobs over the fact that there was absolutely nothing she could do. Colly's doctor had made that perfectly clear. There was nothing any of them could do.

"Curly, honey," K.B. soothed, hugging his daughter and fighting back tears of his own. "June, we'll figure out what to do, and we'll get through this."

They sat together for a long time, never saying a word, simply finding comfort in the company of one another, especially with Colly, cherishing every second. Both constantly thought of what was to come and what they hoped they could prevent, and, most of all, how unfair it was that of all the people in the world, Colly was the one to suffer. It wasn't right, June thought, that a kid so full of life might have his own robbed from him. Though she'd never prayed to any kind of God before, she kept her eyes closed and pleaded for Colly's sickness to be taken from him. If someone had to battle cancer, then she wanted it to be her, take it out of her son and give it to his mother, who was stronger, who had a better chance of surviving. She was more than willing to bear that burden if it meant protecting her child.

After a long moment of silence, deciding that he had to take some kind of action, no matter how small, K.B. rose to his feet after kissing his daughter on the cheek. "Tell you what," he murmured, "I'll go make us something to eat, get the kids to bed, and afterwards, we can sit down with your mother and decide what needs to be done. We'll talk to the doctors, and see what kind of treatment he needs, and do it. The sooner we get on this, the better the results will be. Trust me."

As K.B. made his way to the door, his words sunk in and June sat up, pushing her coiled hair back behind her ears. When she spoke, her voice was full of accusation. "You knew, didn't you."

K.B. froze at the door. He didn't turn around right away, and when he did face his daughter, his expression conveyed the truth.

The look on her father's face was all she needed to see or hear. "That's why you let him eat all that junk food today…because you knew he was… How could you?" June lifted herself from the bed with an energy inspired by fury, her head shaking in disbelief. "How could you not tell me?"

"June." K.B. held up his hands as she came closer. "I didn't know for sure."

"But you *suspected* something! Like Grandma!"

"I thought his symptoms were like my mother's, yes," K.B. regretfully admitted, sadly thinking back to his mother's fatal fight with cancer, a fight that had all begun with a sore throat. "But I couldn't be sure. And if I was wrong, I didn't want to scare you over nothing."

"But it isn't *nothing*!" June shouted, her tear-stained face furious. "He's been sick for a *week*! We could have done something *sooner*, if it weren't for *you*!"

Out of rage and fear and utter devastation, June shoved her father against the door.

K.B. took the beating without anger or blame. Instead, he reached out for his daughter, only to have his hand slapped away. "June, don't—"

"Don't tell me what to do!" June shoved him again, her back to Colly, who was awakening from all the commotion. "That is my baby boy! He is my *baby*, and you didn't tell me! You didn't tell me that he might…he might…" She couldn't get the horrible words out as she broke down into uncontrollable tears.

There was no word for this kind of pain, no way to break free of the black fog that gripped her heart. Her fists pounded her father's broad shoulders as he grabbed her into a hug, whispering loving words into her ear, following her as she sunk to the floor, until she finally relented and gave into his arms. She had no strength, no power. Only sorrow flowed through her veins.

"Mommy?" Immediately troubled by his crying mother, Colly crawled out of bed and over to June. He wrapped his own arms around her neck. "Why are you sad?"

"Collin," June whispered, grabbing her son and bringing him into the hug.

Colly let her hug him, wondering why she was so upset, and how he could cheer her up.

"Papa taught me a new song," he announced proudly. "It's about monkeys. It will make you smile, I promise."

Chapter 18
TICKLE WITCH

In his dreams, a dark figure haunted his every sleeping moment.

The figure was a woman, an old hag with long and matted gray hair that flew all around her head. Her eyes were pointed and bright yellow, and shone down on her long, sharp nose. She was skinny, so skinny that her black dress hung off her bones, so skinny that she was weak and couldn't walk right, instead hobbling down the hallway with crooked legs and arms. But worst of all was her laugh, a high-pitched cackle that hurt his ears and made him feel sick inside.

She kept finding him; wherever he tried to hide, around every corner of the white plaster hallways, tucked beneath neatly made beds, ducking behind shiny metal machinery, she found him. He raced down the corridor, fervently protecting the stuffed animal in his arms as he entered what he thought was an empty room—but there she was, standing at the foot of the bed next to a tray with a big needle and a tube of freshly drawn blood resting atop the surface.

She was everywhere. Even when he closed his eyes and prayed for her to disappear, she was right there, grabbing him, laughing at him. When he opened his eyes again, she was still waiting, and so he kept on running, his bare feet pounding on tile floors. But there, at the end of the hall, he knew she would find him. And when she discovered him, she grabbed him with her bony fingers and tickled him, tickling him until he couldn't breathe and he was begging her to stop and was gasping for air but he couldn't get any and he was suffocating and suffocating because she wouldn't let go even though he was screaming and screaming and screaming and—

"*Stop it!*"

Colly shot up in bed, drenched in sweat. His heart was pounding and his chest throbbed from breathing so hard. He couldn't stop gulping in deep breaths of air despite the burning in his chest. Frantically, he searched his room for the evil witch, convinced that she was hiding in his closet or underneath Tony or Christian's bed, waiting for him to fall back asleep so she could creep out of the shadows and tickle him to death.

"You're not gonna get me, ugly evil witch," he mumbled. He quietly crawled out of bed, weak and clumsy, a tight grasp on his favorite stuffed animal, a brown fuzzy otter named Garth. His first instinct was to go to his mom's room, but she had been upset lately and he didn't want to bother her anymore. Instead, he rushed to Kariss' room across the house and hopped into her bed without waiting to wake her first.

"Colly?" Kariss opened her eyes and rolled over, half asleep, when she felt her brother climb in her bed and hide himself beneath the covers, curling against her with Garth safely nestled between them. "Colly, what's wrong?" Colly only clutched her arm as an answer, and recognizing the look of fear in his big brown eyes, she propped herself up on her elbows. "Did you have another nightmare?"

Colly nodded. "An ugly evil witch kept trying to tickle me to death," he whispered, voice filled with wavering terror. "She wouldn't stop even though I kept telling her I couldn't breathe. Now she's still after me even though I'm awake!"

"Just relax, you're safe now. My room is witch-proof, remember?"

The Tickle Witch wasn't a new nightmare. In fact, Kariss could recall at least fifteen other nights that the witch had tried to kill him in his dreams, and every time he had the dream, she came closer and closer to succeeding. It didn't take much imagination to figure out why.

Colly had been in treatment for three months, and in those three months, he had taken a turn for the worse. Each time he had the Tickle Witch dream, the witch became skinnier and skinnier, weaker and weaker, just like Colly. Each time he had the dream, he came nearer to death. And each time he had the dream, he came closer and closer to realizing that.

Besides the dream itself, Colly hadn't had a decent night's sleep since his treatment started. Nor had he been able to eat, or go to school every day, or play baseball. But despite being in pain, he managed to keep his spirits high. Kariss and her brothers, as well as K.B. and Joyce, suspected that the reality of his condition hadn't yet sunk in, though June chose to believe that he was energetic because the treatment was working.

Kariss moved over so her brother had more room to curl up against her. He kept his head buried beneath the covers. "You know," she offered softly, lifting the comforter just enough so she could see the top of his head, "maybe the witch isn't really evil. Maybe you're just scared of her, so you just think she is."

"She *is* evil," Colly replied, his voice muffled. "And ugly. She's an evil and ugly witch."

"But she tries to tickle you," Kariss continued, gripping her brother's hand. "Momma tickles you too, and she's not evil or ugly, is she?"

"...No."

"And when Momma tickles you, it's because she wants you to laugh and be happy, right?" She waited until Colly regretfully agreed before going on. "So maybe the witch is tickling you so you will laugh and be happy, but you *think* she's evil just because she's a witch and isn't pretty. Maybe she's a nice witch, like Glinda, the Good Witch of the North on The Wizard of Oz."

Kariss waited silently, stroking Colly's arm, until finally he peeked out from behind the comforter. "Better?" Colly nodded, giggling when Kariss picked up Garth and wiggled his whiskers against the boy's nose. "So what happens the next time you see the Tickle Witch?"

"If I see her again, maybe I'll talk to her. And not call her ugly."

"Good." Kariss settled down and put an arm around the boy. "Let's get some sleep."

The next day, as they huddled together on the back porch and watched the rain cascade from a slate-gray sky, Colly told his Papa all about the Tickle Witch dream, and what Kariss thought about the evil witch. K.B. listened without saying a word until his grandson was finished.

"Well, Doodle," K.B. said as he sat back in his chair, "it sounds like Stinker there was right."

"Really?"

"Sure enough. Don't you know nothing about Tickle Witches?" As expected, Colly shook his head. "Tickle Witches," K.B. began, thinking quickly to explain the phenomenon he was about to invent, "go all the way back to Medieval times, back with the fire-breathing dragons and knights that slay them with long sharp swords. No one knows how they came to be, but it is believed that they come only to people who deserve to see them."

"Like Gumdrop Trees?"

K.B. laughed. He'd forgotten about that. "Yes, exactly, like Gumdrop Trees. You see, Tickle Witches come to people who are scared, or sad, or angry, or in need of some guidance, and make them happy. You ever hear your momma say that laughter is the best medicine?" Colly nodded, jumping a bit when thunder pounded the sky in the distance. "Well, it's like that. They make you laugh so you can feel better, and they tickle you to make you laugh. Some legends say that the knights used to pray to the gods to have a Tickle Witch watching over them as they went on their dangerous journeys and fought their death-defying wars."

"Cool," Colly whispered in awe, picturing the Tickle Witch from his dreams. Maybe she wasn't so ugly and scary after all. "But why doesn't she stop when I can't breathe?"

The question of death was one that Colly had been circling around since he began his treatment. It was something he didn't quite understand, yet was fully aware that whatever it was, it was getting closer. And K.B. was not going to be the one to explain it to him. He didn't want to be the one to have to say the words, that cancer was killing his body, that death seemed to be the only end. He couldn't be the one to say those words.

"She tickles and tickles," he answered as best he could, "until she's absolutely sure that all the sadness or fear or anger is out of you. She can't stop tickling until you're happy."

"Oh."

The thought excited him, but Colly wasn't sure if the Tickle Witch was doing such a good job. He wasn't *un*happy, but lately he was so tired and sick because of the medicine his doctor made him take that he couldn't play baseball, and playing baseball made him very happy. So was the witch making him happy, and he was too afraid of her to know it, or was he so tired from all his doctor's appointments that the Tickle Witch just couldn't get him happy enough? He couldn't decide, but he did know one thing for sure—he wasn't getting any better. His doctor had explained his condition, that he had cancer, a sickness that, he was told, was life-threatening. Colly knew what life-threatening meant.

It meant he could die. And if he wasn't getting any better, then maybe that's what was happening. And maybe the Tickle Witch, the one who was watching over him like the Medieval witches that watched over the knights, was trying to keep him as happy as possible as he got sicker. That would be nice, Colly mused. He liked the idea of a special guardian that was there to make him happy, but he was terrified of the reason why he needed a guardian in the first place.

K.B. recognized the expression on his grandson's face. It was one of awareness, of reality sinking in. It was the same one he saw on Joyce and June's face when he'd had his heart attack, the reality that age was setting in, age and everything that came with it. Every day Colly's reality edged its way closer, and every day it moved with more determination and devastation. The cancer was taking his grandson faster than anyone could have ever expected, and there wasn't a single thing he could do for Colly except make him as happy and comfortable as possible.

"You know what, Doodle?" K.B. pulled Colly onto his lap. Colly rested his head on his grandfather's shoulder, exhausted. "I think the Tickle Witch is just here to tell you to smile and laugh, because when you smile, the whole wide world smiles with you." K.B. tightened his arms around his frail grandson, quietly humming the tune to his Monkeys on Flagpoles song.

As he drifted off to sleep to the sound of the falling rain, Colly couldn't help but smile.

Chapter 19
KOWANEECHIHAWA

It was the day of the Annual Sour Orange Derby, and Colly was ecstatic. He hadn't played the Derby in almost four months, four long and miserable months filled with cold weather and endless trips to the hospital, and now that summer was here, the weather was perfect for a day out in the sun.

He sat up at the counter, deciding what to eat for breakfast. He wanted something quick, since he'd overslept and was eager to get outside as soon as possible, but his stomach was grumbling for a big meal, which didn't happen too often anymore.

June stood on the other side of the bar, awaiting her son's decision. While she waited, she took the time to look him over. She had finally reached the point to where she no longer burst into tears at the sight and prospect of what was soon to come. Somehow, she had come to terms with fate, though she couldn't foretell how long she could maintain the strength. The sight of her ailing son was slowly chipping away that wall of courage.

Colly lost the last of his hair only a few days before. Having been born with a head of thick brown hair, this was the first time June had ever seen her son completely bald, and while Colly seemed to be fascinated with his new look, running his hands over the smooth skin and occasionally taking a colored marker to the top of his head and scribbling goofy faces or the name of his favorite sports teams, she longed to be able to run her fingers through the dark tresses once again. Even now, despite the fact that the boy had drawn a bright, round orange on the top of his head that made her laugh every time she looked at it, she would have given everything she owned for her son to look—and feel—like his old self again.

But the loss of hair wasn't the worst part for June. For June, it was the loss of his eyes, Colly's wide, eager brown eyes. Once so vibrant, so full of life, they were now faded, sunken holes of exhaustion and sickness. Her son was so tired, constantly nauseous and in pain, rapidly losing weight, and there wasn't a thing she could do about it.

She was his mother. She was the one who was supposed to be able to fix things. Every cut, every bruise, every tear and fear, she was supposed to make everything better. But this...this was beyond her. This was devastating.

This was taking her energetic baby boy away from her.

"Grits and scrambled eggs, please."

Colly's decision snapped her out of her daze and back into breakfast-making mode. "Cheesy or bacon grits?"

"Cheesy!"

"Cheesy it is." June set out the ingredients and shot her son a smile. "Anything else?"

"Scrambled eggs!"

"You already said that."

"I know. I want lots of them."

June laughed, thrilled by the display of energy. "You got it. Lots of scrambled eggs."

Colly tapped his fork on the counter. "Lots of scrambled eggs for the growing boy!"

June froze, her back to her son. Tears instantly formed, but she recovered quickly, determined to never let Colly see her cry. "That's right," she forced herself to say around the sobs that threatened to rack her body, "lots of scrambled eggs for the growing boy."

Colly scarfed down the meal, still managing to savor every bite, then hopped down from the stool and over to the phone. "Papa?" he said when K.B. answered the other line. "Sour Orange Derby! Sour Orange Derby!"

He hung up the phone. "Papa's coming over!" he howled to June.

"No need to shout, Colly, I'm right here," June replied, but he didn't hear, as he was already out the back door.

Colly raced outside and stopped when he reached the orange tree. He reached up and plucked off the biggest, juiciest sour orange he could find. "You're going over the fence, buddy," he whispered to it, and started to make his pile.

A wave of nausea passed over Colly, forcing him to sit on the grass. He leaned over, head in his hands, silently begging for the feeling to go away. He couldn't be sick, not today. Today, he was going to play in the Annual Sour Orange Derby.

As he walked next door, K.B. kept his eyes on Colly. It was obvious that the boy wasn't feeling well, and K.B. knew that the Derby was sure to wipe out what little energy Colly had left. Because he knew that, he veered directions and went into the house rather than the backyard. He greeted June, who was cleaning up from breakfast, and kept walking straight into Tony and Christian's room.

"Wake up, boys," K.B. ordered, flicking on the light. "Up, let's go!"

"Papa," Tony complained, rolling over onto his stomach. "Too early."

"Up," K.B. said again, opening the blinds to let the bright sunlight stream in. His grandsons grumbled in reply and yanked the pillows over their heads. "We have a game to play, and Doodle's not going to be able to do it by himself. Get up. I'm not gonna tell you again. Don't make me flip those mattresses over and roll you out onto the floor myself."

They would follow his orders. They always did, especially since they knew that he had flipped their mattresses before and was willing to do it again, and so without waiting to make sure they were dragging themselves out of bed, he made his way to wake Kariss.

"Stinker," he opened the door. "Up. Outside. Doodle needs you."

That was all he needed to say, and she was up. K.B. left the house and went to be with Colly, who had managed to get himself to his feet and was unsteadily gathering oranges for the other players.

"Doodle," K.B. called, lowering himself to the ground. "Come sit with me for a minute."

Colly did as he was told, taking a seat beneath the shade of the orange tree and hating that he was already tired. "Ready to play?"

K.B. leaned back on his hands and looked over at his grandson. "Well, that's what I wanted to talk to you about, Doodle...I don't think you should..." He sighed and stared up at the cloudless blue sky. "How about you keep me company today during the game, sit with me in the audience?"

The question confused Colly. "But I want to play."

"I know, I know." K.B. picked up an orange and rolled it around in his wrinkled, work-and-weather-worn hands. "But maybe you'll feel better if you rest, and if you watch with me, we'll be able to come up with new ideas about how to make the Sour Orange Derby even better."

"But it's already perfect."

"How do you know? You ever watched from the audience?"

"No."

"Then how do you know it's perfect if you haven't seen it from all sides?"

"Guess I don't."

It took about ten minutes more of convincing, but Colly finally gave in and agreed to watch the Derby from the audience with his grandfather. He didn't want to, but the truth was that he really didn't feel well, and wasn't sure if he'd even be able to hit the orange at all. And he certainly couldn't let his brothers and sister show him up and make him the loser of the Annual Sour Orange Derby for the very first time, so it would be best to rest for the next game.

June rounded up her kids and ushered them outside for the second Annual Sour Orange Derby in which the entire family was involved. Even Latheena was given a pile of oranges to chew up and roll around in.

"What do you think, Doodle?" K.B. asked as Tony went up to bat. "Should we give him three strikes and he's out, or as many hits as it takes?"

"As many as it takes," Colly answered. "It's funner that way."

"I agree." K.B. cast a sidelong glance at his grandson. Despite the warmth, Colly had a light blanket wrapped around his shoulders, and big sunglasses protected his sensitive eyes. But the old man didn't need to see the boy's eyes to know his feelings, for his body language told it all. Colly wanted to play, and he was miserable on the sidelines.

K.B. wasn't sure which was better or worse, keeping him depressed and dejected on the sidelines so as to preserve his much-needed strength, or letting him play only to have the boy feeling miserably exhausted for the next few days. The decision tore at K.B. and left a bitter resentment in his heart at having to make such a choice.

To distract Colly, even if only temporarily, K.B. thought of an old trick he used to play on his daughter. "Hey Doodle, did you know that I fought in a war?"

"Yeah." Colly kept his eyes trained on Christian, who was on his fifth strike and trying to ignore the teasing jibes from Tony and Kariss. "Momma says you were in the Navy."

"That's right, I was. And you know what I learned in the Navy?"

"No." Colly barely cracked a smile when Christian hit the orange and it exploded in his face.

"I learned how to speak Japanese."

Now Colly turned his head, interested. "Really?"

"Sure enough. You want to know some?" Colly nodded, so K.B. continued. He didn't really know Japanese, but that had never stopped him before from pretending like he could. "*Waydeechima*." He made the word up on the spot. "That means 'friend' in Japanese."

"*Waydeechima*," Colly repeated, instantly fascinated. "What else?"

"Well, the word 'dog' is *sheeshay*."

Colly reached out and pet Latheena. "Hi, *sheeshay*." He glanced up when Joyce cheered for a perfect hit over the fence, but didn't clap with her. Instead, he continued to pet the dog, preferring to learn more Japanese rather than watch the game.

"Baseball?"

"*Babawa*."

"Boy?"

"*Heheeshan*." K.B. hid a smile, laughing inwardly when June caught wind of the conversation and shook her head in amusement. He hoped Colly wouldn't ask the words again, because he wasn't sure he could remember the fake translations.

"Papa?" Colly scooted over and leaned against his grandfather. "How do you say 'orange tree' in Japanese?"

This time K.B. did smile. He handed Colly the orange he was rolling around in his hands. "*Kowaneechihawa*," he answered softly, lifting his head to take in the magnificent sight of the Standridge Orange Tree, the last orange tree of the once-enchanting orange groves that stretched for acres in rows and rows of sweet-smelling splendor.

And then, with that one look at his tree, he realized that he couldn't do it anymore. He couldn't just sit there and watch his youngest grandson sit on the sidelines of the game he loved most in the world. Colly didn't have much time left. That much was obvious, and it was a fact that everyone did their best to deny. But today, in the presence of the Annual Sour Orange Derby, K.B. couldn't deny it any longer.

"Doodle," K.B. rose to his feet, "you get yourself up there to home plate."

Colly tore off his sunglasses. "Really? I can play?"

K.B. glanced at June, who nodded in approval, before helping the suddenly ecstatic boy to his feet. The change in Colly's attitude was both thrilling and saddening. He had no idea if batting would drain the rest of his energy for the day, or likely the rest of the week, but he didn't take the time to wonder. All that mattered to him was that his grandson got to play. "I think a couple times at bat won't hurt."

Kariss handed her little brother the wooden bat, graciously giving up her turn. Joyce, ready with the camera, positioned herself to get the perfect shot. Tony picked out the best orange of all the piles and tossed it to Colly.

"Piece of cake," Tony said with a smile.

"Batter up," Christian put in from behind.

Colly was nothing but confident as prepared to bat. No one was better playing the Sour Orange Derby than him, and he was going to prove it.

As her little brother strutted up to the plate, weak arms struggling to lift the bat, Kariss shifted in her seat upon the grass, unsure how to feel about the situation. She wanted Colly to play; after all, it was his game, his passion. But at the same time, she was afraid that playing would make him sicker, weaker, less likely to recover quickly.

"Don't worry," Tony, as if reading her mind, said from beside her, "he'll be fine. Playing will be good for him."

Kariss stole a quick glance up at her older brother. Every day, Colly was beginning to look more and more like Tony, with deep, almond-shaped eyes and a face full of strong bones. Even now, being sick and thin, she could still see the resemblance.

"What if he's not?" she asked quietly, toying with a blade of grass. "Fine, I mean….What if he gets worse?"

Chewing on his bottom lip, Tony thought about the risk of his brother not recovering. It couldn't be possible, couldn't happen. Not to Colly. His brother was only ten years old. Tony was nineteen, and he wanted his little brother to know how it felt to be nineteen, to drive a car, to go on a date, to graduate high school. To become a professional baseball player, just like Colly dreamed of becoming.

It used to bother Tony that his youngest brother was a dreamer. He was never like the other kids his age. Even at ten he seemed younger than the rest, more innocent, naïve about the ways of the world. Nothing was ever able to keep his head out of the clouds, and Tony felt that his grandfather only made things worse with all his stories. He felt the same way about Kariss, who didn't act like a normal almost sixteen year-old girl either. Rather than hanging out with friends and rebelling against their mother like other teenagers, she was home, writing stories and playing with her little brother. The idea of maturity seemed beyond them, and K.B. was at fault.

But now, the eldest Standridge sibling realized that the innocent dreaming was what made Colly and Kariss so special. It wasn't immaturity driving the fantasies, it was hope, the hope that magic really did exist. And maybe, as Tony came to conclude, magic only existed to those who could remember what it was like to be a child, like Colly. Colly *wasn't* like the other kids his age, who were determined to grow up fast and do adult things. He was just like a little boy should be, a child who loved to have fun and dream big. Innocence and naivety didn't seem like such bad things anymore.

Suddenly, Tony didn't know why he had been so against his grandfather's tricks and claims of magic. If anything, they were the reason why Colly was so strong and full of life, against the odds of death. But if he was going to lose the fight, then Tony would rather his little brother pass with images of magic in his head rather than the harsh realities of the world.

"I...I don't know, Kariss," he finally answered with a sigh. "I don't know what's gonna happen."

Kariss faked a smile when Colly shouted at everyone to watch the master play the game. "It's just...it's not fair. I mean, what did he ever do? He's just a little kid, you know?"

"...I know."

As much as she wanted to, she couldn't stop her depressing thoughts. Hot tears burned her eyes. "And what about Momma? I mean, first Daddy dies, and now..."

"Stop," Tony ordered, keeping his voice low. "The last thing Mom needs is us falling apart. And the last thing Colly needs is to see you cry." Kariss lowered her head until she felt the tears disappear. Watching her, Tony felt tears of his own, tears he had to force back, and he softened.

He put an arm around his sister. "Let's stay positive. No one knows what will happen. But no matter what does, we're still a family, and we're always here for each other. And for now, all we can do is make sure Colly stays happy. Right?"

"Right," Kariss agreed, sniffling and raising her head, hoping no one had seen her tears. She could do that, make sure Colly stayed happy, and to prove that fact to both Tony and to herself, she clapped her hands together and cheered for her brother as he tossed the orange a few times in the air for practice.

"Go Colly! Hit it out of the park!"

"Duh!" Colly called back, sticking his tongue out playfully. He gripped the bat hard, his favorite wooden bat, and threw the orange up high into the air. It came back down fast, his eyes trained on the round, orange blur, and at just the right time, Colly swung.

Like hitting the perfect, game-winning home run, the orange flew over the fence, not a single drop of juice escaping. Lifting his arms in victory, Colly laughed and cheered, then pointed to the woods where the orange had disappeared.

"Still the champ!" he boasted, jumping in triumph. When his brothers playfully teased him as being a sour winner, he stopped, a serious expression crossing his face. For a moment, June thought her son was offended, but when he smiled, a smile that hinted at the mischievousness that boys were so capable of committing, she simply sat back and let the action unfold.

Colly lifted a hand. "*Weeelllll, excuse me while I linger, but I have chicken dookie on my finger!*" He scooped up a pile of orange goo. "*Weeelllll, excuse me while I linger, but I have chicken dookie on my finger!*"

"*And I gotta get it off!*" the three oldest Standridge kids shouted back in unison. Tony leapt up and grabbed Colly by the waist before he could throw the orange goop. They fell to the ground, Tony cushioning the impact, and Kariss and Christian scooped up their own handfuls of sour oranges and covered their little brother with it.

"*We gotta get it off!*" Tony sang loudly, mushing an orange on the top of Colly's head. Colly erupted into squeals of laughter that filled the entire backyard.

"I'm gonna get you!" Colly broke free of his brother's grip and jumped on his back. His pale, bony limbs wrapped around Tony's neck in the tightest grip he could manage. "Take that, enemy batter!" He pulled Tony's hair.

Tony laughed and held Colly by the legs when he heard his little brother's heavy panting, as the boy was already out-of-breath. "Catch us if you can!" he yelled to Kariss and Christian, and took off across the yard.

The adults watched as the kids ran around the backyard, chasing one another with handfuls of juicy orange pieces. Colly bombarded Kariss and Christian from Tony's back, and the two being attacked dodged his aim by ducking behind shrubs and trees. When they reared back their arms to throw a handful of orange goo, June could tell that they were only pretending to miss.

She held on to her father's arm, never taking her eyes off the touching sight. The sound of their laughter soothed her aching heart.

Chapter 20
Annual Sour Orange Derby

"That was the last Annual Sour Orange Derby Doodle ever played," K.B. said quietly, staring down at his worn, black leather wallet after pulling it from his back pocket. "Sometimes I still think of how foolish I was to almost keep him from playing. That kid loved this game more than anything, and there I was, thinking he'd be better off on the sidelines. Goes to show you that you still got a lot to learn even when you're an old man." He pulled a picture from his wallet and handed it to Rod. His hands shook from age. "This is my favorite picture of my Doodle."

Rod couldn't help but smile. The picture magically embodied the story K.B. had just told. A little boy no older than ten, grinning from ear-to-ear with withered arms raised in victory, shone from within the frame of the photograph. His big brown eyes, eyes that seemed double in size against the contrast of his bald head, were lit up with triumph, a wide, toothy grin spread across his pale, innocent face. Colly was a child having one of the best days of his life, but Rod could also see that he was a child who did not have many more of those days left. Yet somehow, the boy's energy and zest for life sparkled through the appearance of his sickness, and the reporter found himself admiring the child for his ability to savor the moment.

"He's adorable," Rod said as he handed the photograph back. "He must have been a great kid."

K.B. ran a finger down the picture. He treasured the photograph now like he once treasured his orange tree. "He was a character," he agreed. "So full of energy and imagination. It was real tough when he died, real tough for a long time."

The group of fans that had gathered around the field cheered suddenly, encouraging Rod to check out the championship game. Amazingly, more than half the game had passed while K.B. was telling his story, and Team Colly was winning by thirty points.

A thought occurred to the reporter. "So this is how you memorialize him? You started the Derby in his honor?"

"We did," K.B. confirmed. "When Doodle died, we were all kind of lost. And June, she couldn't even get out of bed." He gestured to his daughter, who was congratulating a member from the opposing team on his great hit, and fought back the familiar sadness. "It ain't right, a mother having to bury her son."

Rod didn't reply; he just listened. There was nothing to be said after such a stoic affirmation.

"But the Annual Sour Orange Derby...well, my momma was right when I saw her all them years ago. It's the best thing that ever happened to our family."

Chapter 21

IRON MAN

It took only a month after Colly's last time at bat.

K.B. stood in the back of the church, hands in his pockets and eyes trained on the floor. He didn't have the strength to lift his head, to face the truth of what the day had brought. In the front row sat June and her children, and despite the crowd that separated them, the sound of his daughter's weeping pounded into K.B.'s ears. Anger, sorrow, hate, devastation, all tore at him for the miserable fact that he was unable to make things better.

Every night since it happened, every night since Colly's death, he had nightmares of the future. Without Colly, life seemed to have lost its spark for all of them. K.B. felt the same sense of loss and despair he had felt as a child when he lost his youngest brother to pneumonia, only this time he'd been forced to watch death take its course for four months, the longest and most heartbreaking four months any of them would ever experience. The memory of Colly's youthful, innocent face, his growing body changing as it shrunk, paled, and thinned, made him so nauseous and lightheaded that he had to physically make himself think of something, anything, else.

Taking in a deep breath, K.B. found the strength to lift his heavy eyes to the altar. The sight of such a small coffin topped with beautiful orange flowers brought forth fresh tears that burned as they cascaded down his cheeks. Next to the coffin was Colly's fifth-grade picture, taken just days before his diagnosis. A wooden cross decorated with white satin sashes hung behind the casket, and the sun shone through the stained-glass windows, creating a rainbow of light that illuminated the altar. While the minister spoke of the boy, praising his good heart, his precious existence, K.B. scanned the rest of the church. Not a single eye was dry, hands clutching tissues and faces buried into shoulders. So many people had loved Colly Standridge, and so many mourned for his death.

Sitting in the front pew, Kariss stared at her hands, which were clutching Tony's arm. Her black dress was stained with tears. Next to her, their mother swallowed hard every other second, fighting back raging sobs with her entire body shaking from the effort. Christian sat on the other side of June with an arm around his mother's shoulder, giving his best effort to soothe her broken heart, while his own slowly cracked and fell apart.

No effort could heal any of their hearts. For June and her children, they were now faced with not only the loss of their brother, but the reminder of their father's death, and the painful memories that came from both tragedies. As K.B. watched them, he wondered how they would ever find their way out of the darkness.

They'd all been strong right up to the end. On the night of Colly's death, every one of the Standridges had known that he wouldn't wake up in the morning. Perhaps it was pessimism, perhaps it was instinct. Or maybe it was the mere sight of the little boy that fueled their knowledge. All day long he'd been shivering, unable to find warmth in any blanket, in any hug. Only for a few moments at a time could he remain fully awake, and he hadn't been able to eat even a single bite of food for the past two days. They knew that when he lay down for the night, he wouldn't rise again.

In the morning they each said their goodbyes separately, without letting Colly know what was happening. Christian had spent time teaching Colly how to play several different video games until he was unable to hold the controllers any longer. That was their way to bond, in the virtual fantasy worlds of excitement.

Tony gave his little brother their favorite wooden bat. "I'm passing it down, from me to you," he'd said. "You're now the rightful owner. You just make sure it stays safe, you hear?" Colly's face had lit up with pride and he promised that nothing would ever happen to it.

K.B. and Joyce spent their time together with Colly. K.B. held another lesson in Japanese with the boy, reveling in the spark of interest and fascination in the boy's eyes, while Joyce simply listened to his talk of racing friends at school and being the champion Annual Sour Orange Derby player. Colly loved to talk about the Derby, and Joyce loved being the one he talked to.

When Kariss' turn came, she wasn't sure she'd be able to maintain her composure. Entering Colly's room, she sat on the edge of his bed and took a few seconds to gather her wits. She glanced around the room. Baseball memorabilia covered the walls, posters of famous players and banners of his favorite teams. The light on his ceiling fan was shaped like a baseball, red stitches and all. Colly's bed, where he was currently lying as he prepared for his afternoon nap, held dozens of trading cards that were spread around the dark blue comforter, where they remained after he had spent an hour admiring his collection, and tired of the activity.

Taking in a deep breath, Kariss held out a hand. Colly eagerly awaited the surprise as she uncurled her fingers and revealed her gift.

"Remember this?"

"My lucky baseball dime!"

Kariss handed her brother the dime. "I know you gave it back to me after you got to be such an awesome baseball player, but I thought you might want it, you know, for Luck."

"Baseball Luck?"

Clearing her throat with difficulty, Kariss moved closer and laid a hand on Colly's arm. She pressed her lips into a tight line to control her tears before daring to speak again. "You know......our Luck is good for lots of things. Your Luck specializes in baseball, but really, it can help you with just about anything. With baseball, with tests at school...with feeling...better. So if it's with you at all times, you'll always be safe. I just...I thought you should hang on to it for awhile."

"Cool." Colly wrapped his hands around the dime and adjusted his tired head on the pillow, eyes so heavy with fatigue that he didn't notice the struggle Kariss was engaged in to suppress her emotions. "I'm so glad you found my special Luck."

"...Me too, Colly...Me too."

"You're my bestest sissy ever," he murmured as he drifted into sleep, and the moment Kariss heard his light snores the tears tumbled from her eyes.

That night Colly slept in his mother's room. Unable to eat dinner, he'd complimented June on her best-ever smelling lasagna and sampled only a tiny forkful of the saucy noodles, rubbing his belly in approval. Then he snuggled beneath the covers with Garth the Otter gathered in his arms. At the foot of the bed, Latheena lay curled in a fat ball of black fur, ecstatic that tonight she was finally allowed to be on the bed.

June lay down next to her son after making sure the other kids were safely in their own beds, unable to sleep as their minds were dominated with thoughts of the impending morning. Together, she and Colly watched a baseball game that K.B. had taped for his grandson one night when he couldn't watch the game because of a trip to the hospital. The Atlanta Braves were up to bat, and although he was too tired to cheer or reenact any of the great hits, catches, and throws, the gleeful glint in Colly's eyes told June that he was absolutely thrilled.

"Someday, I'm gonna be there," Colly whispered, taking in the magnificent sight of the lush green field lit up with tall spotlights and camera flashes that sparkled among the crowd.

"That's right, Colly, you will be." June put an arm around her son and hugged him close. For the moment, she forgot her tears as her imagination took her into her son's dreams. "You'll be standing on the pitcher's mound, striking out those enemy batters one by one. Then you're up to bat, eyeing the enemy pitcher as he tries to fake you out with them curveballs and fastballs. But you're too smart for that smelly ole' pitcher, and you hit that ball way into the field, over the fence, and it's a grand-slam homerun!"

Colly let out a satisfied chuckle, closing his eyes and listening to the soothing sound of his mother's quiet voice. He hugged Garth tighter to his chest. "What then?"

"What then?" June repeated, lowering her head so that she was whispering into her son's ear. "Then, the best thing of all happens. You run the bases, feet hitting first, then second, and third, and you race to home plate as everyone in the crowd jumps up and down, screaming your name and asking for your autograph. You've won the World Series for your team, and everyone wants to shake your hand and have their pictures taken with you. Then you look up in the stands and see your family, your momma, your Mema and Papa, your brothers and your sister, all cheering for you and telling you how much they love you. And best of all, you're named the MVP, the best professional baseball player that ever lived."

With the Atlanta Braves playing their hearts out in the background and his mother's vivid promises dancing behind his eyes, Colly slipped into a deep, peaceful sleep.

June pressed her lips together, fighting against the angry and desperate scream that was bottled in her throat. She stroked Colly's back as he slept, breathing shallow breaths, grateful that her son had held on to his dreams until the very end.

"And best of all," she whispered to sleeping ears, "is that you got your Daddy waiting for you as you walk off that field." Colly never got to meet his father, and June believed with all her heart that her departed husband was waiting with open arms to greet his son.

"Goodnight, sweetheart," she murmured, resting her head next to his as the power and determination it took to be strong for her son and her family drained from her exhausted mind, body, and soul. Her puffy eyes lifted to the ceiling and her quiet, tear-filled voice wavered when she spoke. "Look after him, Grandma. Give him all the hot dogs and Blutos he wants....And Philip, you keep our son safe. Play the Sour Orange Derby with him, he'd like that. And be sure to tell him how much we love him, and how much we love you. And that one day, we'll all be a family again. I promise."

The ceremony ended, but it took awhile for anyone to rise from their seats. It seemed no one was willing to step outside into the bright sunlight, as though the cheery atmosphere of the day was an insult to the gloom that was housed within the solemn walls of the church.

Eventually everyone, June and her family included, found their way to their cars, and then to the cemetery. There, Kariss joined her grandfather as they hung back from the gathering, holding one another's hands. They stood between two towering oak trees, the sight of freshly placed flowers brightening up the somber hues of the guests' clothing.

"Is it gonna be okay?" she asked, her voice wavering. She sniffled and wiped her nose. She turned and looked up at her grandfather when he didn't answer. "Papa?"

"What?"

Kariss chewed on her bottom lip. Ahead of them, Tony and Christian stood with their cousin, Dewey, who had his hands shoved in his pockets and his dark eyes clouded with tears, and none of them spoke. June was comforted by Joyce off to the side, and Hester, who had arrived with Dewey, was leaving to head back to K.B. and Joyce's house, where she was going to cook the best food she could manage for the mourners of Colly Standridge.

A rock had formed in the pit of Kariss' stomach, painful and determined to serve as a constant reminder of her misery. She had barely been able to eat or sleep since Colly died, and just when she didn't think she had any more tears left to cry, a thousand more raced down her cheeks.

It wasn't fair that her little brother had to die, and she was angry. But her anger couldn't defeat her sadness, a kind of sadness that she didn't remember feeling when her father passed away. She had been young then, only five years old, and didn't quite understand the concept of death, of someone she loved never coming home, never seeing them again. As she got older, she learned how to cope with her father's absence, and over the years it got easier, because she never felt that she had known him as well as her older brothers, or her mother.

But she had known Colly for his entire life. They'd spent eleven full years together, what would have been twelve if his birthday had come just a week earlier, as he died six days before. For almost twelve years she had played with him, protected him from monsters, explored magical worlds side-by-side. Who would eat gumdrops with her now? Who would she save from evil tickle witches? Did magic even still exist, or did it die with her little brother?

She had to know. She had to hear the words, that magic hadn't gone away, that it followed Colly wherever he was and made him happy and safe. She had to know that magic could still exist in a world where the bad seemed to overshadow the good.

"Papa?" Kariss shifted from foot to foot. "Do you think that maybe it's possible that Colly's in ancient Rome, fighting in the Coliseum, being hailed as the greatest gladiator the world has ever known? Like you said?"

K.B. heard his granddaughter, but didn't have the courage to answer. The truth was, he didn't have the answer, because he didn't know if what he said would be a lie. There were no stories in his heart today, no magic, and he couldn't give Kariss the hope she so desperately needed.

"Papa?" the girl's voice broke as a sob escaped. "He's...he can be...he's a gladiator, right? Right?" Her chin quivered, and when she saw the tears in her grandfather's eyes, she couldn't fight her own. She breathed deeply, hands curled into tight fists. "Pa...Papa?"

Kariss took a step back, shaking her head in disbelief. Her surroundings faded into the distance as her reality, as everything she once believed to be honest and true, was threatened by her grandfather's excruciating silence. "No...he's a gladiator...you said...you *said*..."

When K.B. only swallowed hard and lowered his head, refusing to look at her, Kariss ran from his side, past the grieving crowd, across the freshly-cut grass, collapsing on the ground just before the parking lot. She drew her knees up to her chest, not knowing what to think, what to believe. She was old enough to know that her grandfather's stories were just that, stories, but even at sixteen she needed to hear that there was more to death than nonexistence. For Colly's sake, she needed there to be something more. If her brother could be a gladiator, then she wanted him to be a gladiator, even if such a thing seemed impossible. *Someone* had to believe in magic.

"*Osiyo*, sweetie."

Kariss looked up as a man approached her side. He was tall with a big belly, gray hair that matched his beard, round glasses, and tribal tattoos on his arms. He was dressed in a traditional Cherokee ceremonial regalia, a beautiful brown leather outfit with red and black lines patterned across the man's chest, blue-painted bone buttons, and a beaded medicine wheel in the center of the top. A bone belt was wrapped around his waist, and a feathered headband circled his head. He wore tan moccasins with long suede laces and held a wooden cane painted with the colors that matched the cardinal and sacred directions of the medicine wheel—red for east, black for west, blue for north, white for south, yellow for up, brown for below, and green for the center of all things . Around his neck was a leather medicine bag with white feathers hanging from the bottom.

To the Panther Clan of North Carolina, the man was known as Elder Little Feather, a name that contrasted his stature. But to Kariss, he was known simply as Uncle Tony.

"Hi, Uncle Tony. *Osiyo*."

Anthony Standridge, K.B.'s younger brother of eight years, as well as the namesake for June's oldest son, squatted next to his great-niece. "How are you?"

The comfort in his voice soothed the girl. She shrugged. "It's...hard." Kariss wiped her nose with the handkerchief her uncle offered. She looked Uncle Tony over, appreciating the ceremonial outfit. Though many people in her family didn't understand their heritage, and frowned upon his choice of wardrobe for the funeral, Kariss believed that her brother would have loved the sight. He would have believed in it, just like she did. And it didn't surprise her that he was wearing the regalia, for he was an elder of a Cherokee clan and took his position seriously.

"Uncle Tony? Do you think it's possible for Colly to be in Rome, as a gladiator?"

Uncle Tony smiled. "I do. In fact, I think he is there right now, beating up all the bad guys and making fun of them when they cry." The image made her giggle, and she could see her little brother doing just that.

Pleased to see the smile, Uncle Tony reached into his medicine bag and pulled out a small feathered object. "Here, this is for you. It came to me in a vision, and my guide, *Ugugu*, the owl, taught me the ways in which to create it."

Kariss took the object. She peered down at the butterfly, running her fingers over the wings made of bluebird feathers, painted in an intricate pattern with red swirls surrounding black dots. The body of the butterfly consisted of tiny square beads, alternating between green and dark blue. "It's... beautiful. I love it." She clutched the butterfly to her chest.

"I gave it to you for a reason," Uncle Tony said as he carefully settled down onto the grass. "Kariss, I have given you a Cherokee name. Your name is Little Butterfly. In Cherokee, it is pronounced *Usti Kamama*."

"*Usti Kamama*," Kariss repeated. "I like it."

Uncle Tony took the butterfly from Kariss and held it up. "The butterfly is an extraordinary creature, Kariss. It is the only animal able to transform itself from one identity to the next, which means that it is a symbol of change and transformation. When faced with change, whether good or bad, the butterfly can withstand anything, and always comes out triumphantly. No change is too great for the butterfly."

Kariss hoped her great-uncle was right. No change, even the change in her brother, was too great for her to handle, and if she drew on the strength of the butterfly, she too could withstand anything.

Uncle Tony offered the item back to Kariss, who cradled it with both hands. "But more importantly, *Usti Kamama*, is that the butterfly is also a symbol of resurrection and spirituality. You see, the butterfly is the only creature able to travel from the physical world to the spiritual world. The ancient spirits say that if you capture the butterfly, you can whisper to it your greatest desires, and it will carry your wish to the Great Spirit so that it will be granted. In doing so, you help to restore the balance of nature."

Kariss lifted the butterfly in the wind, imagining that it was drifting along with the breeze, visiting Colly in the spirit world. "If I'm the butterfly, does that mean I always help the balance of nature?"

"It does. You are the balance, and if you ever need it, you can find balance right in here." He reached out and gently tapped Kariss just above her heart. "Use your gift well, and it will help guide you, and others, through your life." He cast a glance over toward K.B., the man he thought of as both a brother and a father. K.B. had experienced so much loss in his life, and Uncle Tony's heart ached for his pain.

"*Usti Kamama*, I have also given Colly a name, and I thought that you should know it first." He pulled out a necklace from one of the many pouches on the bottom of his shirt. He held it up in the sun, and Kariss marveled at its beauty. Pure white bones formed a nearly perfect circle, each individual bone separated by a beautiful blue bead that glittered in the light. In the center hung a miniature metal axe surrounded by white egret feathers.

"I named your brother *Talugisgi Asgaya*. It means 'Iron Man,' a man who is strong physically, but more importantly, who has a strong moral character, and who is a great joy to his family. He is his family's pride."

"Iron Man," Kariss whispered, fingering the necklace. She smiled through the tears approvingly up at her uncle. "Colly would have liked that name."

"It will do him good as a gladiator."

Kariss' eyes lit up with hope. "You really think it's possible?"

"Of course I do."

"But...so many people tell me to just grow up, and act my age. They tell me that things like that aren't possible."

"*Usti Kamama*, most people do not know what we know."

"...What do we know?"

"That this world is founded upon magic. Our very existence is written in the history of the earth, in the movement of the clouds. If we do not have our dreams, our beliefs, then we do not have ourselves." Uncle Tony fastened the necklace around Kariss' throat. "Sometimes it is easier for people to give up magic for the replacement of science because it gives them a reason for everything. Science gives them truth. But science does not give them gladiators, or butterflies that transcend worlds. And sometimes, it is hard to believe in magic when our world is threatened by the harsh realties of life, but it never leaves us. Some people may tell you to grow up, *Usti Kamama*, but I say, those people have grown up too much. They have forgotten the old ways, and so death, to them, is merely the end. But to us, to you and to Colly, to *Talugisgi Asgaya*, death is the beginning of a new, exciting life somewhere else."

His soft yet strong words sunk deeply into her heart. Touching the necklace reverently and feeling a powerful, comforting connection to her brother, Kariss gave her uncle a long hug, and together they rose to their feet. Kariss provided the old man a sturdy shoulder to grip as he straightened.

Neither were aware of K.B.'s watchful gaze, or of his deep appreciation for his younger brother's presence. Uncle Tony had a way of bringing peace and hope into people's lives, looking to the spirits of their ancestors for guidance. He could create a magic that made anyone believe in the impossible, one different from K.B.'s but exquisite nonetheless, and his magic was needed today.

Today, K.B. couldn't find any magic for himself, let alone for anyone else.

Chapter 22

KAMAMA

Kariss wandered around the backyard aimlessly, occasionally kicking a fallen pine cone. Latheena trotted behind, a stick held in her mouth and her tail wagging in hopes of a game of fetch. The air was crisp and the sky clouded, the perfect day to wallow in the bitter memories of death.

It had only been two months since the funeral, and those two months hadn't been long enough. None of them had found the strength to heal, to move on. Tony and Christian spent most of their days anywhere but home, desperate to get away from the gloom. Tony used his time outside of work and college classes to look for an apartment, and often took his brother with him. Sometimes Kariss envied their ability to escape, other times she hated them for leaving. June rarely left her bedroom, and ate only when Kariss or Joyce forced food in front of her face. K.B. hadn't told a single story, preferring to watch TV instead. Only Latheena seemed unfazed by Colly's death, and Kariss wondered if dogs really were able to sense the spirits of the dead, and therefore knew that her former owner was safe in his new home, wherever that home may be.

Kariss missed the way things used to be. From the depths of her heart, she missed that life. Each morning she awoke with a deep longing for big breakfasts of scrambled eggs and grits and bacon, for days of school not filled with sympathetic looks and teachers who let her get away with not doing any homework, for Little League games, the sound of her mother's cheerful voice, for the magic of the Standridge family tradition.

But it was a longing that she could not avoid, an emptiness that could never be filled.

Her Uncle Tony's comfort at the funeral had soothed her only for that day. When she awoke the next morning, everything he said didn't seem to matter anymore. She believed his words, did not doubt that the world was founded on magic or that death was only the beginning of a new life some-where else, but having her faith in magic restored did not bring back her little brother. He may be living an exciting life as a gladiator in ancient Rome, but Kariss wanted him here, for herself and for her family.

While wandering aimlessly in the backyard, lost in her thoughts, she came to a stop at the orange tree. Despite the sorrow that surrounded it, the tree hadn't lost any of its glory. Fresh fruit that always seemed to grow no matter the season hung from thin branches, bright green leaves surrounding hues of orange. Wanting to feel happy, Kariss sat in the shade of the tree, wrapping her arms around Latheena when she plopped down by her feet, whining softly and licking her owner's hand.

"I know, girl, things are—"

Kariss stopped short when she saw the monarch butterfly that landed on a milkweed plant only a foot away. Its yellow and orange wings slowly fluttered in the wind as it balanced itself. She watched it for a moment, eyes trained on the tiny creature of transformation. The butterfly was beautiful, delicate and free, and the girl had an immense respect for its unique place in nature. Cautiously, Kariss crawled over on her hands and knees, cupping the butterfly in both hands.

"*Kamama?*" she whispered to the butterfly, glancing around as though expecting time to stand still, nature to turn itself out of balance. She felt the soft wings glide against her fingers, and remembered what her uncle had told her.

"*Kamama,*" she lifted her hands to her lips, "please let me know that Colly is okay, wherever he is. Please let me know that he is happy, and safe, and that he knows that we all love him so much. Please let me know that he found our Daddy, and that they are together, playing the Sour Orange Derby and having fun, and that they have each other, so they don't have to be alone."

With a single tear escaping down her cheek, Kariss rose, lifted her arms toward the sky, and opened her hands, releasing the butterfly. She kept her eyes on the colorful creature as it floated away, carried by a cool breeze through the treetops, eventually disappearing into the sun.

She stood frozen in that spot, squinting up into the sun, wondering if her uncle was right, if she had restored the balance of nature and if her wish would be granted. It wasn't a complicated wish, she didn't think, but really rather simple. She wanted what she guessed most people who experienced loss would wish, to know that their loved one was safe. Her mind's eye imagined the butterfly's path as it journeyed to the spirit world, traversing the different planes of existence, and marveled at the strength it must take to travel so far.

With a sigh, Kariss pushed back her hair and lowered her gaze. She had no idea how long she was supposed to wait, but her wish was one she needed now. If her family was going to heal and learn to move on, then something had to happen soon. Glancing toward her house only to find it dark and uninviting, she slowly and unwillingly made her way toward the back porch, stopping in front of the plastic basket of baseballs that Colly had once so often played with. She reached down and picked one up, tossing it from hand to hand, remembering her little brother, remembering his toothy grin as he ran around the backyard, celebrating his home runs. Kariss laughed softly at the image of Colly wrestling Latheena for the bat, his face scrunched in an expression of desperation and annoyance.

The laughter faded to sadness. She tossed the ball over to the basket, missing and knocking it over. Baseballs rolled across the back porch, Latheena bounding across the yard to chase them, attempting to gather every one in her mouth.

Lowering herself to her knees with a sigh, Kariss gathered the baseballs into a pile and righted the basket, then pulled her hand away in shock when she saw the silver glint at the bottom of the plastic.

With a breath of disbelief, Kariss retrieved the dime from the basket, and brought it closer to her eyes as though not believing what she was seeing. The world seemed to stop spinning when she saw the date on the dime. 1992, the exact date of the original Lucky Baseball Dime.

"It can't be," she said quietly, not able to prevent the smile that was pulling at her lips.

But it was true. She was holding Colly's Lucky Baseball Dime, the dime she had given him for courage on his first Little League game, and for safe passing on the day of his death. The dime was proof that her wish was granted. There was no other explanation. Her wish had been carried to the Great Spirit by the butterfly, by her guide, and now she knew that her brother was in a safe place, that he was happy, and that he knew how much they all loved him. Most importantly, he was with their father, together at last.

She looked up at the sky, where white puffy clouds floated their way into intricate, abstract patterns. "Thank you, *Kamama.*"

Leaping to her feet, Kariss raced through the house and into her mother's room. She found June lying on her bed, curled up beneath a thick comforter. The light on her bedside table cast an orange glow across the room, clashing with the glare from the muted television. A picture of Colly holding Latheena as a puppy was set up on the table.

"Momma?" Kariss climbed onto the bed. She brushed back June's curly hair and waited until she opened her eyes. "Momma, look." She showed June the dime. "I asked for a sign that Colly was safe wherever he was, and that he knew that we loved him, and then I found this. Momma, it's his Lucky Dime. Remember? His Lucky Baseball Dime from Little League?"

June took the dime and observed it. It looked like any other coin she had ever seen. "It's just a dime, Kariss." She handed it back to her daughter.

"No, Momma, it's a sign. Why else would this dime be at the bottom of his baseball basket right after I asked for a sign?" Determined not to be defeated, Kariss tucked the dime into her pocket and rubbed her mother's shoulder. "It was just like Uncle Tony said it would be, that when you catch a butterfly, you whisper—"

"Those are just stories, Kariss. They're made up. You know better than that."

Kariss frowned and looked down at the bed, tracing the pattern of the comforter with a finger. She didn't know how to convince her mother that the dime truly was a sign. If she could do that, then she could get not only June but everyone else to know that Colly was safe and happy. And if Colly really was okay, and if he was happy, then maybe they could be too.

For now, she decided that the best thing she could do was simply be there for June and the rest of her family. She could try her hardest to make things right, though what that meant, she wasn't sure. What she did know, however, was that while June had lost one child, she still had three others.

Kariss settled down next to June and wrapped an arm around her waist. "It's okay to be sad, Momma." June clutched her daughter's hand, but didn't respond. "But you know...I'm still here. And Tony's still here, and Christian, and Mema and Papa. It's okay for us to be sad, but...we can't just stop living."

June lay silently for a moment, wondering how the world would ever be the same. She heard her daughter's words, but didn't have the energy to consider them. "I'm tired, Kariss."

Kariss wasn't going to give up. "But Momma...we still need you. Even if it's just to talk, you know?" June desperately wanted to talk to her daughter, to all her children, but she just couldn't find the right words or the right strength. "We could start by maybe just eating breakfast together, if you want."

After a long pause, June agreed to the suggestion. "That sounds good, sweetie."

Pleased and relieved, Kariss hopped up from the bed. "I'll make some bacon and eggs, and we can have breakfast in bed." She headed for the door, then, as an afterthought, took a few steps back to the bed and set Colly's Lucky Baseball Dime on the table next to her brother's picture. As she left the room and was closing the door behind her, Kariss stole a peek back at her mother, inwardly satisfied when June reached out and picked the coin up, placing it on the pillow beside her head.

Chapter 23
LEGACY

It was a rare day that the old man felt the weight of his long life crushing down on his shoulders. In his mid-sixties, he still enjoyed a brisk walk through the park, a boat ride down the river, a few sunny hours of gardening. He prided himself on keeping his body healthy, his heart strong, his mind sharp; but now, with his thinning dark brown hair, deep lines etched across a sun-roughened face, and arthritic limbs, his age had finally caught up with him.

But this wasn't an old age brought on by time and its unfortunate consequences. This was the old age of bitter sorrow, and for an entire year, that sorrow had beaten him down.

As he sat on the back porch, feeling the warmth of the summer sun against his leathered flesh and keeping his eyes trained on the tall, grand orange tree in the middle of the yard, K.B. reflected on his troubles. It had been just over a year since his world changed, since his family suffered the tragic death of one of their own, and he still, no matter how hard he tried, how hard he searched, couldn't find a way to move forward in life, couldn't find a way to remember the way his grandson deserved to be remembered.

In fact, none of them could.

K.B. often wondered why the mourning process was so difficult. After all, time was supposed to heal all wounds. When his mother died, he'd moved on. When he lost his little brother, he'd moved on. But back then was different, because back then, he'd been forced to move on, as he had a family to take care of. There hadn't been time to mourn when faced with the responsibility of clothing and feeding his younger siblings.

Colly's death seemed so unlike the others. Now, there was all the time in the day and night to mourn, there was time to cry, to sit and remember what was lost. There was all the time in the world to remember, and no time to forget.

It had only taken four months for the cancer to seize the boy's life. It happened so fast, yet as each month passed, the days seemed longer and longer as they witnessed the effects of death. K.B. had hoped that those four months would give them time to accept what was going to happen, so that when Colly actually died his death wouldn't come as a shock. Instead, those four months deceived them, giving them a false hope that the chemotherapy would work, that some miracle would take place and that life would go back to normal. It wasn't until the funeral that the reality set in, the reality of eternity, that they would be spending the rest of their lives without the youngest member of the Standridge family. And it was the funeral that set them back so emotionally, rendering them incapable of moving on. For a year now, a year that passed quickly in their misery, absolutely nothing had changed.

Only Kariss seemed to have found some peace in her brother's death. He didn't know what had sparked the change, but somehow, only a couple months after the funeral, she was able to get out of bed in the morning and get dressed, and go about her day despite the number of tears she cried the night before. K.B. admired her courage and her strength, but still didn't understand how she could miss her brother so dearly, yet smile over each memory of his life. K.B. couldn't find such strength to cherish those memories, and that fact made him feel like he was failing his grandson. He had to find a way to remember.

K.B. rose from the plastic chair and made his way across the grass, feeling every single burden of not only the past year but of his entire life suffocating the air of the world around him. As he neared the house next door, he saw his teenage granddaughter stretched out on a hammock, absently petting the fat orange cat lying across her stomach as she stared up at the clouds.

"Where's your momma?"

Kariss Standridge turned her bright green eyes to her grandfather. The look alone spoke every word that the old man needed to know. These days, his daughter spent the majority of her time in her bedroom. The progress Kariss thought she was making when she encouraged her mother to breakfast in bed upon the discovery of Colly's Lucky Dime had proved to be slow and frustrating, for while that moment did spark some change in June, she was yet to return to her old self. She had returned to work only at the persuasion of her boss, and did her job well, as she poured her mind and body into her work as a distraction for the thoughts of her deceased son. But when June came home for the night that distraction faded, leaving Kariss and her brothers on their own.

Tony had decided to remain living at home while attending school until he could be sure that his mother and siblings would be alright, while Christian was planning his move to whatever college he would soon be accepted to. Kariss did her best to get their mother in high spirits, and at times she succeeded in putting a smile on June's face. It was, in fact, progress, just slower than she would have liked.

K.B. gently and sympathetically patted the girl on her shoulder. He may have felt like his age was catching up to him and the weight of so many burdens was impossible to bear, but Kariss was dealing with not only the loss of her sibling, but the withdrawal of her mother into a gloom of seclusion and loneliness.

"Papa?"

"Yes?"

"Do you think the reason why it's so hard to move on is because we don't know how to stop being sad?"

"...Could be."

"Then how do we stop feeling sad?"

That was the question K.B. had been trying so hard to answer for the past year. How does one stop feeling sad, when all around are constant reminders of an event so painful that happiness seems impossible? He thought about that as he turned his attention to his beloved orange tree, the tree that never lost its beauty despite the ugliness that surrounded it, and he realized he may have the answer. The way to stop feeling sad was not to mourn, but to celebrate, and celebrating his grandson's memory was what they needed to do most, what he needed to do most, and what he had failed to do thus far.

When he turned his attention back to his granddaughter, he saw that she, too, was staring at the orange tree, an expression of hope crossing her young face that told him they were thinking the exact same thing.

"Get your mother and brothers outside," he ordered, heading for the tree. "We got a game to play."

Kariss did just that, though it took a good twenty minutes to coax her mother off the couch and through the back door, and Kariss was careful to be vague as to her purpose for gathering them all together. If her mother knew her plan, she certainly would have stayed beneath the comforter.

Tony and Christian followed simply for the sake of having something to do. When they saw the baseball bat and pile of sour oranges lying on the ground next to the trashcan lid, all three stopped short. June turned to head back inside with a disgusted huff, but K.B. took her by the shoulders and nearly had to shove her into the backyard.

"Give it a chance."

"Dad, this is ridiculous. And hurtful. I can't believe that you—"

"Curly, give it a chance."

"Why?"

"Why?" K.B. crossed his arms as Joyce cautiously entered the yard. "Because for an entire year this family has done nothing but mope around the house and hate the world. Because we lost someone who meant the world to each and every one of us, and we haven't done a damn thing to honor his memory. That's why."

Kariss approached her mother slowly, holding out an orange. "Please, Momma? We have to try."

Biting back tears, June took the orange, running her fingers over the gritty surface. Her mind replayed every Annual Sour Orange Derby her son ever played, every time at bat, every celebratory song. He loved the game and everything it entailed. It was upsetting that so many things had to end with Colly's death—the Annual Sour Orange Derby, baseball games on TV, Little League and pitching practice in the backyard, gumdrop trees and candy arm-pits.

Maybe not everything has to end after all, June thought

Her father was right. It had been an entire year, and they had done nothing to honor Colly's memory. *She* had done nothing. But how could she, when every second of every day was filled with the constant reminder that she would never get to hold Colly in her arms again? She'd already dealt with the loss of her husband, the man she had loved most in the world, the man who always knew just how to make her laugh, and it had taken years for that pain to subside in her heart, a pain that still, some thirteen years later, affected her throughout her daily life. Now she was faced with the loss of her son, and she didn't believe that there was any right way to mourn.

Maybe Kariss was also right, that she had to try. Lying in bed all day, acting like a zombie when she dragged herself to work, wasn't going to bring her son back. Something had to be done.

"Okay," June agreed with an affirmative nod. "We'll try."

"Let the Derby begin!" With an energy half-forced and half-genuine, K.B. picked up Colly's favorite wooden bat and held it out to his grandkids. "Who wants to go first?"

"I will." Tony offered when no one volunteered. "I always used to go first anyway." He took his place at home plate and plucked an orange up from the ground. For a moment he simply stared at it, memories taking over. "Piece of cake," he said softly, sadly, with a hint of nostalgia, and tossed the fruit high into the air.

When the orange burst into tiny pieces, June couldn't hold back the smile that spread across her tired face. It was a smile that everyone welcomed with open arms.

With each pitch, K.B. felt the burden of the past year lift from his shoulders, replaced by the hope that his family could move on with their lives and learn to exist among the memories of the departed, rather than let those same memories burden them down with misery and loneliness. He smiled down at his granddaughter, knowing that the game was exactly what they all needed.

It was as his mother said, the Annual Sour Orange Derby was the best thing that had ever happened to the Standridge family. At the time, he hadn't realized what she meant, figuring that his mother was merely complimenting him on creating a fun game for his grandchildren. Now, he believed that she knew of what was to come, and was sending him a message for the future.

By the end of the game, everyone, June included, was cheering and celebrating with playful high-fives and genuine encouragements. When the last orange sailed over the fence, giving Christian the points he needed to win the game, they collapsed on the grass and looked out across the yard at the scattered bits of sour orange.

"So…now what?" Joyce asked, pouring glasses of sweet tea.

"Dunno. I already missed my class," Tony replied, scoffing at his mother's surprised and disapproving glare. "Hey, I figured this was more important…Ah, come on, Ma," he complained when June kissed him on the cheek, but surrendered to her hug.

"I have an idea."

"What's that, Stinker?"

"The yard's a mess."

"That's not an idea."

"It is in my head."

"So, let's hear it."

Kariss stood, walked over to a pile of orange remnants, and picked up a juicy peel. With a grin and a mischievous glint in her green eyes, she reared back her arm and released the chunk. It sailed toward Christian, smacking him square in the forehead.

"Sour orange fight!"

At their sister's shout, Tony and Christian leapt up from the ground and grabbed as much orange bits as possible, flinging them at Kariss, who ducked and dodged like the agile huntress her grandfather had proclaimed her to be. With a laugh, she hid behind K.B., then yelled in protest when he mashed orange guts into her hair.

"This means war!"

"Bring it on, Stinker! And Curly, I'm coming after you next!"

True to his word, K.B. fought against both his daughter and grand-daughter, and finally against his grandsons, until they were forced to declare him the champion of the fight. Only Joyce escaped his sour orange wrath, since K.B. knew better than to squash oranges into his wife's hair.

Eventually, the orange pieces ended up either in the woods or on the Standridges themselves, so together they headed to the hose to rinse themselves off before entering the house for a shower.

Trailing along at the back of the group, Kariss stopped short when she saw the young boy bracing himself against his bicycle at the edge of the driveway, slightly hidden behind an oak tree. Curious, she walked over to him.

"Hi."

"Hi. You're Colly's sister, ain't ya?"

"Yeah. And you're Jess."

"You know me?"

"I remember Colly's friends."

"Oh." Jess Smith, a tall and scrawny boy of twelve, shyly pushed back his blonde hair. "Cool."

A familiar sadness tugged at Kariss' heart at the sight of her brother's friend, but she fought it back. "Can I help you?"

"Were you playing the Sour Orange Derby?"

"How'd you know about that?"

"Colly...he used to talk about it all the time. He said he was gonna invite us to play sometime." He shrugged and looked down at the handlebars of his dark blue bike. "Guess that's not..."

The sight of the boy touched Kariss. She did remember him, remembered him quite well, in fact. Colly used to race against him, and frequently came home from school bragging about his victory. Jess was a sweet kid, polite, though a little rambunctious. She didn't like the look of regret in his bright blue eyes.

"Tell you what. Next time we play the Sour Orange Derby, you're invited."

"Next time?"

"Next time."

"Can Colly's other friends play too?"

"Of course they can. We'll teach y'all how to be real-life Sour Orange Derby players, Colly-style."

"Awesome."

Three months later, Kariss fulfilled her vow. Fifteen of Colly's old friends appeared in her backyard, though they had only been expecting seven or so, and together with her brothers, grandparents, and mother, they played the biggest game of the Annual Sour Orange Derby that had ever been played. As far as Kariss and K.B. were concerned, they had created a legacy out of her little brother.

And that was only the beginning.

Chapter 24
HOT DOG OFFERINGS

In the light of the morning sun, K.B. finalized the plans for the upcoming weekend. He double-checked the guest list, the times, the safety wavers, and when he finished, he brought the list to Kariss. She added a few names and crossed out others before tallying up the total.

It had taken them seven months, seven tedious months of negotiations and irritating setbacks with the city council, but they finally had a date and a place to play the Annual Sour Orange Derby. The game had become too big for the Standridge backyard as more people, primarily kids though some of their parents were eager to join in as well, asked to take part, and K.B. knew that if they wanted to continue, they needed a bigger yard.

It had been Tony's idea to play at the park by the Rec center on the fields once used by Colly's Little League team. The idea was a good one, but getting city officials to agree to a game in which sour oranges would be spewed across the field wasn't as easy as they'd originally thought. The fact that the field was open to the public made no matter, as any plans for an organized baseball game, particularly one that involved fruit being splattered on the grass, had to be approved by city hall. Kariss' appeal to the mayor of Barton County on the basis of her deceased brother's memory was what allowed them to play the game, but before they could step foot on the field, forms had to be signed and an official agenda had to be approved. But regardless of the hassle, all that mattered to K.B. was that in three days, he would be on that field playing the Annual Sour Orange Derby.

Those three days passed quickly, and at seven AM Saturday morning the Standridge family walked the field, measuring distances to set out markers for points and organizing the batting equipment. Christian had thought it would be fun to use actual baseball gloves and batting hats even though there was no real use for them, and the others agreed. Joyce oversaw the delivery of oranges. Some came from the Standridge backyard, plucked fresh from the last orange tree of the old groves, but there simply weren't enough to play an entire game and so the rest were ordered from local distributors.

Everyone was willing to play along that the oranges were sour, and K.B. certainly wasn't going to tell them any differently.

Around nine AM the players began to arrive. As directed, members of Team Colly, those who were family and close friends of Colly Standridge, wore orange, and members of Team Citrus, those who were new to the game or a friend-of-a-friend, wore green. Parents of the kids filled the bleachers as the players rushed to the dugouts, eager to know how the game would be played at their new location.

Kariss wandered around the field grounds as the crowd began to grow, amazed by the turnout. She had only been expecting the players and their parents and maybe a few spectators, but she was beginning to see people she knew from school, as well as plenty of others she didn't recognize.

"Who are all these folks?" she asked Tony as he stopped at her side.

He shrugged. "Word got out, I guess. I told some students in my classes, Christian told the guys at work. Ma talked to the women she works with. Guess people wanted to see what the Derby's all about."

He walked off to greet a group of his friends, leaving Kariss standing in wonder. She hadn't planned for this; none of them planned for this. She didn't know what to do, if she was supposed to let them play, if she was supposed to meet and greet them all, and worried that the city officials creeping around the fields would be annoyed with the growing crowd, considering she and K.B. had promised a significantly smaller turnout.

"Don't worry about it, Stinker," K.B. soothed his young granddaughter, placing a hand on her shoulder. "This is what we want, everyone to experience the Annual Sour Orange Derby and know how much Colly meant to us."

"But…what are we gonna do with them all?"

"Do with them? Heck, let them figure that out. We got bleachers and chairs. And look, some even brought their own. They get hungry, we got lots of restaurants right down the road. They want to play, they can wait 'til our game is over."

"Should we explain what the Derby is about? So people actually get it, I mean, and don't think we're a bunch of weirdoes hitting oranges around."

"Now that's a good idea, Stinker. I think you should do that."

"Me?" Kariss' eyes widened and her heart leapt into her throat at the thought of speaking in front of all those people. But she couldn't protest, for her grandfather was already herding the crowd toward the bleachers, promising that the game would soon begin. Within minutes, not enough minutes in Kariss' opinion, K.B. was gesturing her over.

"Okay," she whispered nervously. "For Colly. I can do this...maybe." She walked over to K.B.'s side and stood before the bleachers. The crowd quieted, and the Derby players, some kids, some adults, turned their attention to the teenage Standridge who was clutching her hands together and frantically thinking of what to say. She slipped a hand in her pocket, fingers touching Colly's Lucky Baseball Dime as she sought the strength and confidence that her brother once found within the coin.

"Um...hi...I'm Kariss Standridge," she began with a small wave. The people returned the greeting with smiles and nods, as well as a few "hellos." Their joyful reactions surprised her, as she had been expecting a bunch of blank stares and snickers from the back row, which usually happened in school whenever she and her classmates were forced into class presentations.

"Um...well, we're here to play the Annual Sour Orange Derby. For those of you who don't know what that is, it's a game that my Papa and little brother created about four or five years ago. It's basically what it seems, a baseball game with oranges. We...we're playing today in honor of my little brother, Colly Standridge. Colly...um...Colly died...about two years ago from cancer, and this...this is how we remember him. Some of us on the field are his family and some are his friends. Others have played the Derby and enjoyed it so much that they decided to play again. We do play for points, but we're really just here to have fun. So, hopefully y'all like what you see and come back next year. Oh, and if you see a city official walking around here mad because we didn't follow their rules, please feel free to throw an orange at them." She turned and walked to the dugout to the sound of the crowd's laughter and cheers.

"Way to go, Stinker. Got them all interested, can't even look away from the field now. And guess what? You're up first." K.B. handed Kariss the wooden bat, and before heading to home plate, which was the trashcan lid from their backyard, she cradled the bat and touched the carved names with the tips of her fingers. She loved this bat. It would bring her strength and luck today.

Members of Team Citrus had already taken their positions on the field, positions that were all for show and fun. Kariss felt that her grandfather should have been the first up to bat, but during an earlier argument while finalizing the batting line-up he had insisted that she be the one to show everyone how the Annual Sour Orange Derby was played, and so it was now up to her.

The crowd wasn't disappointed. On her first hit, the orange sailed into the outfield with only a single slit. On the second, she slammed the bat into the fruit simply for the satisfaction of being the first player to feel the cool, sticky juice splatter across her face. The sound of laughter met her ears from behind, but it wasn't a mocking laughter that she had been expecting from a group of people who had never seen anything like the Annual Sour Orange Derby. Instead, it was the sound of people enjoying the show.

K.B. watched the crowd as Tony, Christian, and then Jess Smith took their turns at bat. It seemed as though no further explanation was needed in order for them to understand what made the Derby so special. He wondered if part of that reason was because most of them knew who Colly was, and what his death had meant to the Standridge family. Perhaps simply watching made them laugh, and laughing made them feel better about themselves and about life, as it did for K.B. Ultimately, it didn't matter to the old man. What mattered was that he had done it. With help from his granddaughter, he had found his special way to honor Colly's memory.

K.B. had finally found his way to remember.

That fact was on his mind as he took his turn at bat, scoring twenty-three points. His soulful brown eyes took in every sight of that field, remembering each and every detail as though he were planning on returning home to paint that exact scene on a larger-than-life canvas. Or maybe he was hoping to dream about it later that night, because in his dreams he often visited Colly, and he desperately wished to share this moment with his grandson. And he would, someday.

This moment meant that K.B. could die knowing that he left his mark on the world, and that his mark commemorated Colly, celebrated his family, and left behind a legacy.

Intermission came between the fourth and fifth innings. The players used that time to refuel for the remainder of the game, the kids heading to their parents for drinks and a snack and the adults gathering around the cooler of Cokes supplied by K.B. Joyce was ready with pitchers of sweet tea and cups of ice, while June offered chips, cookies, and a variety of sandwiches. Chewing on a bite of roast beef, K.B. wandered around the field, enjoying the aroma of sour oranges that wafted from his clothes. He stopped occasionally to greet his guests or to further explain the origin of the Sour Orange Derby.

"K.B. Standridge?"

K.B. turned and faced the man who had called his name. He didn't know him, not recognizing the short, light brown hair, the hazel eyes, the six-foot-two lanky frame. The middle-aged man was dressed in slacks and a dark blue, button-down dress shirt, and K.B.'s first instinct was to sneer at the figure he guessed was an official.

"Hey, we didn't plan for this crowd. They came all on their own."

"Well...good for them."

"Good for them, good for us. You don't like it, you get lost. This here is our day, and you ain't gonna ruin it for us."

The man frowned, a bit taken aback by the somewhat rude comment, then laughed when the realization set in. "No, no, sir, I'm not from the city. My name's Paul Tison. I own a couple restaurants here in town."

K.B. softened and offered a hand, slightly embarrassed. "Well then, welcome to the Annual Sour Orange Derby, and I apologize for what I said. What can I do you for, Mr. Tison?"

Paul reached into his pocket and retrieved a business card. "My nephew is playing today. Nick, that loudmouthed, bouncy boy over there that's challenging the umpire to a race. He has spoken highly of the Annual Sour Orange Derby, and I thought I'd stop by to check things out. You have quite a game here."

"Always been quite a game. This is something much greater."

"And I'm sure it will grow with each game."

"Meaning what, Mr. Tison?"

"Meaning, I'd like to help. I'd like to be a part of this."

"Ah." K.B. grinned. "We sucked you in too, did we?"

"Most certainly did. I wanted to offer my restaurant services. After all, every great game needs food, right? So how about a concession stand next year? We set up in that little building over there off to the side, bring a big grill and cook up as many hot dogs and hamburgers you could ever possibly want, sell soft drinks, chips, candy, and give all the proceeds to the Annual Sour Orange Derby."

The idea thrilled the old man, but before replying, K.B. took a moment to observe the newcomer to the Derby. Paul seemed genuine, a decent man who truly cared. After all, he'd never even witnessed the Annual Sour Orange Derby until today and already he was volunteering his time and restaurant. Paul Tison could certainly be an asset, as well as a friend, and K.B. certainly wasn't a man to burn any bridges or turn down any offers of help.

"Tell you what, Mr. Tison. You go talk to that woman over there. Name's June, June Standridge. You tell her what you want to do. If she likes your idea, then it's a go for next year." Paul followed K.B.'s gesture, his eyes settling on the woman standing behind the snack table. June was laughing, her entire face lighting up as her thick curly hair blew freely and wildly in the light breeze. His gaze lasted longer than a normal glance, and K.B. recognized the look in the man's eyes.

"And maybe while you're over there, you can ask her to dinner. You know, to talk business."

Paul chuckled, knowing he was caught and a little intimidated by the old man who he was sure would now be keeping a close eye on him. "You're trouble, Mr. Standridge, aren't you?"

"More than you know."

K.B. watched Paul make his way across the pavement and over to June. The man walked and talked with confidence, but the longer he spoke with June, K.B. saw that his charm had no affect on his daughter, and he turned away rejected. Determined, K.B. marched over to his daughter, took her by the arm, and led her over to the shade of an elm tree.

"So, that was a good-looking man."

"So, you sent him over, didn't you?"

"He had a very interesting proposition concerning a concession stand. If a dinner happens to be thrown in, why not?"

"Why not? Because I'm not ready."

"Curly, one year, and you're not ready. Two years, and you're not ready. Three years, you're pushing it. Twelve, thirteen years, you're an old maid."

June's mouth parted in insult. "Old maid? I'll have you know I look very good for my age."

"Which is why available men who own restaurants want to ask you to dinner." June gave her father a look that he remembered from her teenage years. It was the same stubborn, smart-alecky glare that she used to deliver every time she wanted to win an argument, and usually, she did. But this time, he was determined to walk away victorious.

"Curly, do you know anything about the ancient American cultures?"

"No, Dad."

"Well, Curly, in many ancient cultures, when a man wanted to prove his love to a woman, he would come to her father offering a hot dog."

June scoffed and playfully shoved her father. "Yeah, right, Dad. A hot dog is the way to a woman's heart."

"Don't you laugh at me, Curly. I'm serious. You see, one hot dog means he truly cares for the woman. Two hot dogs means he wants to spend the rest of his life with her, and only her. But if the man brings a grill and offers as many hot dogs as anyone could ever possibly want, well, that man is considered a god on earth and must be snatched up as soon as possible." He lifted a brow at his daughter, who was shaking her head and averting her eyes. "You think I'm kidding? There is documented proof that hot dogs are the supreme offering of true love. You don't like it, you have yourself a little conversation with the ancient gods, but I promise, they won't let you get away without a fight."

They stared at one another, a silent showdown between father and daughter, until June finally broke the connection and rolled her eyes. "Fine, you win. I'll go to dinner."

"Good girl." Satisfied, K.B. stood his ground until June found Paul among the crowd and accepted his offer. Somehow, for some reason, K.B. knew that this man was the one to fill the void and complete his daughter's life.

The game resumed, and K.B. went back to the Annual Sour Orange Derby feeling fresh and renewed, and nothing could bring him down. His grandchildren were happy, his daughter was moving on, and for the first time since Colly's death, life seemed normal again.

Chapter 25
Annual Sour Orange Derby

K.B. took a break to drink, also making sure he didn't miss the end of the game. Without a doubt, Team Colly would come out victorious. Not a single year had passed in which Team Colly didn't win. Maybe Rod was right, that the other teams let them win because they were the founders, the family of Colly Standridge. Or maybe they simply played harder, with more passion and love than anyone else, because Colly was a part of them and they played in his memory and honor. Regardless, it wasn't winning that mattered at the Annual Sour Orange Derby. What mattered was that they were here, and that they were playing.

The crowd was already cheering and congratulating the players of Team Colly. When Sam finished his turn, walking away with thirty-five points, everyone, both players and spectators, started piling onto the field.

"What are they doing?"

A wide grin spread across K.B.'s face, emphasizing the deep wrinkles at the corners of his eyes. "The Annual Sour Orange Fight, of course."

The two chuckled as everyone, adult and child alike, raced around the field, picking up handfuls of orange bits and throwing them at one another. Joyous, chaotic pandemonium ensued, blurs of people crashed into one another, laughing as they fell to the ground, screaming as orange juice was squeezed into their hair, soaking their clothes. The juice slicked the grass, causing many to slip and slide as orange pieces flew through the air.

"It's the clean-up process," K.B. informed with a grin. "First we play, then we celebrate, and finally, we clean."

"Looks like fun."

"Smelly fun," he corrected. "The best kind of fun there is."

"Hard to believe that this all started in your backyard."

"Sometimes, I think back and wonder how we got it this far. Then I remember that when Stinker sets her mind to something, she does it with her whole heart." The pride for his family was evident in his voice. "That girl over there," he pointed to Kariss, who was wrapped up in Sam's arms as he threatened her with orange guts, "she'd found it. She'd found our way to heal." He leaned back and sipped his Coke.

"Things seemed to be unraveling for awhile," K.B. continued, waving to an old friend who was passing by the bleachers. "On that first game ever played without Doodle, not one of us walked away without some crying. But you know, we did it again, and again, and here we are. We got teams, we got pamphlets, we got a concession stand. We got everything we ever dreamed of." He slapped the reporter on the shoulder. "This thing's been going on for years, and will continue for many years to come. Lots of things have come to change in those years. Stretch, that'd be Tony, runs a mechanic shop a couple towns over. Bubba, that'd be Christian, owns a chain of shoe stores, still plays basketball with the guys when he has time, married his girlfriend from high school, got two kids. Stinker over there became a writer, spends her time here and at her place in the Carolina mountains. June even remarried, to Paul, as I knew would happen." He pointed to the middle-aged man who was leaning against the chain-link fence, clapping and whistling.

K.B. leaned back. "But one thing sure ain't changed," he continued. "Every year, you'll find this old man sitting right here, cheering them on.... Crazy how things work out."

"Definitely," Rod agreed. It took quite a person, quite a family, to create something like the Sour Orange Derby. Even more, it took quite a love. Kariss and K.B. and the rest of the Standridge family weren't out at the field for themselves. Perhaps they had been in the beginning, finding their way to heal, but now they were there for Colly, for his memory, and for so much more.

Rod closed his notebook, shocked at the amount of pages he'd filled with quotes and stories. "Well, I have to say, you definitely found that family tradition you were searching for."

The statement warmed K.B.'s heart to the core. "You know, it never ceases to amaze me how something so beautiful could have emerged from such a tragedy. This, all of this," he held out his arms wide, "is so amazing. It's exactly the kind of thing that Doodle would be a part of. And he is." K.B. nodded, casting a glance up at the bright blue sky. "As sad and as heartbreaking as Doodle's death was for us, we're here today, able to celebrate him, because he was a constant reminder of what family truly means."

It was so poetic, so tragically loving, that Rod found himself longing to be a part of the Standridge family. Even in the loss of one of their own, they never forgot their name, their heritage, and they didn't let pain tear them apart. Instead, they let it make them, their bonds, and their love, stronger than it could ever have been before.

"Your way to remember Colly...no one but the Standridges could have ever thought of this."

"Well, that's because we understand the concept of magic." K.B. took a deep breath. "It soothes my ancient soul, knowing that I can die having left something behind." At the reporter's frown, he offered a soothing smile. "I'm an old man, Mr. Jenkins, much older than I look, and I'm tired. My heart just ain't as strong as it used to be. When we first started this game, I knew we'd made our mark, and I was satisfied with that. Only thing that's been keeping me going so much longer, especially now that my Joyce has passed on, was needing to know that they would be alright without me. All of them. And they have needed me over the years, 'cuz we certainly ain't perfect. Tony's had his share of conversations with the cops, Christian's went through a struggle with alcohol, Stinker quit graduate school when her writing career took off, much to her mother's disappointment, and they had one heck of a spat over that. I was there for them every time, and we've gotten things back on track after some time. So now, something tells me I needed to be here, talking to you today, to complete the circle. And now...now I'm not needed any more. I've done my part. I've raised them to be strong, and independent, and to love as strong and as long as they can. I've given them a tradition to uphold, to cherish, and now...now I can join Doodle and Joyce in the land of my ancestors."

Rod thought about the testament, saddened by the thought of a world without K.B. Standridge. But then he remembered that K.B. lived on in Kariss, in June, in every person the man had ever touched with his words and his magic. Perhaps K.B. was right. He had completed his mission in life, and could retire in the peace he always longed for the world to find.

The reporter chuckled as a child taunted her father with a handful of orange goop. "One thing's for sure. The Standridge family has left behind a legacy."

"Every—whoa! Hey there!"

K.B. jumped and covered his head as the Standridge kids, June included, rushed at him from behind, slathering his face and arms with oranges. "Whoa, whoa, whoa! Have mercy on an old man!"

"No mercy! You can never escape the sour oranges!" Christian shouted, rubbing half an orange in his grandfather's hair. "No one escapes the wrath of the SOD Squad!"

Rod had to admit that the sight of five grown adults, some young, some old, attacking one another with oranges was charming, and somehow, perhaps because of the circumstances or because it was just plain fun, it seemed right.

It seemed perfect.

K.B. gathered his grandkids in his arms, his daughter hugging him from behind. "Every family leaves behind a legacy," he said, grinning as Kariss kissed him on the cheek, celebrating as the crowd milling all around them rejoiced and continued their fun.

Kariss winked. "Ours just happens to be The Sour Orange Derby."

Epilogue
ORANGE TREE PROMISES

Resting beneath the shade of the last Standridge family orange tree on an old cedar swing, Colly and K.B. sat side-by-side, sharing a pitcher of sweet tea and a bag of Blutos. It was a rare moment for them, as Colly's time was now spent either sleeping or being with everyone in his family. The reality had finally set in, and for Colly, there was no more denying his fate. No amount of imagination or stories or tricks could make it better.

What Colly didn't know, however, was that his time was coming to an end now rather than later. K.B. did, though, which was why he had taken the time to bring his grandson out to the orange tree. He needed that time alone with Colly.

All around them, nature was full of life. Squirrels jumped from tree to tree, a light breeze rustled the leaves, Latheena chased the fat orange cat around the colorful flowerbeds. Colly didn't seem to see any of it. Instead, he appeared to be focused on the long wooden object he was clutching in his hands, running his tiny, weakened fingers from end to end.

K.B. observed that object carefully, wistfully. Colly held in his hands his father's baseball bat, scarred over time, now carved with the names of all the Standridge kids. The sight was both endearing and poignant, and the old man sighed, not wanting to waste precious time.

"Doodle, I brought you here because I wanted to talk to you." He tried to catch Colly's eye, but Colly wasn't interested in looking up. "I brought you to the orange tree because this spot is special. You know why?"

" 'Cuz it's the orange tree."

"Not just that, Doodle, it's special because of much more than just being the last Standridge orange tree. It's because any promise made beneath the shade of the orange tree is a promise that is always kept, no matter what. So...I wanted to make you a promise." K.B. put a hand beneath Colly's chin and lifted his head so he could see his face. Colly's eyes were tired, sleepy, and his breaths were shallow, but he struggled to concentrate on his grandfather.

"Doodle, I promise you that no matter what happens, no matter where anyone in this family goes, or moves to, no matter what jobs they have, no matter what they are doing, that we will never stop loving you."

K.B. couldn't keep himself from tearing up. At the promise, and at the sight of his grandfather crying, Colly's own eyes watered. He clutched his bat, feeling the scars, the smooth spots. He didn't say anything for a long time, couldn't say anything.

Only a few yards away, June also found herself teary and speechless as she watched the scene from her bedroom window. It was hard, so hard, for her to give up her son, if only for an hour, because that was one less hour she got with him. One less hour to hold him, one less hour to hear his voice. It was selfish of her to want his every moment, both waking and sleeping, but she didn't care. She wanted, and needed, every moment.

"Momma?"

June turned, holding her arms out as Kariss approached. "Hi, honey." She hugged her daughter tightly before returning her gaze to the window. Kariss followed her mother's eyes to see her grandfather and little brother sitting beneath the vibrant sour orange tree. Neither was speaking, but both looked sad. She wondered what they were talking about.

"Momma?' Kariss said again, shifting from foot to foot as sobs threatened to rack her body. "Momma…is there any chance that Colly…"

She couldn't find the words to finish, but June understood the question. It was the question she'd been asking herself for more than three months, the question she despised, the question she couldn't avoid.

She swallowed hard, a tear slipping down her cheek. "…No, Kariss," she whispered, kissing the top of her daughter's head. "I'm sorry, honey…it's just…" Her voice trailed off as she lowered her head and wiped her eyes.

Kariss didn't push her mother. Now wasn't the time to dwell on the harsh facts of reality. Now was the time to love, to reminisce about all the joys of the past, all the fun that was had, all the laughs that were shared. Now was the time to be strong, to make sure her little brother was as happy as he could be, to make sure her mother had a sensitive shoulder to cry on.

Colly would never be forgotten. No one would ever stop loving him; no one would ever forget his toothy smile, his bright brown eyes. Kariss would find a way to commemorate him, would find a way to let the world know just how great a little brother Colly Standridge was to her.

Wrapping her arms around her mother's waist, Kariss focused her attention on the orange tree and its occupants, and although June remained silent, she cherished the feel of her daughter next to her.

Still toying with the heavy bat, Colly thought about his future. He knew what was coming, and had accepted the fact that his treatment might not work, though he did wholeheartedly believe that good things happened to good people and that the world may let him live. He just hoped that whatever happened next would be fun and exciting, and not at all painful or scary.

Then something occurred to him.

"Papa?"

"Yes, Doodle?"

Colly sighed heavily, a sigh filled with exhaustion. "Did you really die?"

He wasn't going to lie, not now. "I did."

"Did you really see your momma?"

"I did."

Colly wiped his eyes, and for the first time in awhile, thought to himself that he really liked the smell of the oranges and the warm sun shining all around the tree.

"Papa?"

"Yes, Doodle?"

"What's heaven look like?"

K.B. put an arm around his grandson, who rested his head on his grandpa's shoulder. "Heaven, Colly, looks like a giant baseball field. Tall spotlights that light up a bright green field that's surrounded on all sides by huge Gumdrop trees and lots of Acorn Cities, dugouts with every kind of baseball bat and glove and uniform you could ever want, hot dogs and ice cream sold at the concession stand, and a huge crowd all cheering your name."

"Cool." Colly smiled and closed his eyes to rest in the warmth of the summer sun. "I'll bring the sour oranges."

Acknowledgements

The Sour Orange Derby has been, quite literally, a lifetime in the making. I wrote the first draft of this novel in my head when I was in middle school, when it began simply as a collection of random bits of our childhood. Over the years, it has transformed into the story of heritage, a celebration of family, and a showcase of imagination and magic.

Magic is, perhaps, the biggest theme of The Derby (how I affectionately refer to the book), and that magic is the direct result of the *real* K.B. and Joyce Standridge, also known as Ken and Evelyn White, or Papa and Mema to us grandkids. When I look back on my childhood, I remember all sorts of outings with both sets of grandparents, family vacations to exciting new destinations, independent adventures that shaped me into the person I am today. But one thing shines brightest of all—the steadfast faith my Papa had in having fun, and remembering the joy of being a kid no matter how old we may be. From something as simple as a Lucky Dime to the intricacies of the Sour Orange Derby, magic was always at the core of our childhoods. And for that, I thank you, Mema and Papa. Some people may say that magic isn't real, that some dreams are too big, that imagination is for children, but we know the truth—that all things are possible, if we just believe in them enough.

Along with Mema and Papa, many more people helped realize the dream of The Sour Orange Derby. I must take this time to thank my parents in their endeavors to keep imagination and magic alive; my family members for indulging me in my talk of things "not possible" in this world; my husband for always being willing to lend an ear when I need to talk through a scene; Kelly Hall for once again creating a wonderful cover while putting up with my anal-retentive demands; Anna Aughenbaugh for giving an honest review of the initial draft; Randi Whittington for donating her time and skills to edit the manuscript; and Melissa DeSimone for continuing to give me the kick in the butt I need.

I feel I must also take this time to add a little disclaimer. Although The Sour Orange Derby is inspired by true people and events, I did take some liberties with the facts of my family history. My little brother, the real Colly Standridge (otherwise known as Lathan Circelli), is still very much alive and continuing to make his presence known—and is not very happy to have been killed off. Sorry, dude, it had to happen. But to make up for killing you off (figuratively, of course), I promise a book with aliens, swordfights, or gunfights—or possibly all three—in the near future.

www.ingramcontent.com/pod-product-compliance
Lightning Source LLC
Chambersburg PA
CBHW031335170626
46807CB00002B/715